Soul Purpose

For Beattie

Soul Purpose

Nick Marsh

Stafford, England

Soul Purpose
By Nick Marsh

Cover by Vincent Chong
Design by Kid Charlemaine
Typesetting by Storm Constantine
Editor: Suzannah Runnacles

Set in Souvenir

First edition by Immanion Press, 2006

0 9 8 7 6 5 4 3 2 1

An Immanion Press Edition
http://www.immanion-press.com
info@immanion-press.com

ISBN 1-9048-5331-5

Immanion Press
8 Rowley Grove
Stafford ST17 9BJ, UK

PROLOGUE

Four billion years ago…

It all comes back to here. It's as good a place to start as any. Back here, things are different — not only a foreign country, but a foreign world. If you were here, there would be little from your world that would make sense. Of course, you wouldn't be here. Or rather, if you were, you would be too busy asphyxiating, boiling, getting zapped by lightning, fried by lava and generally having too much of a rotten time of it to sit down and take in the local scenery. Not that you'd enjoy it much if you did. What isn't red hot and melted is boiling hot and steaming. The ground is covered in black slag dissected by molten rivulets of the still-forming world. The air is filled with the crackle of lightning, and the mists and fogs of numerous unpleasant gases. Staring up into the primordial sky is like trying to watch an Andy Warhol film from the back row of a smoky auditorium. Barely visible through the gloom is the distant haze of a virgin sun, ancient beyond measure and yet long before its prime.

Still, this is your world. And this is where it begins.

When it starts, it starts with a simple chemical reaction — and to be honest, in all this chaos, chemical reactions are ten a penny. Acids forming proteins forming complex tertiary structures that become unstable and melt away, collapsing in upon themselves and dispersing, drifting away to do it all over again. This reaction, however, is different. Not in a flash-kerbamm-zoooom chemistry-set kind of way, but in a subtler, quieter and altogether more important way. Another protein is formed. It maintains its shape. It is not the first to do so, but there is something unique about it. This protein can make copies of itself. It can replicate and propagate and spread. It can recruit nearby unsuspecting proteins, rope them in, force them to conform. It knows nothing of its destiny, but its descendants will rule this world.

Proto-life has arrived on the young planet. And with it, something even more significant.

The first soul.

Chapter One

I

— Ring Ring —

At first, he didn't have a clue where he was, or what his name was. Slowly it dawned upon him that he was in a bed, and the noise was the telephone ringing. Everything else remained a mystery. Instinct sent his arm scrabbling towards the phone, and when his outstretched fingers felt it he picked it up, studying the receiver with a puzzled look, as if it were an iguana that had unexpectedly been handed to him for lunch. Then he remembered what to do. As he placed the phone to his ear and his mouth began to form the first tentative syllable of a sleepy 'Hello?', his memory decided that he was awake enough to release some relevant information to him. He wished it hadn't.

- He was twenty-seven years old.
- He was a vet.
- He hated his job.
- He was absolutely, completely bloody sick of being called out in the middle of the night.
- He was being called out in the middle of the night.

There had been no response from the phone in his hand. He examined it, cursed, turned it the right way around and said 'Hello' again, praying that if it was a call out, it would be a nice, warm one. Perhaps the euthanasia of an elderly cat with kidney failure, peacefully passing away in front of a log fire. Or an epileptic dog. Even a collapsed hamster would do. Anything where he didn't have to think. Anything that he could examine in the comfort of the surgery. Anything that wasn't a cow.

II

'Hello?'

'Is that the vet?'

'Erm... what?'

'I said, is that the vet? I'm phoning for the vet.'

'Erm... yeah. Yes, it's Alan here. Who is it I'm speaking to?'

'Hi, Alan. It's Mike White here, out at Quayle's farm. I've got a problem with a cow.'

'What kind of problem?'

'Buggered if I know, Alan. That's why I'm calling you. Could you get out right away?'

III

One of the few things Alan Reece had learned since he had started practising was that it was entirely possible to go out in the night, see and treat an animal, discuss the case with the client and only wake up on the drive home. It was then, of course, impossible to get back to sleep, leading to him being wide awake for the rest of the night and half-asleep the following day. He was, therefore, only mildly surprised to find himself pulling the terminally ill Astra his practice had supplied him with into the yard of Quayle's farm with no memory of the preceding fifteen minutes. He turned off the engine, which coughed and shuddered to a halt like a tuberculotic sprinter after a hundred-metre dash, and stared miserably out of the windscreen at the dismal rain, which was blattering everything that could be blattered into a soggy pulp. The rain stared miserably back at him, and then got on with the job of covering everything in cold muddy water, and basically making everything in the county as thoroughly unpleasant as possible, a job at which it was astonishingly good.

With a sigh as deep as an ocean trench, Alan opened the door, trudged round to the boot and manoeuvred his feet into his Wellies — managing, as he always did on nights like these, to get his socks soaked through before getting them in the boots, thus utterly defeating the point of putting them on. He was in the process of wrestling with his waterproof top, working out where his arms were and wishing he had washed the top at some point in the last month so that didn't smell quite so much of rotting lamb, when Mr White arrived. Alan squirmed his way into the top (inside out, as usual, ensuring he would never again be able to wear his shirt in polite company, or even impolite company, come to that) and blinked as the farmer flashed his torch into Alan's eyes. Alan tried to smile as the beam was lowered.

'Hello, Mr...'

Something in Mike White's face stopped Alan. His round cheeks were as white as his name and looked as if he'd just been diagnosed with the sort of thing that gets publishers of medical textbooks excited and reaching for their digital cameras.

'Through 'ere,' was all Mike said before turning to the barn.

Alan was normally worried when on call. He hated it. The stress of it was almost too much for him to bear. It was certainly too much for his digestive system to bear. You could always tell a weekend when Alan was on call, his ex-fiancée had told friends, because he got through at least two and sometimes three double-quilted toilet rolls. The expression on Mike White's face got Alan wondering whether this weekend was going to be a treble-roller. He followed Mike towards the barn, his Wellies squidging mournfully with every step.

IV

The barn was an old building, rickety and wind-blown and, at this time of year, ankle deep in cow shit. It had a thin scattering of straw on the ground as if in an attempt to disguise the dirt. It didn't work. The beam from the nervous farmer's torch bounced around the room as if it would rather be at an all-night rave. The acrobatic lighting added to Alan's feeling of discomfort and displacement. It should have been a relief to be out of the driving rain but at this moment Alan would have gladly stood out in it naked until sunrise if it meant he could avoid seeing what had turned Mike White, who had calmly held prolapsed uteruses up on his knees and sawn rotten heads off stinking lambs to get them out of the ewe, as pale as his cows' milk.

'What... er... what have you got for me, Mr White?' Alan asked nervously.

Mr White turned to Alan. He had been a farmer all his life. He had seen just about everything nature could throw at a person, most of it before he was twelve. The horrible pulsatings and hideous smells of nature gone wrong held no fear for him. Alan wasn't at all sure that he wanted to know what it was that had shaken him, but thought he should at least have some warning about what he was approaching.

'It's the damnedest thing, Alan. Never seen anything like it in all me born days.'

'What is it, exactly?'

'I was 'opin you could tell me. Maiden heifer, just calved. See for yerself.'

Mike turned back again, and trudged forwards, his torchlight illuminating a cow-shaped form in the corner of the barn. Alan followed, squinting, trying to make it out. It was a Friesian-Holstein heifer, slightly on the thin side, and as Mike had pointed out, obviously just calved. She was standing and licking forlornly at a small pale object lying in the straw. Alan's mouth formed the 'W' of 'what' but whatever else he was planning to say was lost to posterity because at that moment Mike shone his torch directly onto the object. The word retreated from Alan's mouth and hid, quivering, down by his diaphragm.

The thing the cow was licking was a calf. Of sorts. Alan had seen foetal monsters before, strange furry blobs of flesh with the odd foot, tail or even head protruding. Accidents of nature, never meant to live. This was different. Externally, it looked normal. Four legs, head, tail, everything seemed in place. At least, Alan thought so. It was hard to make out, because the torchlight shone right through the calf, illuminating the bloodstained straw beneath, which reflected the light right through the calf again as if it wasn't there. The calf was transparent.

Alan's brain didn't quite grasp the concept as it zapped through his neurones the first time, so he tried thinking it again, more clearly this time.

The calf was transparent.

He could see its ribs, its beating heart, its lungs, which were twitching and contracting as the neonate fought for breath. Alan watched in astonishment as the calf gave a feeble cough and a blob of pleural fluid travelled out of the lungs, up the trachea, and into the mouth, where the calf swallowed it.

The mother briefly glanced at the two intruders and then turned back to licking her miraculous calf.

V

Alan's heart skipped a beat. A moment later, it skipped another one. It was preparing to skip a third when it received an urgent communiqué from his brain, suggesting that if it did so, there would be trouble. Reluctantly, it started up again, but decided to make up for lost time by hammering away at double speed.

Alan took a cautious step towards the calf. Mike stayed where he was.

'What d'you reckon, then?' the farmer asked.

Alan couldn't tear his eyes away from the creature in front of him. He wondered if he was still asleep. Half of his brain was gibbering with sheer incomprehension. The other half was running through his notes, searching for the section headed 'photo-transparent idiopathies'. Either he had forgotten all about them, or no such section existed.

The heifer looked up at him again. Alan had never been

very good at reading bovine expressions, but as far as he recognised that a cow could look reproachful, this is what she did.

'Did she calve all right?' he asked automatically, buying time so that his brain could stop gibbering and start working.

'Reckon so,' said Mike. 'We didn't help her out or nothin', anyway.'

Alan was at a loss for what to do. Surely he should be gathering evidence, taking photos, something. This was obviously a whole new disease. He switched himself onto autopilot, clinical exam mode while he wondered what the bloody hell he was going to do.

The cow herself seemed fine. Normal heart rate, normal temperature. A little bruised, but nothing out of the ordinary. She had cleansed quickly. The shrivelled mess of placenta lay on the floor next to the calf. It was normal.

'Er... aren't you going to look at the calf?' Mike asked from his safe distance.

'Oh... erm... sure,' mumbled Alan. He moved back around to the front of the cow and looked down.

It didn't make any sense. How could it be alive? Weren't there... reactions and things that had to happen in the skin? Didn't it need to absorb light or something? Alan wasn't clear on the specifics. Biochemistry was not his favourite subject.

Slowly, he knelt down beside the creature. It turned its head to him, making a weak mewling sound. Alan could see its larynx vibrate as it did so. It was clearly dying. The calf's heart had slowed its beat since he had first looked at it, and the wretched thing was almost too weak to hold its head up.

Alan felt strangely reluctant to touch it. At the back of his mind a quiet but insistent voice suggested that it would be a really bad idea. The cow nuzzled her calf again. Slowly, trying to shake the feeling that this was all a dream, Alan reached his hand out to it.

VI

It was mainly the noise that Alan remembered when he thought back on it; a tremendous burst of screaming noise, like an out-of-tune television on full volume. It filled his world, so loud it seemed to leave no room for anything else. He couldn't see, he couldn't feel, he couldn't think. He simply stopped as the tidal wave hit him, waiting for it to pass. He was aware of a feeling of enormous pressure, and for a moment the small part of him that could still think was terrified that he was going to burst. He had a brief mental image of himself popping like a balloon in front of the mystified farmer. Then, the pressure eased, as if something has just passed *through* him and popped out on the other side. The noise stopped instantly.

Slowly, he came back to himself. He was still kneeling in the straw, on the ground, behind the cow. His arm was still outstretched.

Sitting in front of him, coughing and mewing softly, was a perfectly normal Friesian-Holstein calf.

Chapter Two

I

Kate leaned back and rubbed her eyes as the shapes spun and danced crazily in front of her, and came back to herself. She hadn't realised it, but she had entered into the weird trance of the habitual computer-junkie. She must have been staring at the screen for ten minutes. She blinked several times and rubbed her eyes again but the dull ache behind them remained. Time for a break.

She reached out for the cup of coffee that had been standing on her workbench and peered into it. An unpleasant brown skin had grown over the surface of the drink, and it wrinkled as the cup rocked in her grip. She took a sip anyway, swilled it around her mouth, swallowed it thoughtfully, and took another one. Yep, she thought. Undrinkable.

Standing up, she rolled her head from side to side. Her neck made several disturbing cracks, so she stopped and peered back at the computer screen.

No progress. The algorithm must have been flawed. It always seemed to get stuck at this point. What the bloody hell time was it anyway? She must have been up all night fiddling with the thing, trying to figure out what she had done wrong. It was frustrating work, frustration that was always compounded for Kate whenever she worked with computers by the knowledge that computers only do what you tell them to, and so if anything was going wrong it was basically her fault.

Crap, she thought. They don't always do what you tell them, anyway. Hadn't she spent about twenty minutes screaming 'Oh come on, you bastard!' at it a few hours ago. It didn't do what she had told it then.

She looked at her watch, but her monitor-frazzled eyes couldn't make out the tiny digits on its face. It must be pretty late, though. It felt late. In fact, it felt so late it was probably early.

She sighed, running her fingers over her head, slightly surprised, as always, to find the short spiky strands that sat there, instead of the long flowing Rapunzel-style of her previous life, and looked at the computer again, in case it had done anything in the few milliseconds between now and her last glance. It hadn't.

What was wrong with the bloody thing? It should be a relatively simple program. Simple for her, anyway. It had seemed an ideal problem too, combining her studentship in particle physics with her degree in computer programming. Ideal, simple, and completely bloody impossible.

She was trying to use her computer system to model the effects of the new particle accelerator being built in Kent, designed to model heavy ion impacts at high speeds. The accelerator had little fanfare surrounding it. It was a massive machine, an impressive feat of engineering, but because it neither had exciting flashing lights on it, nor could anti-abortionists try and complain about it, it had interested the general press not at all. Even *New Scientist* hadn't been all that interested. Kate had. Not because of the accelerator itself, but because the way it was set up was exactly what she was looking for to test out the new modelling system she had designed. She had researched, worked for months to get her model of the accelerator just right. Everything that conventional physics (if you could use that word when dealing with objects smaller than most people could comfortably imagine and still get a decent night's sleep afterwards) accepted was there. She had got it right, she knew it. She had spent all night debugging, rerouting, retesting, but could find nothing wrong.

So why wasn't the bloody thing working?

She shook her head. Time for a break.

'Time for a break,' she said out loud, hoping that this would somehow make it sound more professional. Strangely enough, it worked. Of course, there was no one in her flat to say it to at this time in the morning. The fact that there wasn't, of course, was largely why she had spent the whole evening fiddling with her computer. If there was, she doubted very much she would be sitting up all night with her silicon chum. Then she thought of Trevor, and decided that maybe Windows XP wasn't such bad company after all.

She turned from the computer and headed through the bomb-site of a lounge to the kitchen, where she turned on the cold tap, letting it run for a moment before she cupped her hands under the stream and plunged her face into the water. By the time her sleepy hands had informed her that she had actually turned on the hot tap rather than the cold, she had already covered her face with it. Cursing, she grabbed for the tea towel that hung from the hook nearby, and rubbed her stinging face with it. The tea towel had been bought by her mother and was inexplicably covered in pictures of small smiling teddy bears, due to her mother's mistaken belief that Kate had the mental maturity level of a three-year-old.

She turned off the tap, dropped the towel on the floor, flicked the kettle on and stared at the wall in front of her, blinking and trying to focus. The shapes from the computer screen still danced across her vision, and her mind felt cloudy and dull. Why wasn't it working?

She rubbed her eyes again roughly with her knuckles, feeling the first ominous thuds of a headache deep in her skull. She sighed. She had no painkillers in the flat, of course. That would be too simple. She didn't get a lot of headaches, not any more, at least. She had used to get a lot, in her old life. But that had been years ago.

She stared at the wall as the kettle hissed and bubbled, and thought about her old life, because it was that sort of time in the morning. Had she been happy? She supposed so. She had never really thought about it back then. It wasn't a profitable vocation, being a medium, but she had felt like she was providing a service. Certainly she had been popular, in her way, with the more open-minded or gullible people of Bristol. She had an ad in the paper: her face, looking as serene and peaceful as a Buddhist, with the words 'I see dead people,' written underneath. She had thought of that herself, and had been proud of it, until that bloody Bruce Willis film had come out and stolen her catchphrase. People even started accusing her of stealing it from the makers of the film, so that she was forced to change it to the less catchy, in her opinion, 'I see souls'. This was made worse by the misprint that meant she had to spend a week being phoned up by marine mammal enthusiasts asking where she kept the seals.

By then she had already started to lose her faith anyway. It wasn't that she didn't believe, particularly. How could she not? She had seen the things. At least, she thought that she had. It all seemed so long ago now. It wasn't that, anyway. No, it was that she slowly began to realise that perhaps whatever it was she had been able to see, it wasn't what people thought it was. It just seemed... wrong. It seemed... oh, she didn't know.

Anyway, as if they could sense that she had lost her faith, Kate found it harder and harder to see the... whatever they were. Eventually she couldn't see them at all. It didn't matter by then. At least she didn't get the headaches any more. She had decided she wanted to spend her life doing something useful, something concrete. Something that didn't involve sitting in a darkened room lying to old dears and grieving mothers. She decided to become a scientist.

Still, that had all been a long time ago. The click of the kettle brought her back to her senses. Distantly, Kate watched herself make a coffee, her mind on the problem. She wondered if she should give up, but she knew she wouldn't sleep until she had sorted it out.

Down on the kitchen floor, Roger the cat shrugged off the tea towel which had landed on his head, and rubbed up against Kate's legs, purring hopefully, and looking pointedly at the fridge, where it knew several lumps of chicken and sliced pig were crying out to be eaten before the mould that was invading the fridge from its beachhead in the vegetable tray overpowered them. He received no response. Oh, he thought, she's in one of those moods. Fair enough.

Slowly, with the air of a professional at work, he stalked off toward the office to piss on the speakers.

'One more try,' Kate muttered to herself as she headed back to the computer.

II

She knew something had changed even before she looked at the monitor. The room felt different, expectant. Either that, or the shapes on the screen had stopped moving and reflecting off the window. It was a good sign, whichever.

As she settled back down into the chair she could see she was right; the calculations had stopped. The equation had either got somewhere, or it had crashed. Well, at least it was something. Kate put the coffee on top of the computer's tower case, and clicked the mouse a few times. She frowned and clicked it again. Then she tapped at the keyboard for a few seconds, frowning even more. Her next action had the most positive effect, on herself at least.

'Shit,' she said, loudly, but not quite shouting. Not yet.

The simulation was working. Or at least, it had been, but something in the way the accelerator had been set up created some kind of chain reaction in the program she had written to model its behaviour. The chain reaction rapidly gobbled up all her computer's spare processing power without actually telling her what was going on, so that now the program was locked, unable to continue.

She tapped away at the keyboard a few more times, then moved the mouse in a circle, watching the little hourglass shape on the screen whirl as she tried to think. Not enough processing power. Any more options? The computer was stuck. So was she. Surely there could be some way to…

She stopped moving the mouse as the answer came to her. Why not try the new routines she had been working on? Part of a completely different project, but this was exactly the sort of thing she had designed them for. They could boost a program's power by giving the processor numerous back doors; ways of looking around the equations for areas where it could fudge and cheat its way through. The routines used fuzzy logic as their starting point, giving the computer choices. She didn't like to say it to anyone, even herself, because it sounded so dramatic, but the routines basically gave the computer a very limited degree of intelligence and independent thought. Nothing much, of course, certainly nothing approaching HAL-9000. Not even approaching Roger, come to that, but they may be just the thing she was looking for.

She minimised the current program and hunted around her directory for the routines. They weren't quite finished yet. What the hell? What did she have to lose? It was do or die at this point. Well... do or bugger off to bed, anyway. If it didn't work, she would simply have to try on the computer at work. Give it a go, she told herself. She hunted around for the icon that started them up, which for reasons she could no longer remember resembled a large strawberry, and pointed them in the direction of the accelerator model.

The effect was instantaneous, or at least as instantaneous as Windows got. The model began working again, and a few seconds after that Kate saw what had gone wrong. It was nothing to do with her programming. It had to do with the reaction itself.

'Oh, shit,' she said. She felt her heart rattle in her chest, and the back of her throat seemed to have swelled. There was that horrible sinking feeling in her stomach, familiar to her from years of exams. She couldn't believe it. There had to be a flaw somewhere. She had to show this to someone, maybe Professor Lattman. She had to get it checked.

Eyes on the screen, she reached down to the case to open the CD drive. There was a clunk of metal on porcelain, a hot sensation on her hand, a yowl and a terrible fizzing noise. The smell of hot coffee mingled with the odour of cat urine and that peculiar burning smell only an electrical component that has had something terminal happen to it can make, and the monitor blinked off.

'Shit,' she said again.

Chapter Three

I

The storm clouds were gathering. Alan floated amongst them, flew and spiralled like a bird. He could feel electricity in the air, could feel the clouds heavy with potential. There was a dull buzz at the back of his mind, the kind that a light gives off before it explodes. The clouds were ready to burst.

Alan knew he was dreaming; at least, he knew it on some level. It was the strangest dream he had ever had. It had no structure, no form except for the clouds, the clouds that were waiting for... for what?

The buzz intensified, until all the clouds were throbbing with the noise. Alan thought he could hear voices under the hum. He tried to close his eyes, to cut out some of the sensory overload, but he had no eyes to close. He opened his mouth to cry out, but he had no mouth. He could do nothing but float and try and scream. The buzzing got louder, and then louder still. This time Alan did scream. He screamed and opened his eyes and...

II

The noise of the alarm clock filled his bedroom. Within seconds the dream vanished from his memory, and he found himself for the second time in only a few hours lying confused in his bed. His hand slapped the top of the alarm clock automatically while he struggled to think, but the clock continued to buzz. Alan had become so adept at turning off his alarm clock in a semi-conscious state that he had been forced to buy a novelty one from a catalogue — the novelty being that the clock had a small jigsaw puzzle on top of it that ejected its pieces all over the room when it rang. The thing would only shut up when the jigsaw had been correctly reconstructed on top of it. Unfortunately one of the pieces had fired itself right out of Alan's open window on the second day he had used it, and so he was now forced to climb out of bed and rip the batteries out of the wretched thing every morning. This seemed to work just as well as the jigsaw idea, though, so Alan had never bothered to find the missing piece.

Alan pulled the curtains open a crack as he sat up in the bed. The weary light from a flaming ball of hydrogen seventy million miles away ended its long journey on his purple carpet, wondering if it had been worth all the effort. Alan ignored it as he fumbled with the back panel of the howling alarm clock and ripped the batteries out. One of them fell from his hands and rolled under the bed. The alarm clock shut up. Ah! Sweet relief. He sat with his eyes closed for a moment, then opened them again, looking at the clock. The buzz had not stopped, at least, not entirely. Puzzled, he looked into the battery cavity at the bottom. Empty. He brought the clock up to his ear but the buzz got no louder. It was not coming from the clock. Great. Now he had tinnitus to add to his troubles.

Alan had been wide awake by the time he returned to his house in the early hours of the morning. Sleep had been impossible, so he had spent an hour looking through his notes and trawling the Internet for anything like what he had just experienced. Nothing. In fact, the sites he started discovering even when using seemingly innocuous words such as 'transparent' in his search engine put him off the whole exercise. Deciding to leave any more thought of the cow and its calf until the morning, he had gone to bed in the hope of getting some rest before his morning's work.

He had eventually got to sleep forty-seven minutes before his alarm clock woke him up. Sleep was a mystery to Alan. It always seemed to be in reverse. How come he always woke up in the morning feeling like he couldn't keep his eyes open for another second, yet he could never get to sleep in the evening?

Muttering to himself without realising that he was doing it, Alan staggered into the shower to face another day at work, hoping it wouldn't be as bad as all the other days at work thus far.

He was right. It was going to be worse.

III

George was already up and eating breakfast by the time Alan had arranged himself, with shirt and tie, so that he looked, if not every inch a professional, then at least three-feet's worth. That was good enough for him.

'Morning, George,' Alan mumbled as he shuffled in the kitchen and switched the kettle on, then leaned by the sink staring out of the window into the grey morning. He was actually feeling much better after the shower, despite the buzzing in his ears, but it was his natural instinct to act more tired than he was. It had been a hell of a night. He deserved sympathy.

'Busy night?' George asked through a mouthful of Cinnamon Grahams.

'Hn,' said Alan.

'Want to talk about it?'

Alan shook his head, rubbing his eyes.

'Working all day, then?' George said.

Alan turned from the window, yawning. 'Till seven,' he said. George scrunched his face up in what would have been a sympathetic wince if he hadn't had milk dribbling down his chin.

'You working today, then?' Alan asked. George worked roughly one day in seven, his parents being wealthy enough to indulge him in whatever hopeless dreams he was currently chasing. George classed himself as a 'seeker of truth' whenever anybody asked him, but did it with such a glint in his blue eyes that most people assumed he wasn't serious. Whether he was or not was something Alan had yet to work out. George had been staying with him for just over three months. Alan had originally lived in the house with his fiancée, but she had left him six months ago. She couldn't stand the strain of being a partner to a vet. Alan couldn't find it in himself to blame her. He just wished she had taken him with her when she left.

George was in his mid-twenties, and handsome in a laid-back, surfer-dude kind of way, except that his hair was a mousy brown instead of blond. The house belonged to Alan's boss, and he had rented a room in it to George, whose parents were friends of his. It was a beneficial arrangement for everyone. George got the independence he craved without the stress of actually having to live for himself, while he indulged his current career craze of working as a journalist for some *Fortean Times*-wannabe magazine, and his parents got to keep an eye on him through Alan's boss. Alan's boss got the rent money. Everyone was happy. Everyone except Alan.

It wasn't that he disliked George. He was weird and annoying but as roommates go there were a lot worse traits to have. It was just that Alan felt he had done it all at university. It felt like a step backwards.

'What are you doing today, then?' he asked George, more out of politeness than any real interest.

'Got a text this morning,' George said, ejecting a fair portion of his breakfast on to the table in front of him as he did so. 'Hector has got me a few jobs lined up today, few people to interview.' He raised an eyebrow. 'Lots of weird things happening in Bristol today,' he said, enigmatically.

Alan sighed. Weird things, as far as George was concerned, generally meant that someone thought their kettle had been possessed by aliens, or that they had seen the face of Liberace in a baked potato. Then he remembered the calf from last night. He cleared his throat.

'Erm... what sort of things?' Alan asked, as disinterestedly as he could, but George shrugged, wiping his mouth. 'Ah, y'know. Usual.'

For a second Alan thought of sharing the night's experience with George, but as he watched his flatmate noisily consume the rest of the cereal he thought of himself on the cover of next month's 'World of Mystery' magazine, or whatever it was called, and decided against it. He looked at the toaster, but his stomach protested that it didn't think it could cope with much before midday. George was already heading for the door, mumbling a muffled 'G'bye' over his shoulder. Alan shook his head, and poked his little finger in his ear for the seventeenth time this morning, but the buzzing noise persisted.

IV

Thoughts of the previous night were temporarily forced from Alan's mind as he walked through the doors of Chestnut Vale surgery and was deluged with messages from clients, and notes from nurses about inpatients that he needed to check. He waded his way through them on autopilot, putting off whatever he could until tomorrow, phoning the people who needing phoning, and smiling at the people who needed smiling at.

It was his ops day, so he only had to do a few consultations in the morning. After five years as a vet, he couldn't work out why speaking to people about their animals was called 'morning surgery', while actually doing surgery on animals in the morning wasn't. At university, like every other vet student, he'd been terrified at the thought of consulting, of actually meeting the public and having to tell them what was wrong with their animal. He wasn't long into his career when he realised successful consults mainly consisted of smiling, frowning and sounding either stern or reassuring at the appropriate moments. This morning was much like any other.

It wasn't that Alan didn't care about the people, or their animals. In fact, he was quite proud of himself that he still cared quite a lot what happened to his patients. It was just difficult to vaccinate animals with the same degree of enthusiasm every day without resorting to faking it.

Three boosters and a cat bite abscess later, Alan managed to escape to the prep room. Cameron was there, just arriving from an early morning call to take over consults from Alan, while he got on with the morning's operations.

'Morning, mate,' said Cameron, a huge smile on his face. He was washing blood off his arms in the sink. It was also all over his face.

'Hi,' Alan said.

Cameron frowned. 'You look like crap,' he said to Alan. He wasn't one to mince his words. Cameron was a large Australian vet, frustratingly cheerful and effortlessly handsome. Even washing blood off his hands in a sink, wearing waterproof trousers covered in God-knew-what, he looked like he had just stepped out of the pages of the Freeman's catalogue. Alan liked Cameron, mainly because it would have taken a great deal of effort not to like him. He had a kind of inner glow about him that reassured you that everything would be all right. He got a lot of calls from young, female horse-owners who made sure they put their make-up on before he arrived. The inner glow also seemed to affect his body temperature because he wore shorts every day of the year.

He finished washing his hands and stripped off his waterproofs. Sure enough, he was wearing shorts today, even though it was December, and cold with it. However much he liked Cameron, Alan always found him depressing company, because he seemed to enjoy the job so much. There was no calving too horrible for Cameron, no rotting lamb too rotten.

'Crappy night?' he asked Alan.

'Erm...' said Alan, as the bizarre incident on Quayle's farm replayed itself again in his head. 'Erm... not too bad, no. Just a late night, that's all.'

'No worries,' said Cameron, and for a moment Alan almost believed him. Cameron headed to the cloakroom where he picked up the largest consulting top, and put it on. It was still too small for him. For all his charm, Cameron was not designed for small animal work. He didn't look comfortable in a green top, and he managed to loom in a consulting room, however big it was, and however much he smiled. A hamster, in Cameron's hands, looked like a tiny speck, an inconvenience that Cameron might swat at a second's notice. He tended to frighten the old dears. Still, it was his turn. He wriggled his shoulders in the top, trying and failing to get comfortable, then headed to the consulting room for morning surgery while Alan relaxed with a few gentle cat spays.

His mind wandered while he worked down the board, as he tried to make sense of what he'd seen last night. He was finishing off his third cat spay when Mike White called him.

V

'Morning, Mr White. Sorry about the wait there, just stitching up a...'

'Never mind about that, Alan.' Mike's voice was quiet, with the same subdued quality that it had last night. 'I'm just ringin' about that calf you came to see.'

Alan's mouth went dry quicker than a man with a mouthful of crackers.

'All fine. Wouldn't know there had been a thing wrong with it,' Mike said.

'Oh,' said Alan. He struggled for something else to say. 'Oh,' he said again, and gave up.

'Thing is,' said Mike, slowly, 'thing is... I'd rather not go through all that paperwork, have the ministry round or anything. You know how it is.'

It suddenly struck Alan that he probably should have notified the Department for Environment, Food and Rural Affairs about the calf. Why hadn't he thought of that already? Probably because he was still coming to terms with it himself.

'Alan? You there?'

Alan thought about it, and found that he agreed with the farmer. He didn't really want the hassle, particularly not when it would involve talking quite slowly to one of DEFRA's phone-an-idiots. He didn't really want the conversation. And besides, what could he tell them, really? What, exactly, had he seen last night? How could he prove it? Better just to do some research on the quiet, and mention it if it seemed important later.

'Yes,' he heard himself saying, 'I think you're right.'

'OK. Good,' Mike replied. 'You all right, Alan?' he said, after a pause. The farmer didn't really want to ask, and Alan didn't really want to answer, but you couldn't see something like they both had without at least saying something. As Mike spoke, Alan felt the buzzing in his head again. He didn't know if it had got louder or if he had simply noticed it again.

'I'm fine,' he lied. 'You?'

'Fine,' said the farmer. Another pause. There was nothing else to say. 'OK,' said Mike. 'Well, see you then, Alan,' he said, suddenly trying to sound cheerful.

'Yeah, bye, Mr White.'

VI

Alan hated doing bitch spays almost more than he hated being on call. The dog booked in today was a particularly fine specimen; a great fat Rottweiler, being spayed so that it could have no more puppies to expand its already massive brood, and only then because the last two times the bitch had whelped it had needed caesareans, cutting into the owner's profit margin.

Alan sighed as he looked into the brown eyes buried in the rolls of skin. Poor bloody dog, he thought, just an innocent in all this. But it's you and me stuck with the difficult part.

His sympathy for 'Athena' lasted until he tried to anaesthetise the animal. It was wriggly, fat, and vicious. It took Alan and three nurses to hold it down, even after its hefty pre-med, and when it was finally asleep he failed several attempts at placing the ET tube. On the fourth attempt at peering into the fleshy mass of the throat he finally visualised the larynx. Great, he thought, as the tube slotted down into the cavernous trachea. Easy bit over. Now for the spay.

He was, as he got older, becoming increasingly of the opinion that owners of fat dogs should have to come in to spay their own animals. It made the surgery ten times more difficult — harder to see anything, much harder to tie any ligatures as fingers slipped on the slimy catgut, and fat had a tendency to ooze blood and a horrid milky fluid throughout such operations, making the surgical drape look like the wrapping from a vampires' fast food shop.

He sighed deeply as he began to scrub up, watching Sam and Alice manoeuvre the dog between them onto its back and start to clip its massive belly. He wasn't up to this. He wasn't in the mood. He'd been putting it off all morning hoping Cameron would come through and do it with his usual fearless enthusiasm for surgery. It wasn't that much different from operating on a cow, after all. Unfortunately, Cameron had been called to an unspecified horse emergency only ten minutes before (Alan was willing to bet it wasn't such an emergency that the owner had forgotten to put her eyeliner on) and there were now no other ops on the board.

Alan rubbed his hand under the chlorhexidine wash and sighed once more. He'd been feeling strange all morning, and the buzzing had only been part of it. At first he had thought it was due to lack of sleep but it seemed now to be something more, something stranger. He remembered the way one of the owners had looked at him this morning. It was a young woman who had somehow managed to pour coffee all over her cat while simultaneously frying her computer. The cat was not badly burned. Alan had given out some anti-inflammatory cream and told her to come back in a few days for a check, but the woman had been acting very strangely, avoiding his gaze. When he turned back from his computer after booking the consult, she had been staring directly at him, her face a mixture of puzzlement and concern.

He shook his head as he opened the brush. What a weirdo. He'd make sure he wasn't around when she came back in a few days. Still, something about the way she'd been looking at him...

The thoughts vanished from his mind as the mammoth task ahead came back to him. Shaking his hands, he stepped into theatre, looking dejectedly at the enormous beast on the table.

'It'll be all right,' said Sam, cheerfully, but Alan knew she was trying to convince herself as well as him. The last one like this had taken nearly two hours, and Alan must have broken the world record for profanity during that time. Still, he nodded back and tried to smile. She opened his kit for him and he placed the drape over the rottie's abdomen, then clipped a fresh scalpel blade into place.

He was feeling stranger than ever. Maybe it was the heat in here — the giant surgical light, and the poor ventilation, with him in his gown and gloves. It didn't usually get to him this much, though.

'OK,' he said. 'Let's get it over with.'

He made the first incision. Blood welled up immediately, not stopping despite Alan holding a swab on the wound for over a minute. Great, he thought. Von Willebrands, knowing my luck.

Laboriously he cut his way down through the fat to the external abdominal oblique muscle. The buzzing was stronger now. As he cut through the muscle and opened the abdomen he thought he felt the scalpel blade wobbling in the holder. He opened his mouth to ask Sam what size blade it was when the scalpel suddenly leaped forwards, out of his hand. As he watched with his mouth open, the blade hovered above the wound in the giant dog's abdomen for a heartbeat, then plunged its way forward into Athena's spleen.

Chapter Four

I

Somewhere else...

There is a vast sea in another place, a vast and terrible sea. It is a place you have seen before, and it is a place you will see again, although no one alive would recognise it.

It ebbs and flows as if with a tide, although there is no moon above it, and it bubbles like a cheap prop in a student production of Macbeth.

Above the bubbling sea, storm clouds are gathering. There is a feeling of immense pressure, like a valve that is about to blow. Energies are building up here, second by second. The sea begins to froth with frenzy. The energies need to be released, but there is nowhere for them to go. Something is stopping them. A balance that is as old as life itself has been upset.

The souls are trapped.

II

Kate swore as the bus cut in front of her little Metro and headed off down Union Street. The traffic was getting worse, of course. It always was. Bristol was going the way of all the cities. Kate had decided several times to get a bike for work. It was cheaper, greener, healthier, just better in so many ways, but she never did. She knew deep down that whatever arguments she could muster up for biking to work, they always came up against one that she would probably never surmount. She simply couldn't be bothered. She'd actually rather spend her mornings swearing at bus drivers and gripping the steering wheel, so long as it meant she could spend it in her own private little world, with her own music, shut off from humanity, happily burning sticky bits of long-dead animals and plants and converting them into a gas that would turn the planet into a gigantic storage heater.

As she thumped the steering wheel in annoyance and anger, a cooler, more reflective part of her despaired at the nature of humanity.

'Use your mirrors, you stupid twat!' she yelled.

She didn't know why she was getting stressed anyway. It wasn't as if she was in a hurry. She had all afternoon to get to work. No one was expecting her to be there, after all. The only reason she had to go in was to try and recreate her experiment of last night. The computer was completely ruined. Not only that, she had also managed to pour coffee all over Roger and had to rush him to the vets. Now the car had the odour of a vehicle that has contained an unhappy cat, which made Kate unhappy as well.

It was probably that making her impatient. That and the headache, which still hadn't left her since the early hours of this morning.

Oh... and the end of the world, of course. Mustn't forget that.

III

There weren't many students around this time of year. Most of them were back home, revising for exams in the New Year, but a few lost souls still made the trip to the library every day, even this close to Christmas.

There was a security card system in place at the physics building, a new introduction, presumably in case terrorists felt the pressing need to hijack a mass spectrometer, or to get up to date with the more obscure aspects of superstring theory. Kate was not, in any sense, in favour of the new identity cards the present Home Secretary seemed so keen on pushing forwards. Not only was she unsure of how a small strip of plastic could prevent some lunatic leaving a bomb in a bin, but she also knew that she didn't want a card that identified her down to her dental records and DNA, because she would lose it almost immediately. She knew this because she had lost her security card for the physics building three times already, and consequently had to go through the same charade with the security guard on the door as she had to every morning, even though it was the same guard on the same door.

'Good morning,' she said, smiling to the besuited man standing in front of the doors, as she had done one hundred and thirty-seven times before. The man showed not a glimmer of recognition when he looked at Kate.

'Can I help you, Miss?' said the guard, not smiling.

'Erm, yes... it's me, again, Kate Schekter,' Kate said. There was no response from the guard. 'I was here yesterday, you see, I've lost my...'

The man interrupted her. 'Have you got a card, Miss?' he said, painfully slowly.

'That's what I'm trying to tell you,' Kate replied.

'Visitor, are you?'

'No,' Kate said, hearing the echo of this much-repeated conversation in her mind's ear. 'I'm not a visitor.'

'Could I see your security card, please?'

'I'm trying to tell you. I haven't got one. Look, you let me in yesterday. Can you just...'

'I thought you said you weren't a visitor?' the guard said. Lines of suspicion were creeping across his face, very, very slowly.

'I'm not. Look, yesterday, remember, I showed you my picture, just behind the desk. If you'll just...'

'Can't let just anyone in,' the guard was saying, ignoring her. 'Can't be too careful, nowadays.'

'Yes,' said Kate, impatiently. 'You can. I have lost my card. I lost it three weeks ago, and I'm still waiting for a replacement. If you remember...'

'If you lost your card,' the guard said, glacially, 'you should 'ave a temporary one.'

Kate was quiet for a moment. She looked at the floor and muttered something.

'Pardon?'

'I said I lost it!' said Kate. 'I work here! My picture is on the board not ten feet behind you! I showed you it yesterday, and the God knows how many yesterdays before that! Let me in!'

The guard was silent for a long time. Kate wondered what help this brain-donor would be if a terrorist actually did turn up. The whole world had gone crazy since that terrible day in September, but it was going crazier still if it thought anything like this would stop some lunatic doing whatever they liked whenever they wanted. The ones who had taken over the planes had used pottery knives, for God's sake! Anyone with the strength of conviction to destroy the most famous buildings in the world with pottery knives was unlikely to be stopped by this lemon in a suit.

'Hmm,' said the guard, then there was another pause. 'Well,' he said eventually, with a this-may-lose-me-my-job-but-just-for-you sigh, 'let's have a look at this picture then.'

IV

Kate's office was a mess, of course, as all of them were. The professors and their students took great pride in the amount of clutter. The messier the office, the unwritten rule went, the greater the science being carried out in the office must be. Kate's office was of intermediate mess, somewhere in between untidy and chaotic. She knew if she worked hard her office could be chaotic within a year or two, and she would be able to hold her head up with the greatest clutterers in the university.

It wasn't the clutter that was on her mind today, though. She had to rerun the experiment. She had to check the results. She found herself hoping that it was true — how exciting would that be? Then she remembered what it would mean if they were, and decided a little sadly it would probably be better if the simulation was flawed. She sat down in front of her PC. The disk with the back-up copies of her algorithms on it had been a coffee casualty along with the computer and the cat. She couldn't remember if she had had the presence of mind to back them up on her computer at work. She could remember thinking that she needed to, but that didn't guarantee it. She drummed her fingers impatiently on her desk as the machine went through its interminable start-up sequence, which seemed to get a little longer every time she did it. It always took just exactly long enough for Kate to think the whole thing had crashed. In fact, the act of her saying the 'Oh…' or 'Oh, bloody hell' always seemed to be the trigger it needed to spring into action.

It seemed to be taking an extremely long time today, even by its own poor standards. The screen went black. Nothing happened. Kate drummed her fingers again. Still nothing. Surely it didn't normally take this long. Again her fingers tapped the desk. The computer did nothing.

'Oh, bl…' Kate said. The computer sprang into life.

V

She hadn't saved it, of course. The hard disk was empty of her algorithms, and of the simulation. She'd known it, of course, but she hadn't wanted to believe it until she could see for certain. All gone. Two months' work completely wasted. It was possible that something could be recovered from the hard disk of her espresso computer at home, but most of it had been on the CD, which had simultaneously been electrified, melted, and sprayed with cat urine. Kate wasn't sure, but she thought that might invalidate the warranty.

She leaned her head against the cool, bright monitor, and closed her eyes. What now? She still needed to tell someone, but she had no evidence. Was there time to write it all again, to confirm the result? She thought about sitting, starting over, typing and fiddling and staring at the monitor for hours and hours, while her brain pounded as if it was trying to escape via her eye sockets. Not a happy thought. What, then?

She had no choice.

VI

The faded legend 'Professor Lattman' was just about readable on the grimy smoked glass of Will's office. Through it, Kate could just about see a figure hunched over the desk inside. She knocked on the door and the figure jumped.

'Kom,' came the voice from inside. Kate opened the door slowly and entered.

Will, being the head of department, was entitled to far more clutter than Kate, a lowly PhD student, and he took his clutter seriously. Kate considered him her mentor in this at least, though he did occasionally help out in matters of physics too.

He was sitting behind his desk, looking uncomfortable. He had recently bought one of those chairs which looks like a curious device intended for either torture or exercise; the idea being that you knelt on it, sitting on a seat perched above the knee rests. Will had claimed, with the enthusiasm he brought to anything he worked on, that the chair was ergonomically designed and was the most comfortable object ever designed by any member of the human race. It was good for your back, too. He had spent several weeks trying to look happy in it but had obviously finally given up the charade and was now resigned to looking uncomfortable. It didn't really help that he had the kind of frame that didn't kneel down tremendously easily, being several stone overweight, and had reached the age that the word 'creaky' had been designed for.

His face brightened into a smile as Kate entered the room.

'Ah, Kate!' he said, his north-German accent still strong despite twenty years at the faculty, 'So good to see you. I would shake your hand but…' he gestured at the torture device below him, indicating it would take some minutes to extricate himself from the most comfortable chair in the world. Kate smiled and nodded, sitting herself in the more traditional chair in front of the desk, having first swept several pages of equations, two textbooks, a calculator and a shiny metal thing that looked a little like a carburettor onto the floor.

Kate was slightly touched to see Will run his large knobbly hand through his thinning hair, rearranging it into a less chaotic fashion, for her benefit. She had a great liking for Professor Lattman. He was friendly and approachable, acceptably weird, and possessed none of the arrogance or aloofness that most people in the small university world at his level usually thrived on. She thought of him as a sort of benign Van Helsing figure, though she would never say as such to his face. He beamed at her; his thin, half-moon glasses perched on the very tip of his wide, red nose.

'So, my dear, how are those delightful children of yours?' Will said.

'Erm… non-existent,' Kate offered.

Will frowned. Chit-chat was not his forte. He gave up on the attempt.'So, my dear,' he said, smoothing over the awkward gaffe he had made by simply ignoring it. 'What can I do for you today?'

Kate leaned forwards onto the desk, but leaned back again when she felt her elbow enter a patch of something sticky and wet.

'I've lost my work, Professor.'

Lattman raised his eyebrows in polite incomprehension.

'You know I've been working, just to test my programs, on this new accelerator they're building near London? The Relativistic Massive Ion Collider?'

Lattman's face relaxed and he smiled and nodded, pushing his thin glasses back up his nose, where they began again their slow slide to freedom.

'Ah, yes. The RMIC. In Kent, I believe?'

'Well, I was working on it last night, trying something new, just to see if I could refine the projections, correct for some random factors, and… something happened.'

'Oh,' said Lattman. 'What was that?'

Kate shrugged. 'Well, I spilled my drink all over the computer, that's what happened. But just before I did, the projections started to work, to predict what would happen when the accelerator is switched on.'

Kate paused for dramatic effect, but the professor, still not completely at home with English, rather rudely refused to say 'And...?' so she just had to carry on as if she'd forgotten something.

'Professor, have you ever heard of strangelets?'

This time the professor frowned a little. 'Hmm. I believe so. A blob of the most fundamental matter, so I believe. Theoretically made up of strange quarks, as well as the more usual up or down variety. There is a chance, though I believe it is very small, of them forming with any heavy ion collision, such as when cosmic rays smash into the moon.'

Kate nodded. 'Right. Or when someone switches on a relativistic massive ion collider.'

Lattman's eyebrows rose slightly. They would have risen more, Kate suspected, had they not been so large and bushy as to require more muscular effort than the professor's brow could muster.

'Kate, I don't think...'

'Professor, in my simulation last night, just before it crashed, the accelerator produced a strangelet after only a few hours of becoming operational.'

Lattman leaned back in his chair, smiling indulgently. 'Yes, as theory would predict. But such things are not to be worried upon. The strangelets are not stable.'

'This one was, Professor! Stable enough to convert the matter next to it. To create more strangelets!'

Again she paused for dramatic effect. Again Lattman failed to indulge her.

'Don't you see what that means? A chain reaction! The next strangelet survives long enough to convert the matter next to it and before you know it... you wouldn't be able to stop the reaction once it started!'

'You are saying these strangelets would eat the world,

yes?' Lattman asked. Through his accent Kate couldn't tell quite what his tone of voice implied, but his expression was enough. She suddenly felt stupid, unsure. Perhaps it was wrong. She'd only had time to run the simulation once. If only she hadn't spilt the bloody coffee. She nodded slowly.

'You have the figures, then?'

Kate opened her mouth, then closed it again, feeling very foolish. Something approaching pity crept into the old professor's eyes. He steepled his hands together in front of him on the desk, in a very Van Helsing moment, looking at them rather than his student.

'Kate, you know the chances of what you propose. They are very slim.' He had reverted to his lecturer's voice now.

'Yes,' Kate said gloomily. 'Less than twenty chances in a billion. But, Professor, it happened! I saw…' Kate caught Lattman's expression, though he was still staring resolutely at his fingers.

'I suggest you rerun the analysis. When you have proof, come back to me.'

Kate nodded, and tried to smile. She wanted to point out that the RMIC would become active before the New Year, and it would take her months to reprogram all her work. She wanted to shout and scream and run around in a panic, and get Lattman to do the same. It would be futile. What could the professor do without any evidence? Certainly he couldn't risk his academic reputation on the say-so of a PhD student who had drowned her end of the world prophecies in hot coffee and cat piss.

As they exchanged pleasantries and Kate left the office, she found herself reminded of the story of Superman. Superman's dad had found something out, some terrible secret that would end the world of Krypton. He had tried to warn everyone then, and look what happened to him. Laughed out of the community. Branded insane. The same thing would happen to Lattman. OK, his son probably wouldn't end up a superhero in pants on some distant planet, but the story was broadly similar. He had been ridiculed. And Krypton had still exploded.

Feeling thoroughly despondent, Kate worked briefly on reprogramming her equations then spent most of the rest of the afternoon playing Minesweeper. She managed to beat her own time on expert level, so the day hadn't been a total loss.

VI

She found it hard to sleep that night. Her headache, which had been her constant companion all day, had got much worse as darkness fell. Driving home, she found herself thinking of the vet she had seen today, in the morning with Roger. She had seen the things again. She hadn't seen them for years, but when he had entered the room they were all around him, a ghostly shifting shroud of colours and lights.

Back in her days as a medium she had grown used to them. She didn't have a bloody clue what they were, of course. They never spoke to her. She didn't even think they were human. Perhaps they never had been. But they always seemed to surround the bereaved, or the desperate. She had told the people their loved ones were near, were talking to them, all the time wondering what she was actually seeing.

In time, she had become disillusioned with the illusions she offered. She knew there was something there that few others could see, but she became tired of profiting from something she didn't really understand herself, of offering false hope. That was when the visions had begun to fade. Slowly at first, but they became harder and harder to distinguish as the weeks went by. She couldn't remember the last one she'd seen. But today, there had been the headache, and then the vet, surrounded by so many, so thick, that it had been difficult to see his face, as if he was walking around with his own personal smoke generator. She had barely listened to what he had said. Fortunately Roger seemed OK when she got back to her flat. Perhaps she wouldn't take him back. She could see that the vet had been a bit confused by her reaction. Probably sees a lot of weirdies though. Just another one. Another weirdie.

Sleep was elusive. Her brain was in active mode; running thoughts round and round without actually taking them anywhere, the same worries over and over. She turned over, hoping this would somehow dislodge the thoughts. It didn't work. There was a brief lull and then the treadmill began again.

worry worry Roger worry end of world worry worry strangelets worry computer insurance worry worry phone mum birthday soon worry worry strange vet worry worry TV licence worry worry what's that light?

She opened her eyes. There was indeed a bluish light creeping in under the door. It hadn't been there before. She knew she had turned the lights off. Brilliant, a voice in her head said, bringing with it a shot of adrenaline and a dose of fear. Burglars.

Her first thought was to shout 'Hello?' Her second thought was of all the young women in horror films who had followed this course of action and had wound up regretting it, albeit not for very long. She sat up. The light was definitely there, a bluish glow, which seemed familiar to her, though she could not say why. It seemed to be getting brighter.

What if she got out bed, and investigated? That seemed a bit close to slasher movies too. But what option did that leave her? To just sit and wait? Didn't seem such a great option either.

While numerous scenarios ran through her own personal simulator inside her skull, the glow continued to get brighter. Whatever was causing it must be right outside the door.

Kate swung her legs out from under the sheets, still unsure of what to do. It didn't matter anyway. The glow became brighter still, and suddenly the light intensified, seeped around the door like radioactive fog, and coalesced into a form on the other side. Kate's side. The form was one that Kate knew well. Something she had thought was gone forever.

She tried not to scream. She failed.

Hanging in front of her bedroom door, formed out of a glowing cloud of smoke, was the image of Kate's recently deceased personal computer. One word filled the monitor screen in large, white, alarmed letters.

'ESCAPE'

Chapter Five

I

George swore imaginatively as his car swerved off the road onto the pavement, back onto the road, and then once more onto the pavement. He slammed his brakes on and came to a halt half an inch in front of a surprised sycamore. The tree was totally shaken up by the event, and didn't really get back into the swing of photosynthesising for a full forty-eight hours.

George, on the other hand, was more blasé about the whole affair. He glanced down at his lap, where the gloopy liquid that he had bought as part of his breakfast had escaped its plastic carton. The McSludge, or whatever it was called this week, had seeped through the map of Bristol which it had been perched on, narrowly missed his mobile phone, and was now working its way through his jeans. He stuck his finger into the goo, and then sucked it thoughtfully. It was probably, he reflected, because he was trying to interact with all the objects on his lap at once that his driving had not been up to par, and had nearly caused a painful interaction with the poor sycamore tree in front of him.

After another moment he peeled the map off his jeans, stared at it trying to work out where he was, and sighed.

It had not been a good day for paranormal activities. There were never any around when you wanted them. And George wanted them all the time. They were his bread and butter—or, more accurately in George's case, they were his bacon double cheeseburger meal. He lived for them. Yearned for them. Thrived on them. He stayed awake, late at night, just knowing, deep down inside, that there was something going on with the world. Something humming away at the corners of reality.

He didn't know what it was, of course, but he could feel it. He could see the shape of it. It was somewhere in there, he knew, in the fish rain and the flying saucers and the men with large beards and clipboards huddled around a spoon, trying to see if it would bend. Other people had religion. George had the paranormal.

He had been fascinated for as long as he could remember. It embarrassed his friends and his parents, even, if he was honest, himself, but he couldn't let it go. It was his life. He knew that one day, underneath one of these mysteries, he would find THE ANSWER. The answer to what, exactly, he wasn't quite sure. He would know when he found it.

The problem was the reality gap. The acres-wide gap between the mystery of the strange and unknowable, and the humdrum, dismal stupidity of actually investigating such events.

He thought that working for 'Mysterious World' magazine would be the window, the stepping stone to true understanding. He somehow thought that within a few months, THE ANSWER would come to him. It wasn't like that, of course. Every 'mystery' he investigated shook his faith a little bit more. However excitingly he wrote the stories up, however many question marks and exclamation marks he crammed into the last paragraphs, he knew that it wasn't 'it'. Often he convinced himself while he was writing, but there would always some scientific, rational (what a horrible word) part of his mind that looked in utter disgust at what he was doing. You know what really happened, it said. No arcane fields, no aliens. Simply a lot of lost people and some blind faith. Why do you do it?

He ignored the voice as best as he could. He preferred the part of his mind that tantalisingly whispered THE ANSWER to him in the darkest times of the night. He allowed himself to be lulled by its siren call. It was simply a shame that it buggered off when he was talking to these people, and he was left with Mr Rational (ugh!).

Take this morning, for example. Martin (Robart, his boss, a Frenchman who claimed to be a direct line descendent of Jean D'Arc, and who instituted a no smoking policy in his office) had given him three assignments. Already George had investigated the first two and was wondering how the hell he was going to write them up in any way spooky or mysterious, or even interesting.

The first had been the unusual disappearance of a cat belonging to a lady in the Clifton area. The cat in question had been with the owner, a squat fat woman with a ruddy face and greying hair, for twelve years, and had never wandered off before. The woman reported seeing strange lights in the sky several days before and after the moggy had vanished, then one night the feline never came home. The owner had asked around all the vet surgeries and animal charities in the area, but no one had seen it. The woman then had heard the cat whispering to her in the darkness one night, telling her it was now in a better place, far from the cares and worries of this planet. The woman had naturally come to the conclusion that aliens had taken her cat from her, to give it a better life amongst the stars.

When George arrived the first thing he had discovered was that the cat had disappeared on the Fifth of November. The second was that the cat had a propensity for sleeping in warm, damp-smelling places — a large pile of wood, for instance. The third was that the night the woman had seen the cat reappear, she had been sharing her grief with a large bottle of gin. He had filed the story under 'Alien Abductions (subset: pets)', thanked the lady for his appalling cup of tea, and headed off to cover the second story.

It had been little better. He was covering the story of a young woman who had discovered she was the reincarnation of Richard Burton during a hypnotherapy session to cure her obsessive counting disorder. The interview had been hard to conduct for George, as the woman spent most of her time shouting out the numbers on George's Dictaphone as they counted up during the interview, and spent the rest of the time asking if he knew Elizabeth Taylor's telephone number. The minimal research George had done for his task had prepared him enough to notice that the lady had been born four years before Richard Burton had died. When he pointed this out the lady had got quite hostile, and he had only escaped by throwing a matchbox open on the floor, and heading for the door while she frantically counted the spilled matches out loud. Probably not one for the magazine there.

He was now on his way to the site of the third 'paranormal' experience to strike Bristol in the last week or so. At least this one's in a pub, he thought, as he folded the soggy map up and restarted the car. I could really do with a drink.

II

The pub was called 'The Merrie Tudor', and had an awful plastic picture of a large fat man with a beard, a grin and a large pint of beer alongside its name. It was one of the medieval theme pubs that had sprung up recently, the latest craze since the 'Irish' theme pub. George seemed to remember it had used to be a grimy pub called 'The Friendship', though its clientele had been anything but.

The pub was clearly upwardly mobile at the moment. The windows had been washed, and the hideous plastic bearded Tudor figure purchased. Presumably, George thought, this was to tempt a better class of patrons within. He stepped through the door and breathed in the ambience.

Whatever the owners may have hoped, entering 'The Merrie Tudor' was not like stepping into another world. Well, not the kind of world it would be worth leaving the old one for. The pub had been given a lick of paint over the grime, and several mock-medieval items hung from the walls and ceiling. The benches had been specially modified to medieval style, with the effect that they looked very similar to normal benches but were surprisingly uncomfortable. With Christmas approaching the thoughtful bar staff had hung tinsel and light from some of the more offensive items of medieval weaponry and torture. The air smelled quite authentically medieval, too. George saw, to his surprise, that it was working. The pub was quite full, even thought it was a weekday lunchtime.

He looked around the pub for a moment. The place was full enough that it took him a few seconds before he spotted the fireplace. Aha, he thought. Therein lies a mystery. There was no fire blazing in the hearth, despite the December chill in the air. No one seemed to be sitting at any of the tables by the fireplace. George felt a little thrill traverse his spine despite the morning's disappointments. Perhaps this was it. The story was certainly bizarre enough to seem unlikely that anyone would have made it up or imagined it.

He crossed the smoky lounge, found a patch of bar that wasn't wholly sticky, and leaned across it, with the half-hopeful, half-expectant expression that everyone else waiting at the bar had. After a while the barman (short, fat and bald, in line with stereotypes everywhere — he even had ruddy cheeks) looked at him.

'Ar-harr, me merry hearty,' the barman said in a dismal tone. 'What can I get yer now?' His idea of a Tudor barman was obviously based upon a suicidally depressed pirate. George thought for a moment about responding in kind, but dismissed the idea. He could see the fat man's heart wasn't in it, despite the Henry VIII-style hat perched on his head. It looked like a long-dead suet pudding. George looked down the bar at the pumps of local ale. There was one with a picture of a large cockerel at the end. That would do. He squinted to make out the name.

'Oh... Erm... Bishop's Cock, please,' he asked, trying to smile as if he enjoyed the joke name. The barman didn't bother.

'Flagon or tankard?' he asked.

'What's the difference?'

'Tankard's eight quid,' said the barman.

'Oh... flagon, then, please,' said George, hoping this was the cheaper option.

The barman nodded and wiped his nose across his arm, leaving a thin stream of mucous glistening along his forearm. 'Anything else?' he asked, as he pulled the humorously named beer into a large metal jug.

'Actually...' said George slowly, 'I was hoping to ask you some questions about the fire.'

The barman, who had been watching the beer pour into the jug, looked up at George, his deep-set eyes narrowed.

'Oh, yeah?' he said, 'You the reporter lad, then?'

The tone of voice of the barman irritated him. Slightly condescending, slightly disbelieving. Why didn't people respect reporters any more? What had they ever done to anybody? Still, he couldn't be bothered to get annoyed today. He'd been through enough this morning. Get it over with quick, have a drink, then he could moan about it to Alan, in order to prevent Alan moaning to him all night about how much he hated being a vet, as he did every night.

'That's right,' he said, nodding and smiling brightly as he took the jug off the barman. The beer sloshed over the side of the jug onto his hand. He quaffed the beer, as he believed you were supposed to in places like this. Quaffing is very much like drinking, except that most of the drink ends up on the quaffer's cheeks and down his front rather than in his mouth.

George wiped his cheeks and smiled at the barman, who didn't.

'So,' the fat man said, doubtfully, 'how do you want to do this?'

George put down the jug on the table and fished about in his pocket for his Dictaphone. He took the small plastic shape and plopped it down on the soggy bar towel. The barman looked at it resignedly.

'You not makin' notes, then?' he asked as George flicked the switch to 'record'.

George shook his head. 'Not a fast enough writer, I'm afraid. Now,' he said, settling back on his stool, and picking up his jug of beer, 'tell me what happened.'

'Will that thing work with all this noise in 'ere?' the barman said, frowning at the Dictaphone.

'Oh, sure. No problem. Very sensitive,' George said

reassuringly. He looked around the bar. Actually there was no chance of the Dictaphone picking up any meaningful conversation with all the other sounds in the smoky lounge, but as George was pretty sure he hadn't loaded a tape in this morning he wasn't unduly worried. He never listened to the tapes anyway, as most of his reports were complete fiction. Maybe one day he would cover the story where the fine details actually made any difference at all, but he doubted that it would be today.

The barman shrugged, then leaned in to George, his voice a conspiratorial whisper.

'Happened last night, it did. Not so many people in 'ere, of course. Everyone out shopping this close to Christmas.' He nodded sagely, as if he had just imparted one of the mystical truths of the ancient world.

'So what actually happened?' George asked, impatiently.

'Just a few people in last night, but we were havin' a special. Tryin' to get more customers in, you see. Nothin' people like more than a pig on a spit. Thought it'd get 'em through the doors.'

George's mind presented him with several suggestions for what it might prefer than a pig on a spit, but he remained quiet.

'Didn't work, though. Bloody shops are all open too late nowadays. Had a few executives in, few regulars but nothin' more. We decided to go ahead anyway. Didn't want to waste the pig, did we?'

George shook his head, mumbling, 'Course not,' through a mouthful of Bishop's Cock.

'So we spits it, takes it out and puts it above the fire. That's when the trouble started.' George was finding it difficult to concentrate through the man's mangling of his tenses. He could almost hear his English teacher spinning in her grave. Probably the only reason he couldn't was that his English teacher was alive and well. Wherever she was, she was probably spinning.

'The fire wouldn't light?' said George, who had heard most of the story already from his editor.

The barman shook his head. 'That wasn't it. We got a fire lit all right.'

George put down the beer and rubbed his eyes. Terrific. Three in a row. Here he was supposed to be covering the story of a pub fire that mysteriously refused to light, and he'd fallen at the first hurdle.

'I see,' said George, finishing the last of his drink.

'We got a fire lit, all right,' the barman repeated, his eyes narrowing even further, his voice even lower. 'There was somethin' wrong with it,' he breathed, looking over at the fireplace. 'It was…' He blinked, and passed a meaty hand over his eyes. His ruddy complexion had paled. George was intrigued despite himself. Whatever had happened had certainly unnerved the barman.

'What?' he asked.

'P'raps you should come and have a look for yourself,' the barman said.

'It's still there?' George said.

The barman shook his head. 'No. But it'll do it again. I've tried three times this morning. Just the same. It doesn't last long but…' his voice tailed off into silence. He turned, and headed off from behind the bar towards the fireplace.

George dropped his jug on the bar, grabbed his pointless Dictaphone, and followed the barman.

III

The fireplace was one of those that was trying to both look as Olde Worlde as possible but also to comply with all relevant fire safety regulations. Unfortunately, George suspected, it failed on both counts. It was large; large enough to fit, say, the carcass of a disembowelled pig within its confines, and surrounded by brickwork, which had been painted black with shields on it in a feeble attempt to make it look like it had stood there for five hundred years, rather than only three. The fire itself was surrounded by dark cast iron. Several logs were piled in the hearth, and a metal grate stood in front of it. The logs were unburned.

The barman hurried over to it, then turned to wait for George. By now several people were watching the spectacle. The barman started to speak, and then stopped, seemingly waiting for something. George held the Dictaphone out in front of him and pressed one of the buttons at random.

'Go on,' he said to the sweating man in front of him.

'S'better if you just watch,' mumbled the barman. 'Haven't you got a camera or anything?'

George thought of his digital camera, sitting on his bed-side table at home.

'Erm... I'm just here to cover the story,' he lied. 'They're sending a photographer along later.'

The barman grunted, and turned to the fire. George looked at the logs stacked in the fireplace. 'I thought you'd lit the fire today. Have you changed the logs?'

The barman said nothing but fumbled around the side of the fire for a long box of matches. There were several fire-lighters stacked in between the logs, all as untouched as the wood. By now a small group of people had surrounded them. The bar seemed suddenly very quiet.

The barman very slowly struck a match, presumably to try and instil a sense of awe and wonder into the proceedings. Unfortunately he struck it so slowly that it didn't light, and he was forced to repeat the procedure. The match lit, and the bar-man plunged it into the stack of fuel with one last mysterious glance at George.

The fire lit immediately. George frowned, and opened his mouth, a sarcastic comment in his throat.

It never made it past his larynx. He looked again at the flame that had sprung up. It was pale white, flickering and shimmering in the way that fire should do, but that was the only thing that was right about it. Everything else was wrong. It felt wrong. It smelled wrong. George could quite clearly see through it to the fireplace behind. He struggled to remember if fire was normally transparent. He didn't think so. It appeared in some strange way not to be whole. Lifeless.

The flame was already sputtering out. Wordlessly, without taking his eyes off George, the barman thrust his pudgy hand straight into the fire. A gasp arose from the impromptu audience, but George was already half-expecting the result.

The barman did not wince with pain. He held George's gaze levelly. As the fire slid away into nothing, he pulled his hand from the fireplace, and held it up to the people gathered around him.

It was untouched.

Chapter Six

I

Alan breathed a sigh of relief as the door to his consulting room closed behind the woman with her Border terrier and her extremely unpleasant child.

In the seven minutes that they had been in his room, the awful kid had managed to reboot Alan's computer, empty his clinical waste bin all over the floor, break his otoscope and stick its hand as far as it could into his sharps bin. Fortunately the sharps bin had not been full enough to cause the child any damage. Alan had watched the infant whirlwind destroy his room. So had the mother of it. She had not said one word to it during the whole time, and so Alan felt he couldn't either, though he decided to change this policy when the sprog began to pick up scalpel blades with a dangerous gleam in its eye.

Didn't matter. They were gone now. Alan hated school holidays. Christmas was usually a quiet time for him, at least on the small animal front. Farm animals were a different matter. No one seemed to have related the story of little baby Jesus to cows and sheep, and so rather rudely they obstinately persisted to give birth, or develop twin lamb disease, or allow their internal organs to fall out of various orifices, and then tread on them for good measure. Poor bloody things. The kinds of awful things that happened to farm animals were the stuff of nightmares, this association being made stronger because they usually happened at night. In fact, most of the time Alan saw cows, sheep and pigs something so horribly unpleasant was happening to them that his memory associated them with bad things. It was getting to the stage where he got the shivers just from looking at a beef burger. And that was before his see-through calf. He closed his eyes. He wasn't supposed to be thinking about that, was he?

If the nights were still horrible, at least the days were becoming quieter as people went Christmas shopping. Most of his consults were vaccinations at this time of year, and Alan was getting sick of hearing himself make his little joke about giving the animals their 'Christmas presents' as he stuck the needle in. It was a nice line, a client-pleaser. Fundamentally this is what Alan was. He just wanted a quiet life. If the client and the animal could leave a little bit happier than when they came in, so much the better. Never mind if the animal actually needed to be treated or not. He'd often find himself nodding and reaching for the antibiotics just because the owner insisted, and he couldn't be bothered to argue with them.

The tragedy was that he could see what he was doing, and on some level he despised himself for it. Every time he went to a continuing education lecture, read a veterinary journal, or (more commonly) watched an episode of ER, he would come in fired up and ready for working the next day. Bring 'em on, he'd think. Bring on your diseases, your mystery medical cases, for I will cure them! He was going to save some lives today, damn it! After the second or third itchy dog, or anal gland, or dog that panted a bit, he would find his enthusiasm evaporating. By half-ten it would have vanished completely and he would sleepwalk through rest of the morning's work, dreaming of his coffee.

It wasn't that he didn't care, of course. Or even that he was terrible at his job. He knew plenty of vets worse than him. He knew he was his own worst critic, that he beat himself up about his working practices far more than anyone else would, but he also knew he would probably never change either. It was just... just that he felt he was wasting his life. When he was younger he had been deeply troubled by an overactive conscience, as he saw it. It would nag and bother him constantly about the state of the world, of humanity, about the exploitation of animals, about their silent suffering. Eventually, he had given in, and decided to become a vet, in an effort to shut the bloody thing up. If he could keep his conscience quiet with his day job, then in the evenings and weekends he could get on with enjoying himself.

It hadn't quite worked out like that, of course. One of the main problems was that he never seemed to have any evenings or weekends that weren't wet, cold, smelly and stressful. The other problem was that being a vet wasn't enough for the voice that nagged him. It knew he was just trying to fob it off, trying to fool it into thinking he was making a difference. It knew the truth, deep down. It constantly reminded Alan that there were animals in far more need of treatment than the ones he saw every day. It nagged at him. He did his best to ignore it.

All in all it would have been fair to say Alan was unhappy in his work. This Christmas he was even more unhappy than usual. Partially because of the fact that he had somehow managed to end up being on call for both Christmas Day and New Year's Day. Partially because his fiancée had left him a month previously. His parents lived several hours away and would be having Christmas with the rest of the family, and so Alan was facing the terrifying prospect that his only face-to-face conversation on Christmas Day would be with a farmer. Or, which was far worse, a horse client.

The other fly in the ointment of course, he thought as he opened the door to call in the next patient, was that he seemed to be possessed.

II

It had been little things, at first: The scalpel that seemed possessed of a mind of its own, which had decided to attempt a splenectomy unguided by human hand during his last bitch spay. Sam, his nurse, had fortunately been monitoring Athena's breathing at the time, and Alan had managed to extract the offending implement and stop the bleeding without too much swearing, though it had seriously reduced the enjoyment of the rest of the operation (something that he wouldn't have believed was possible). He had managed to explain it to himself as fevered imaginings because of his interrupted sleep, and had largely forgotten about it. But later that afternoon his computer had switched itself off and on several times, and at one point during a long discussion with a lady about her elderly, incontinent, violent shih-tzu, he had watched in horrified amazement as the words 'Put the little git to sleep!' had typed themselves across his computer screen. Fortunately Alan managed to interpose himself between the monitor and the myopic old dear, and subtly switch it off. Feeling strangely guilty, even though the woman had not noticed, Alan had given the dog every form of treatment possible in order to stop it pissing all over her house. The dog promptly bit him and the old woman for good measure. Alan had made sure her next appointment was for his one day off that month.

Even this incident he tried to ignore, but there were more like it. The next day he had been kneeling on the floor with a German shepherd dog when the lights in the room suddenly turned off. This would not have been such a problem had he not been expressing the dog's anal glands at the time. As it was he had to shuffle round awkwardly in the darkness with his index finger inserted into the animal while he searched around for his paper towel. This would still not have been the disaster it turned out to be if the man holding the dog had not also been wandering around in the darkness, and had he not managed to kick over Alan's bottle of lubricant then Alan probably would not have slipped in it and managed to express the whole contents of the dog's infected glands onto his own face.

As he lay on the floor, covered in revolting fluid, silently retching, he wondered, not for the first time, if there were any alternative careers he could pursue at his time of life. Dog and owner had been very good-natured about the whole incident, especially when the man had stopped laughing.

There were the voices, as well. Out of everything, that was what worried Alan the most. The buzz at the back of his mind had slowly turned into the hum of conversation. There were words in it, although Alan couldn't make out what they were saying, if they were saying anything at all. It was a constant low susurration, like the excited whispering of theatre critics before the show opens and they pounce. In the daytime he could just about ignore them, but at night... well, it was worse than being on call.

He was getting frightened, because none of the explanations for the incidents were good. It boiled down to two possibilities, as far as he could see. Either he was insane, or he was possessed. He honestly wasn't sure which scared him most. It wasn't as if he could tell someone, as if they had noticed anything. Demonic possession was not generally easy to talk about. The other vets, nurses and receptionists that he worked with were really just that; people he worked with.

He remembered once, when he had been a new graduate, unaware of just how truly unprepared for work he was, getting called out to some sheep that had been savaged on the edge of the Mendips. Some had been killed, and several had had large, nasty cuts on their faces, sharp thin cuts, always in threes. The farmer had been convinced that the sheep had been killed by the beast of the moors, and Alan could see no reason to disagree — it had certainly looked like the work of a big cat to him rather than a dog.

When he had arrived back at the practice, a dead sheep in tow, he had told everyone about the sheep that had been killed by the beast of the Mendips. He was a vet, and that was his diagnosis.

Everyone he told had developed a sort of half-pitying, half-glazed expression, even when the sheep, along with the wounds, was pointed out to them. They had been polite, but completely and totally unbelieving of his story. It was the pity that had worried him more than anything. The look in their eyes. Even if they wanted to, they couldn't believe him. They were simply unable to. It was easier for them to assume he was mistaken. Over time, he had convinced himself the sheep must have been attacked by a dog, even though no dog bite he had ever seen had looked like those on the sheep.

Whenever he thought of trying to tell someone about his

current predicament, the expressions of the people at his last practice came back to him. Did he want everyone to think he was insane?

Things were getting beyond a joke now. He couldn't remember the last decent night's sleep he'd had. He would have to tell someone. He thought of his parents, his ex-fiancée, his few friends now scattered around the country. No. No good. Who would believe it? Who could believe it? The calf was normal now, and what else could he say? That he was hearing voices?

What was he going to do?

III

It was one of those afternoon surgeries. The ones that seemed to drag on and on into the horizon, with no prospect of ever finishing. The kind of surgery that got worse with every consult. The kind of surgery where every other person in the waiting room had 'no better' in the little box marked 'complaint' on the computer. The kind where all the others had 'worse' written in.

It was the kind of afternoon that could drop a grown vet to his knees, praying that the next consult would just be a simple booster, and not the kind of one where the first thing the client says when they walk into the room is 'Well, he's just not right.' The kind where the other vet who is supposed to be giving consults has been called away to an accident involving a cow and a milk tanker.

The surgery, already fully booked, was running late, of course. There is some kind of strange universal law that the only time people will just wander in off the street hoping their animal can be fitted in is the time that the vets are already running at least thirty minutes behind.

Alan was working his way slowly through the procession of very ill animals, admitting, injecting, blood sampling, catheterising. He had spent the last twenty minutes with a tortoise, attempting to feed it and slowly coming to the realisation that it had been dead for several days. He checked the computer quickly. Eight people waiting. His weary eyes masochistically scanned down the complaint list:

Off Colour
Worse
?PTS?
Worse
No better
Poorly
Check-up

He blinked. Check-up? A simple check-up? Surely not tonight, of all nights. He gritted his teeth, determined not to get his hopes up, but every time he saw it flickering on his computer screen, a little ray of hope inside him whispered seductively 'Maybe we could make up a little time with that one.' He put his head down, ignored the voice, and got on with it.

Interminably, the consults wore on until he reached the (glittering, now, in his own mind, despite his efforts to prevent this) 'check-up'. There were still several people to see afterwards, but he was getting there. If this was a quickie, he told himself, he might still get home in time to eat something before he went to bed.

He walked out into the waiting room. The animal was called 'Roger', the owner 'Schekter'. As he walked, his mind, as it always did, underwent the brief internal struggle of deciding how to call the next client in. Simply saying 'Schekter' seemed a little public school, brusque and rude. Saying 'Roger' was a risky strategy — not only did it seem too familiar, there was always the risk of there being two Rogers in the waiting room, with all the attendant embarrassment that could cause. Saying 'Roger Schekter' could provoke a slightly confused look from most clients, followed usually by a polite laugh, which Alan always felt was at his expense. The only other alternative was generally the worst option — ie saying Mr or Mrs Schekter. This was an absolute minefield of social discomfort. The computers at the practice gave no indication of the sex of the owner who had brought in the animal, which meant a snap decision on viewing the client. Calling someone a Mrs when they were a Miss was stressful enough, but having to spend ten minutes with someone who you have mistakenly called Mr when they are, in fact, a Mrs, was, for Alan, more skin-achingly embarrassing than doing a loud fart in a packed lift.

The hell with it, he thought. Tonight, I don't care.

'Roger?' he called out. Three people in the waiting room stood up, animals at the ready. Alan sighed. 'Erm… sorry. Roger Schekter?'

A low chorus of titters rippled through the waiting room, but not from the owner of the correct Roger. Alan saw his hopes of an easy, quick consult evaporating as the strange young woman, who had done nothing but stare at him through the whole appointment two days ago, stood up. She stared at him.

IV

'So,' Alan said, in his jauntiest possible tone, 'How's Roger getting on?'

The woman, who had been peering at him as if he was naked and painted blue, blinked, and put the cat box on the table. 'Erm…' she mumbled.

Alan turned to the computer. Not to read the notes — he could remember this one all right. The girl who liked feeding her cat hot coffee. Topically. He turned in the hope the girl would stop looking at him.

'How has he been?' he called over his shoulder, fixedly studying the notes he had written last time, even though he had read them twice already.

Young cat, scalds dorsal aspect mid-lumbar region. Sore but not severe. Caused by coffee. CARE.

He remembered, now, that the care had been to warn him of the owner, not of the cat. As he turned round the woman was fiddling with the door of the cat box. He reached over to help. The woman gave a little gasp of surprise and pulled her hands away from his. Alan tried his best to ignore it, and opened the door. Roger walked out of the box, and began to purr.

'He's... he's doing very well, I think,' the woman said. Now she was staring at Roger, and Alan got the distinct impression it was to avoid looking at him. He held the cat, and it pushed its face into his. At least Roger's sane, he thought. He stood from his crouch and parted the hair over Roger's burnt back.

'Looks very good,' he said, hoping he sounded cheerful. The wounds were, in fact, healing fine, but there was something about this strange young woman that disturbed him deeply. That something was her reaction to him. What did she think he was, a leper or something? It would have been easier, he thought, if he didn't find her attractive. If she had been a mad old bat with halitosis and a crystal around her neck, he would find it easier to cope with, but here was someone whom he would have been attracted to if he met her socially, and she was reacting to him as if he were dressed in full SS uniform.

'Should all be healed in a week.' Normally at this point he would suggest one final consult then, just to check, but he decided against it in this case. 'I think we can sign him off,' he said.

The woman nodded, gratefully. 'Ah... good. Good. Stupid thing to do, really.' She glanced up, and for a second their eyes met. Alan tried to smile.

'Well,' he said, but couldn't think of anything to follow that up, so left it hanging in the air. Miss Schekter seemed about to speak, but the seconds ticked by and she didn't, so Alan pointed Roger back towards the open cat box again. Roger obliged by walking into it. Alan closed the door.

'They always go in a bit easier after I've seen them,' he

said, still smiling, hoping to keep the atmosphere light with one of his standard jokes. Miss Schekter reacted not at all. Alan locked the box. Miss Schekter blinked and looked at the floor.

'Erm...' she said. Alan looked up. 'Erm... are you all right?'

Alan suddenly felt cold all over. He had thought he had got away with it. He cleared his throat, and lifted the basket from the table.

'I'm fine, thanks. Thanks for asking, though.' He smiled again, and waved the Roger-filled basket at the woman. She took it from him, and turned to the door. Alan was about to breathe a deep sigh of relief, when the woman turned around.

'I'm... I'm not normally this weird, you know,' she said. Alan didn't know what to say to that so he nodded indulgently. The woman could see she wasn't convincing him. She lowered her eyes, and then raised them one last time.

'I can see them,' she said in a low, urgent whisper. 'I can hear them. Maybe I can help you.'

Alan's jaw dropped open, and he stood, stunned, by his table. His jaw jiggled a little as he tried to assert control over it, then dropped again as he failed.

Kate smiled, briefly, and left the room. The lights switched themselves off, and Alan stood in the dark, his mouth gaping and his eyes wide, like a concussed cavefish.

Chapter Seven

I

It has been stated by many people, frequently and quite correctly, that space is a hostile environment. It would be difficult to imagine an environment more hostile than open space without bending one's mind to black holes, and the interior of suns, and other such places, but the only people inclined to do that sort of thing are physicists and struggling science-fiction authors, neither of which are viewed as useful, or even sane, members of society.

However, this statement is only really true of members of our society, or, more specifically, of humans. The universe is a vast place, and for the most part, despite areas of extreme beauty, wonder, hostility, pressure, light, heat and so on, it is astonishingly dull. Vast tracts of almost nothing, with only the occasional galaxy to break the monotony. Yes, you could argue that on the extremely small scale there are all manner of exciting things happening; things zipping about, spontaneously creating, wobbling, annihilating and so forth, but as the net result of all this effort is absolutely nothing it seems like a bit of a waste of time, cosmically speaking, and as a result only the aforementioned physicists get really excited about it, and they don't count (see above).

Although open space is extremely unpleasant for certain fragile carbon-based creatures, it is entirely possible to make a successful, if not necessarily exciting living out in the vacuum.

Many and varied creatures scrape an existence in the coldness and sparseness even of deep space. Nar-Quanga was such a creature. Nar-Quanga was not its real name, of course. It would have found the concept of names bizarre, very alien, and slightly disturbing, though it is possible, given the choice, that it may have picked Nar-Quanga as its name. In an infinite universe, anything is possible.

Nar-Quanga would not have been visible to human eyes,

had there been any there to attempt to observe it, although if there were, the brain to which they would have been connected would have been somewhat preoccupied, and not in the best mental state to be examining the local flora. Nar-Quanga was, in the simplest sense, an enormous patch of charged spacetime, floating through the universe feeding upon the pitifully small background energy, the remnants of the thirteen-billion-year-old explosion which has been the cause of a lot of trouble ever since.

Nar-Quanga experienced consciousness, in a way. It was aware of time passing and things changing. It remembered a time, long ago, when it had been much larger, and the universal pickings had been much less scarce. It even had a distant memory that there had once been other creatures such as him, and they had drifted far and wide throughout the universe.

Those times were long ago. Nar-Quanga was mostly left with its thoughts, such as they were, and its scenery, such as that was. It was, it must be said, more or less happy with its lot. A few of its wormholes out on its periphery twinged a bit more they used to, and it could have sworn that absolute zero seemed to get a little colder every millennium, but on the whole it enjoyed its life.

Slowly (Nar-Quanga did everything slowly. It didn't see the point of rushing — at least, would not have done had the concept ever occurred to it) it became aware that it had drifted, with the aid of its wormholes, out of deep space and into another galaxy. It watched the suns float past it as it travelled through in search of energy. Suns themselves were far too intense for a universal bottom-feeder such as itself to contemplate nibbling upon, but it dredged up from its memory the thoughts of what had happened the last time it had been in such an energy-rich place. It had found, floating around a sun, some small chunks of rock, which had been quite high in the tastiest bits of energy. It had dined on one the last time it had floated through a solar system, and although the experience had given it indigestion for several million years, it had not been entirely unpleasant. Go on, it thought. Let's enjoy ourselves. It's naughty, but nice.

It twisted its various wormholes this way and that, manipulating the continuum of which it was a part so that it arrived at the closest, juiciest looking sun it could find. This looked promising. There were nine large chunks of rock around the sun, as well as numerous smaller ones. Nar-Quanga dismissed a few of the chunks of rock, as they were all covered with gas, and feeding on large quantities of gas tended to make it feel nauseous, and so instead drifted as close to the sun as it dared. It wanted a rock that had enough energy to be tasty, but not so much as to upset its delicate digestion. Somewhat arbitrarily it selected the rock that lay third most distant from the sun. A small bluey-green rock. It looked a bit sickly, but its wormholes rumbled as it drifted closer. Just this once, it thought.

It wrapped its invisible tendrils (actually fifth-dimensional projections in space-time that would have made any earth physicist gibber with excitement had they had any way of knowing about them) around the rock. If Nar-Quanga had had a mouth, it would probably have been dribbling very slightly.

It took a bite of the energies.

'Urgh,' it thought as it spat them back out. 'Bloody hell,' it said to itself, unable to get the taste out of its wormholes. 'Bloody rotten.'

There was something seriously wrong with that ball of rock, it thought. Anything that had energies tasting like that wasn't going to be around for long.

As far as it was possible for a vast tract of space-time to shudder, Nar-Quanga shuddered as it flexed its wormholes and drifted back into the comforting cool of deep space.

II

Christmas day arrived on Earth. To Alan, it was just another day, made worse than most by the fact that nobody else seemed to be working. In compensation, he got a lot more apologies when he actually did get called out.

The day had started badly. He had already had to go out this morning to lamb a sheep. In retrospect it had been very festive, pulling a newborn lamb from its mother as the sun rose on Christmas day. But that was only in retrospect. At the time the season had not been jolly, and presents were not at the forefront of his mind, even though Mrs Atkins, who owned the sheep, the lamb and the field, had given him a mince pie and a cup of tea for his troubles.

Still, it had gone well. All the participants of the scene remained alive by the end of it, which was generally a good sign. The problems had started when he was driving back from the lambing.

Foolishly, he had decided that being covered in blood and amniotic fluid may not be the best way to appear to any clients he might have to see at the surgery, and he had decided to nip home for a quick shower before driving in to the practice to check on all the inpatients. There wasn't much to check on, he knew. A cat recovering from having its abscess lanced and a guinea pig suffering from diarrhoea. Nothing immediately urgent. Cameron, the vet who had been on the previous evening, had kindly popped in to the practice during Alan's lambing, and had phoned him to say they were both doing well.

Alan lived several miles from the practice, along winding country lanes. The house was a practice house, of course, and the car he drove was a practice car (a nasty blue Astra with a habit of leaking diesel all over his drive, no matter how many times the mechanics at the cheap garage to which his boss kept sending him told him this could not be possible with the new seal they had just installed). He and his fiancée had been planning to get a place and a car of their own until she had stopped being his fiancée, and started being his ex-fiancée instead. The drive normally took around fifteen minutes from the practice, which was on the outskirts of Bristol, near the suspension bridge. One of the only benefits of being on call was that Alan felt justified in pelting down the lanes at top speed in the middle of the night. Never in the day, though. You couldn't drive fast in daylight hours, because you could never see the oncoming cars without their headlights. Not until the approaching car had announced itself in a painful crunching of metal, anyway.

It being daytime, Alan drove slowly and cautiously down his lane, and arrived at his house. Being a practice house it was small, square, cold, and wholly unpleasant to look at, from its drab grey pebble-dashed exterior to the hideous bluey-green colour of the bath. It was home, though.

He hated having a shower when he was on call. Not for any reason in particular other than he hated doing anything at all when he was on call. There was no way he could relax without the constant horrible feeling that at any second, any second just like this one now, the phone could ring and he would have to shoot out of the house, heart pumping and brain screaming. All he really wanted to do when he was on duty was sit in an armchair with the lights turned off, feeling miserable. This did not make for a good relationship when it happened three nights a week, and was a large reason that his fiancée was now his ex-fiancée. Alan couldn't really blame her.

George wasn't in. He had left the house two days previously to spend Christmas with his parents. Alan rushed inside, and showered, as quickly as he could, ears tense and expectant, waiting for the sound of the phone. It didn't ring. The shower passed without incident, and it was a cleaner and slightly more relaxed Alan who stepped back out of the house ten minutes later, got into his car, and set off for the practice.

Finally, he was starting to feel like things were under control. The morning call was done, over with, and he was on his way to check the inpatients with no outstanding work. Even the... whatever it was that had been bothering him seemed to have given him a day off. Nothing unusual had happened at all since he went to bed last night. Even the voices seemed to have quietened. Everybody's off but me, he thought.

As for what the young woman... Kate was her name,

wasn't it?... had said, well... he would wait and see. If he was still being bothered by the New Year, maybe he would give her a ring.

It was at this point in his thoughts that the steering wheel of the Astra suddenly took it upon itself to jolt to the left, taking the wheels, the car to which they were attached and the unfortunate Alan inside straight into a muddy ditch.

III

'Bugger bugger bugger piss cock bastard bugger' Alan opined as he surveyed the damage.

'Sod wanking cock piss arse mangling willy sucker,' he added, after a moment's reflection. The car was stuck, well and truly. Alan had gone through the time-honoured rituals of attempting to extricate his car from the mess — reversing slowly, reversing quickly, rocking the car backwards and forwards, accelerating hard and suddenly releasing the handbrake, pushing the car from the back, pushing the car from the front. This had, of course, had the result that this sequence of events always had whenever they occurred anywhere in the universe; that is, the car was now much more stuck in the mud that it had been ten minutes previously, and Alan was now wet, cold and covered in mud. He was also in a very bad mood, and he hadn't been in much of a good one to start with.

He beat his head against the bonnet for a few moments, then got back inside. For a second he sat in silence, then he leaned forward and bit the steering wheel in frustration. He sat there, mouth around the wheel like a teething crash-test dummy, then leaned back in his seat, feeling a little better.

It began to rain.

Alan closed his eyes, then dug the mobile phone out of his socket, flipping open the glove compartment to get the number for the RAC recovery service from the inside of the owner's manual. He couldn't help feeling guilty now that he was calling someone else out. He was determined not to think about why the car had driven off the road in the first place.

The girl on the other end of the phone was very patient, and told him there would be someone to help him within the hour. Alan simply felt relief. He had exhausted his rage on the car and the mud. He sank back into his seat, hoping that the phone wouldn't ring, and closed his eyes.

The phone rang, the jaunty Batman theme-tune that whined out of it long since having lost its amusement value. Alan jolted up, bashing his knees on the steering column, fumbled with the phone, dropped it into the footwell, swore, picked up the phone, held it to his ear, said 'Hello', realised it was still ringing, pressed the right button then finally got the correct phrase out.

'Chestnut Vale emergency service,' he said.

'Hello?' a tremulous, questioning voice said on the other end of the phone, 'Is… is that the vets?'

'This is Alan, one of the vets, that's right.'

'Oh. I hope I'm not bothering you too much,' said the voice. Alan sighed.

'What can I do for you?' he asked, as calmly as he could manage.

'I'm only phoning to see how little Bubbles is getting on,' the voice continued. Alan's mind quickly flipped to the section marked 'inpatients' in his memory, leaving his mouth on autopilot for a while.

'Oh… erm…' it managed before his mind reasserted control. Bubbles, the guinea pig with the less than satisfactory poo. 'Bubbles is doing fine at the moment, Mrs… erm…'

'Oh, lovely,' Mrs Erm said, 'Can I come in and see him, do you think? Is he eating now? Has he done anything?'

'Erm… yes, it looks like he's eaten a little,' Alan said, wincing with displeasure at having to lie, hoping Bubbles had managed to take something down. 'I'm just in the middle of something at the moment, Mrs… erm… Could I phone you back in about an hour? It shouldn't be a problem to come in and see him.'

'Oh, thank you,' Mrs Erm said, sounding considerably cheered. 'I'll wait to hear from you. Merry Christmas.'

'Merry Christmas.' Piss off, he thought. He lay back in his seat and managed to fall asleep.

IV

The phone did not ring again. The RAC man arrived and dutifully towed Alan out of the ditch. The man was actually from the local garage, and had been about as friendly and cheerful as Alan would expect from someone who had been called out on Christmas Day to pull some idiot out of a ditch. Alan had tried some feeble explanation about a rabbit jumping in front of him but had soon given up when he realised he wasn't even convincing himself, let alone the man from the garage.

It had taken the man around five minutes to pull the stranded Astra from the mud pit, and slightly longer for the man to frown at Alan through his bushy eyebrows while Alan signed the required forms.

'Merry Christmas,' Alan had said as the man got back into his truck.

'Piss off,' said the man, and drove off.

Fifteen minutes later, without further incident, Alan was getting out of his Astra in front of the practice. At least there was nothing waiting. He could just quickly check the inpatients then... then what? Did he want to risk driving home again? Could he risk driving at all today? He toyed with the idea of ringing his boss, telling him he couldn't work today, but he knew he would have to have a bloody good excuse, and he wasn't sure simply being possessed was good enough.

He unlocked the door of the practice, deactivated the alarm at the panel just inside the door, and headed to the small animal ward.

Rags, the cat who until recently had an abscess, yowled at him through the doors of the cage. Alan opened the cage and ruffled Rags' head. The cat purred. Alan glanced at the wound on its side. Healing fine. No sign of a problem. He would get Rags home tomorrow. No need to bother the owners today. He ruffled Rags' head again. Rags bit him. He picked the cat up by the scruff and dumped it back in its cage, deciding to bother the owners today after all.

He walked down the ward and looked through the bars into Bubbles' cage. The little tray of freshly picked grass and grated carrot lay as he had left it the day before. Untouched.

'Bum,' he thought to himself. Bubbles hadn't eaten, after all. It was then that he noticed why. Bubbles was lying on his side at the back of the cage, little legs pointing out stiffly from his body.

'Shitbags,' Alan whispered to no one in particular, pulling open the cage. Perhaps he could revive him, perhaps... The faint hopes vanished as he touched Bubbles' sad, stiff corpse. The guinea pig was stone cold. It had been dead for hours.

A horrible vision materialised in his mind. It was of him, standing in front of a long wooden table, at which were seated several severe looking men and women in suits. Mrs Erm was with them. The words 'professional negligence' floated in the air like a nasty smell.

The phone rang in his pocket, startling him in the silence of the ward. His heart did a quick lap of his stomach before returning to its accustomed position.

'Chestnut Vale emergency service,' he said, dumbly, once he had fumbled the phone to his ear, staring at the recently vacated body of Bubbles.

'Oh... hello,' a familiar tremulous voice said, 'Is that the vets? I'm just ringing about my guinea pig, Bubbles. The person I spoke to said I might be able to visit him?'

Pissing bugger flaps. It was Christmas day! Wasn't it supposed to be joy to the world, and all that? Why did Bubbles have to choose today to wing his way to the land where guinea pigs are eternally happy? He thought quickly.

'Ah... hello, Mrs... erm... I was just about to ring you.'

There was a slight pause on the other end of the phone, as Mrs Erm picked up something from Alan's voice. 'Is he OK?'

'I'm... I'm afraid he's not doing so well.' Think! Think! 'He's... I'm afraid he's taken a sudden turn for the worse.'

'He's going to be OK, though, is he?'

Alan remained silent for long enough for Mrs Erm to realise that he wasn't.

'I don't think he is, I'm afraid.' What now? 'He seems to be in some pain. I don't think he's going to make it. I think...' He heard his voice begin to drip with sentiment, as it turned into his 'I'm afraid I think it's time' voice.

'I'm afraid I think it's time to end his suffering. I think we should put him to sleep.'

Another pause. Slightly choked. 'I don't want him to suffer,' Mrs Erm said.

No risk of that, Alan thought. 'Of course not,' he said, caringly. 'I think it's for the best.'

'Yes,' said Mrs Erm. 'Do what you have to. Don't let him suffer.'

Thank Christ! Alan thought. The image of the table, with its severe, besuited people, vanished from his mind. 'I'll do what I can,' he said.

'I'm coming right over,' Mrs Erm said urgently. 'I want to be with him!'

The phone went dead. The table and the suits swam back into vision. The word 'negligence' had been replaced with 'misconduct'.

He wrestled the phone back into his pocket, his mind swimming with panic. What was he going to do? There was a cheap stethoscope hanging on a hook on the wall. With almost superhuman optimism Alan picked it up and listened to Bubbles' chest.

There was a thud! His heart leapt. Another thud! And another!

After a moment Alan realised he was hearing his own

blood race around his ears looking for somewhere to bail out, and the reason he was hearing this is because there was absolutely nothing to hear from the mortally challenged Bubbles.

He hung his head for a moment, his eyes shut, but it didn't seem to help so he stopped doing it, and instead took the consent form off the front of the cage. Mrs Erm was actually Mrs Stapleton, and she lived... where was the address... she lived... argh!

Alan dropped the consent form in panic. She lived about five minutes walk away. He didn't know how long it would take her to run. He picked Bubbles up and raced out to the prep room, arranging an anaesthetic machine, a tube and an oxygen mask around the furry body. As a bit of colour he arranged some used syringes, ET tubes and even a urinary catheter beside it all. He stood back, surveying the situation. It looked like a scene from ER, provided the doctors in ER had finally got sick of Americans moaning at them and had decided to work on small mammals instead. He could almost believe he had just failed to save Bubbles himself. Good.

Then his eyes fell on the guinea pig, its thin legs poking out like spines from a hedgehog. He touched it again. Even Mrs Stapleton could not fail to recognise that rigor mortis had set in remarkably quickly for an animal that had died while she was hurrying to be with it. What was he going to do?

Bugger it, he thought. I'm going to have a coffee. I deserve one.

He strolled next door, into the kitchen, and flicked the kettle on, then leaned over the sink and splashed water in his face. He was trying to calm himself down. It didn't work.

The kettle clicked off, and he looked up. His gaze fell on the microwave, which stood next to the just-boiled kettle.

He stood up. He looked out of the door, across to the table, and the small body on it. He looked back at the microwave.

'No,' he murmured to himself. Absolutely not. No way.

There was not a chance he would even think of… he found that he was halfway to the table already. 'No,' he murmured again as he frantically picked up the guinea pig and ran back to the kitchen.

'I'm not doing this I'm not doing this,' he said as he opened the door to the oven and placed Bubbles inside. He shut the door, turned the dial and pressed 'Start'. Just in time he flicked the switch from 'High' to 'Defrost'.

He left Bubbles going for thirty seconds, unsure of what the heating-up time for an average guinea pig was. The microwave pinged. The doorbell rang.

Nerves jangling, Alan removed the now realistically warm guinea pig from the microwave and deposited it on the table amidst his ER set-up, then ran and opened the door.

IV

One of the peculiar things about being a vet was that people only ever seemed really happy with you once you had actually killed their pet. If they had a dreadful disease that you fought tooth and nail to get the animal through, the owners were pleased but not effusive in their praise. It just seemed to be expected that the animal would get better. If, in the end, the animal failed to get better, the owners seemed much more praiseworthy of Alan. He had received far more bottles of wine for killing pets than for saving them.

Mrs Stapleton was very thankful for everything Alan had done for her, and for Bubbles. She understood, as Alan explained, that things happened very quickly in guinea pigs, that Bubbles hadn't been suffering, and was not really aware of what was happening to him in the end (which was definitely a good thing, since in the end he had been microwaved on defrost for thirty seconds). She thanked him for all his hard work, told him that the practice was lucky to have such a caring and kind vet working for them, and left, a small towel under her arm with the still-warm Bubbles inside. Alan watched her leave, knowing this was worth a box of chocolates at least. He hated himself.

He shut the door, leaned back on the reception desk, gave a long, weary sigh, phoned his boss and resigned.

Chapter Eight

I

Alan felt good about leaving his job for as long as it took him to remember that the car he was driving was not his, and the house he was driving towards also did not belong to him, but to the practice. Ah, never mind, he thought. It's worth it. It's worth it even to be homeless and carless.

He thought about phoning his boss back, but the prospect of any more days like he had just had filled him with a dread that would require probably at least half a toilet roll if he dwelled upon it for too long.

For so long he had dreamed of quitting, of returning to the sort of life he had before being a vet. From his first day at work he had realised he simply wasn't cut out for the job. That lying bastard James Herriot had seemed to suggest amidst all the muck and vomit there was a shining golden centre to it all, something magical that made up for all the inconveniences, the compromises, the frustrations, the countless tragedies. Well, if there was, Alan hadn't found it yet, and he was buggered if he was going to spend the rest of his life looking for it.

Take last month. He had removed a tennis ball from the small intestine of a Labrador, which had unwisely decided that it would be a great thing to snack on. The operation had gone fine, the dog began to eat; the owners were happy and promised not to feed their dog any more racquet-sports-related objects. The case had given Alan a warm glow inside, one of those where he thought 'Well, they don't all end badly.' For a few days he had actually been happy to go to work, thinking of all the animals he might be able to help.

A week later the Labrador had chased after a tennis ball out on a walk and had been squashed by a bus. Splat. Dead. Alan had done what he could when the mess had been brought in, but there was no way the dog could have been saved. It had been terrible, truly terrible. Upsetting, and very unfair for all concerned, especially the dog. Although, strictly speaking, it had been the dog's fault, was it fair that it had been killed because it had failed to learn the lesson 'Don't eat tennis balls'? What kind of crime was that to be punishable with death?

It wasn't an isolated case. Though extreme, something like it seemed to happen to all of Alan's happy endings. Every cloud may have had a silver lining, but eventually all silver tarnishes. If he'd stopped to think about it, he might have realised this happened because all the ones that got better and stayed better didn't come back to see him. It was only the really bad cases that he saw again and again.

Alan didn't stop to think about it. He was sick; sick and tired of the whole bloody thing. He felt as if a great weight had been lifted from him. The weight had been building up for five years now, every day another stone to his burden. Now that was gone. True, he no longer had a job, and shortly would no longer have a car or a place to live, but the very fact that even this could not destroy his relief suggested to him that he should have done it a long time ago.

His boss had been very understanding, surprisingly. He had told Alan he was technically on holiday, and gave him the rest of the week to think about it. If he still felt the same in the New Year, then that would be that.

Alan buzzed with a won-the-lottery warm glow. He had to stop himself from singing out loud, then he realised he was in the car on his own, and there was no reason to stop himself.

'Beelzebub has a devil put aside for me... for me... for meeeeeee!' he screeched, almost in time with the radio, head-banging as much as he could manage while still keeping his eyes on the road.

He wondered what he would do with the rest of Christmas, such that it was. He toyed with the idea of driving home, all the way home to see his parents. Too far, he decided. The thought of the drive reminded him of the problems he had on the way to the practice, and reminded him that not all his problems were solved.

His hands, bent crookedly from trying to play air-guitar while simultaneously gripping the steering wheel, sagged a little. The… things that were happening to him. Could they all be work related? Maybe, now he had quit, it would all stop, like a bad dream. A tiny part of his brain nagged at him, trying to remind him of the calf, telling him it had something to do with all of this, but he managed to ignore it.

All too much stress, he thought. Well, no more of that now. He would go home, take a long, relaxing bath, ring his parents, leave a nasty message on his ex-fiancée's answerphone, cook himself whatever he found in the fridge, and spend the rest of the evening relaxing and watching Christmas telly, even though it wasn't as good as it used to be. By tomorrow, he would be so relaxed, that all his strange symptoms would have disappeared. No more voices. No more accidents. The voices had quietened already. That low, buzzing hum that he had been half-aware of for days now, had fallen silent. He smiled. Now if only the other things stopped happening…

'So you think you can stop me and spit in my eye!' he yelled to no one in particular. He thought that he might be smiling, but he wasn't sure, because he didn't think he had done it in a while.

It was unfortunate that the new voice in his head chose this moment to start communicating with him.

II

'Erm… hello?'

Alan stopped singing. He looked down at the radio with a sinking heart. It was sinking because it knew, even if Alan didn't, that the stereo was playing a tape, not a radio station, and it had never said 'Erm… hello?' at this point before. So either there was a very unconventional traffic report beginning, or Alan was still mad. His heart didn't want to hang around to find out, so it descended to the level of his shoes, where it cowered, and felt wretched.

Alan caught on a moment later, after he had already jabbed his finger at the 'off' button on the radio. He realised because the voice said

'Hello?'

again, and the radio was now silent. Alan was only minutes from home. He closed his eyes.

'Excuse me,' the voice came again, 'Do you think you could keep your eyes on the road? I've only just returned, and I've no intention of leaving any time soon.'

Alan jerked his eyes open again just in time to avoid driving into an oncoming Peugeot. He stopped the car and reversed into the passing place he had just driven past. The driver of the Peugeot shook his fist at him in a workmanlike way, and then shot off down the lane.

Alan took a deep breath. He let it out. He took another one. Nothing else happened. He looked around the car, stupidly craning his neck around to peer into the footwells of the back seats, in case there was a very small man hidden in there. There wasn't.

'You know where I am, of course,' the voice said, echoing around the corridors of his mind. Alan was horribly aware that if there was someone else in the car, and he had said 'Did you just hear that?' to them, that they would have looked at him with a puzzled expression and said 'Hear what?' There wasn't, and he was glad that this at least saved him from some embarrassment.

'Who... who are you?' he said aloud, reluctantly. Speaking to the thing was, in some way, admitting that it was there at all.

'Ah, you've got me there,' the voice replied. 'No idea.'

The voice sounded familiar to Alan, and he wasn't sure why. It was the voice of a man, rich and well-composed. It sounded as if it held all the wisdom in the world. Which was why he was a little surprised by the answer.

'You don't know who you are?' he tried again.

'No. Sorry, not a clue. Used to know. Or, at least, I

think I did. So difficult to be clear. It's good to be back, though. Well, I think it is.'

Alan suddenly realised where he recognised the voice from. It sounded just like Sir Michael Hordern, who had played Gandalf in his old audio tapes of Lord of the Rings, which he liked to listen to on long journeys. It was a voice he associated, in consequence, with the pinnacle of wisdom.

'Are you... is your name Michael?' he asked, hesitantly.

'Erm... could be,' the voice replied. 'As I say, I've no I idea.'

Alan decided to go for another tactic. 'Where are you from?'

'Well, that's a tricky one too, I'm afraid.'

Alan sighed. If I'm going to go mad, he thought, I could at least be a little more imaginative about it.

'Something is going wrong,' the voice said, as ominously as Gandalf revealing to Frodo that his latest piece of jewellery was, in fact, the One Ring.

'Where?' said Alan, looking around. The road was empty.

'Not here,' said the Gandalf-voice. In an even more ominous tone, it added, 'Not yet.'

'Erm... where, then?'

The voice ignored this. 'I have come to you, after my long period of absence. How long I have been in that other place, I do not know. Time is different there. Memory is different there. All I know is that I was once, like you, an occupant of this world. Many things have changed.'

This was more like it, Alan thought. He was starting to think he had no imagination at all.

'I have come to you, because you are the connection. The conduit. There may be others, but you were the first. I have come to warn you. Things are changing in that other place. Something is gathering its strength. The changes have already begun to occur. There will be more. Many more.'

'Erm... I see,' said Alan, not seeing.

'You don't see, yet. How could you? I'm only learning, myself,' said the voice. It sounded put out at the interruption, the ominous tone replaced with the irritated sniping voice used to chastise hobbits for dropping noisy objects down deep wells.

'Sorry,' said Alan, quietly.

'I don't know if, even now, it's too late,' the voice continued, getting back into its stride. 'But we can try. I think I will need your help.'

'So where exactly is all this trouble? The place where things are spilling over from?' Alan asked.

The voice paused for a moment. When it spoke again, it spoke slowly, perhaps unsure of itself. 'The place that I have inhabited for as long as I can remember. The realm of the dead.'

III

Alan drove home the rest of the way in silence, internally as well as externally. The Gandalf-voice had lapsed into silence for the moment, saying it just wanted to observe, to get its bearings, and Alan wasn't going to argue if that meant it was going to shut up for a while, so he could do the same.

He parked outside his home, noting with some surprise that George's Golf was in the space in front of his. He unlocked the door and went inside.

'Hello?' he said.

There was a grunt from the general direction of the living room. Alan took his coat off and headed towards the grunt.

George was lying on his back on the horrid green sofa that inhabited the living room, holding a can of Stella on his chest. His eyes were fixed at the television. They prised themselves off the screen for just a second to flick at Alan, then jumped back to the screen again. The corners of his mouth twitched in a lazy greeting.

'How was your morning?' he asked.

Alan didn't know where to begin. George probably wasn't fully aware of the complexity of his question, and so while Alan was still trying to think of a reply that made any kind of sense, George jumped in with his own.

'Mine was bloody awful,' he said, still watching the telly. On it, Steve McQueen was bouncing a baseball across a small room and catching it repeatedly with his mitt.

'A...' said Alan, but got no further.

'Bloody family. Bloody Christmas. Don't you hate bloody family Christmases?' His eyes managed the quick journey from the screen to Alan again. 'You're lucky you're on call; don't have to deal with families. Sick of the whole bloody lot of 'em, so I decided to come back here and keep you company.'

He flashed Alan a handsome grin, but it was wasted because Alan wasn't looking at it. He sat down in the hideous brown armchair next to the horrid sofa, and allowed his eyes to drift over to the screen.

'I've left my job,' he said.

George jumped up from the sofa, covering himself with warm lager. 'Shit,' he said as he jumped up further and wiped his top, then looked at Alan. 'Bloody hell,' he said. 'You've had a crappy morning too, then.'

'That,' said Alan, 'is putting it mildly.'

IV

One hour and several cans of Stella later, Alan felt he was beginning to relax. Gandalf had been quiet since he had first spoken to him in the car, and here, sitting in the armchair watching Donald Sinden slowly grow blind, he could almost pretend he hadn't heard it at all. Almost.

'So,' said Alan, from inside his warm glow (as on the screen, Gordon Jackson accidentally said 'Thank you very much', thus revealing himself to be an escaped English POW, and not a German citizen after all) 'how's work?'

George groaned.

'Not so good?' enquired Alan.

'You'd think,' said George, sitting up suddenly, and spilling yet more beer from the can in his hand on the sofa. This did not improve the appearance of the thing, but it would have had to work hard to make it look any worse.

'You'd think,' repeated George, as he slowly walked over to the kitchen and opened the fridge, 'that it'd be pretty bloody good, wouldn't you?'

Alan wasn't quite sure what George was getting at. 'Erm... well, I suppose so,' he said, non-committedly.

'I mean, it's not like things are hard to find at the moment, are they? I mean...' his voice became muffled as he popped his head inside, looking for another can. He pulled one out, then realised he still had an open can in his other hand. He shrugged, and placed the new can on top of the fridge as he closed the door.

He turned to Alan and took a swig from his can. Alan raised his eyebrows, hoping that this would help to make George make some kind of sense. He had discovered, unfortunately, that the point at which George and some kind of sense parted company was roughly around the same time that George began to drink lager.

'With everything that's started happening, you'd think it'd be a great time. Finally, something seems to be going on! I had the exclusive! I was there, in the pub, when it happened! I thought I'd be made up! But the bloody big boys have got it all, haven't they? You slave away for years looking for the great scoop, then the minute it happens the bastards come along and steal it from you! A bloody week, I spent, writing that story, then look what was in the papers this morning!'

He was waving his arms around as he spoke, and sloshing his beer onto the nasty beige carpet. He lifted the can for another swig, but realised it was empty. He turned back to the fridge again.

'George,' said Alan.

'Mm?' George said, as he plucked the new can from the

top of the fridge and settled down in the sofa. He pointed at the screen, his tirade defused for the moment.

'Do you know,' he said, as Steve McQueen flew off his motorbike and landed in a barbed-wire fence, 'that this, the quintessential Christmas movie, has only been actually shown on Christmas Day once before.'

'George,' Alan tried again, 'what are you talking about?'

George waved his hand at the television. 'Oh, yes, it always gets shown around about Christmas time, but never actually on Christmas day.'

Alan shook his head. 'No, not that. Not the film.' George looked at him. There was something in Alan's voice, a strained, desperate tone. 'I mean, what are you talking about, all this stuff that's happening? What was in the papers this morning?'

George did a double take. 'Don't you know? Don't you listen to the news?'

Alan shook his head, feeling foolish. Inside his head, there was no noise, but he could sense something was listening very carefully to the conversation. 'I've... I've been busy lately.'

George rubbed his chin. 'Well, you're missing it, mate. Something's going on! All over the place.'

'What do you mean? What's going on?'

'That's the beauty of it!' George smiled, warming to his subject. 'No one knows! But it's happening, all round the world. I knew I was on to something with that fire, but by the time I'd finished my report it was all over the newspapers! Broadsheets too, so I knew it must be something big!'

George's words had punctured the warm glow that had started to surround Alan. It leaked away, leaving him feeling cold and scared. He rubbed at his temples, which had started to throb. 'Fire?' he managed.

'Listen,' George said, carefully placing the can on the floor, where it fell over and burbled its contents into the carpet, 'I went to cover this story, right, pretty feeble one, to be honest, about this pub in Bristol where the fire didn't work right.'

'The fire didn't work right?' Alan asked, looking sceptical.

'Yeah,' said George, taking another swig, 'That's what I thought. Needed a bloody engineer, not a journalist. But when I got there, I could see what he meant. There was something wrong with the fire. It was a wood burner, ordinary wood, ordinary fireplace. But very extraordinary fire.'

'What was wrong with it?'

'Well, it wasn't hot, for one thing. It looked weak. I checked it with other stuff, and it turned out it was just the logs he was using. Something funny about them. Other wood worked fine. But the fire that came from this wood...' George shook his head. 'It's difficult to explain. But when you touched it, it actually seemed to make you colder. It felt like it was draining you. Like it was dead.'

He shuddered.

'When did this happen?' Alan asked.

'Just a few days ago,' George said. 'Getting my story ready, wasn't I, getting my research done, checking there wasn't some unusual chemical that could have been put on the wood, made it burn like that. Took some of it to a chemist friend of mine at the university, said he never seen anything like it. I mean, you can get fire that isn't hot, but not like this. Ever. He couldn't explain it. That's when I knew, this was it, my big story. But before I could even get it written, it happens again!'

'What happens again? The fire?'

George shook his head. 'Not the fire this time. Some puppies, born in Berlin yesterday. Surely you must have heard?'

Alan shook his head, a prickling feeling creeping up the back of his neck. He knew what George was going to say next.

'Well, they were born just like the fire was. Transparent, weak. When I say transparent, I mean it! You could see...'

'I know what you mean,' said Alan. George stopped. 'What happened to the puppies?' Alan asked.

'They died, few hours later. But it's happening all over.

Not just puppies. Goats, sheep, pigs. It hasn't happened to a human yet, but it can only be a matter of time. I mean…' He tailed off, noticing Alan's expression.

'You know something, don't you?' George said, journalistic instincts a-quiver. Alan didn't hear him. He was listening to something else, something only he could hear.

'I need to make a phone call,' he said after a moment, and headed out into the hall like a newly condemned man.

Chapter Nine

I

The sea had shifted and changed. How long it had been going on, the memory did not know. How it had held itself together through the storm, it did not know. It simply was, and it continued to be.

Barely aware, the memory drifted towards the nexus. It had been drifting towards it for some time. Or was it already there? Was this just a memory of the journey? Things were so confusing, and had been for as long as the memory knew... except for... something. On the edge of its awareness. It had been something more, once. It had been someone. No, that wasn't right — it had been more than that. More than someone. Had it been more than one person? Before the storm, that terrible storm...

The conduit grew in the memory's awareness. The conduit was a connection, a point of contact with something that the memory knew was important. The nexus floated above the sea, a brilliant light above brilliant lights. Intermittently, shafts of thought and consciousness reached out from the sea, and struck it. The sea was nothing more than a random wash, but still it somehow knew the conduit was important. As each thought struck, the conduit reacted with fear and confusion. It did not belong here. It did not wish to be here. But it could not escape.

The memory approached. Within the confusion of the conduit, the memory could make out images within. Images that stirred something within it, reminded it of what it had once lost. The conduit was the key.

Far off in the distance, far across the endless sea, thunder rumbled. The storm was coming again. The memory had to find refuge. It could not survive the storm a second time. There had to be a place of refuge, a place to hide where it could recover its myriad thoughts, to become what it had been before the terrible winds.

And there, suddenly, was an escape route. Not the conduit itself, but something nearby. The memory did not know if it had the strength any longer, but it had no time to prepare. The storm was coming back. He was coming back.

The memory entered the refuge.

They remembered, and were reborn.

II

Kate drank the sherry. It was not a delicate, polite sipping of the drink, such as the vicar made in terrible Eighties sitcoms when he unexpectedly popped round for a drink while, for hilarious reasons, the house was full of naked French exchange students. Nor was it the congenial swig of the professional partygoer. Kate DRANK the sherry, in such a way as to indicate to the pourer of the sherry that Kate would like another glass, right away please.

Kate's mother poured her another glass. 'Everything all right at home, dear?' she asked, as placidly as she could.

Kate eyeballed the freshly filled glass in her hands. The sherry eyed her back, nervously, having noted what had happened to the previous occupant of the glass, and the three tenants prior to that.

Kate put the glass on her mother's coffee table in front of her. The glass of sherry would have heaved a hearty sigh of relief if it could have done. Instead, it settled for twirling itself around the glass in a relieved sort of way.

'Fine, fine,' said Kate absently, staring at the table.

Kate's mother glanced at her father, who shrugged, and decided it was time to go and check on the roast potatoes.

Christmas at Kate's parents' was not going well. For the third year in a row Kate had arrived without any men to show off, something which never went down well. This year, Kate had dumped her boyfriend just before Christmas, rather than the other way round as with the two previous occasions. Kate had done this because she had decided that, on balance, her parents meeting no one at all would be better than her parents meeting Trevor.

Trevor fitted the bill of being tall, dark and handsome, but somehow managed to be almost terminally boring. Kate would have brought him if only she could have guaranteed he wouldn't speak. Trevor had an almost magical gift of making any subject about which he spoke sound about as interesting as a lecture on the development of the trowel. Not only this, but like some kind of verbal vampire he had the ability to suck the life out of anyone else's conversation too, by dropping in phrases such as 'Yes, mm, now something very similar happened to me once,' or 'Really, now I read recently that studies have suggested…' Trevor could have made an armed robbery with violence sound like an especially dull afternoon in a tea room with the aunt you never really talked to.

The compounding problem was that he, along with most men who suffered from this affliction, had another flaw, in that he was be completely blind to how dull and depressing he was to be around. He treated conversations like a huge bowl of overdone porridge, something to be slogged through relentlessly, ignoring or not noticing the glassy-eyed stares, the throat-clearing and the people not only looking at their watches, but shaking them to check if they'd stopped.

Kate had spent several increasingly urgent weeks trying to tease out Trevor's interesting side, only to discover, when it finally emerged, that it was no more interesting than his boring side. Finally, she had given up, and dumped him, although she had a nagging suspicion that Trevor hadn't quite grasped this yet.

And so, Kate was alone again for Christmas. That wasn't the cause of her sherry marathon, though.

The visions were back again, all the strange things she had used to see, things that she had consigned to the part of her life marked 'Over'. It seemed they had not finished with her. There was something different about them, something…

wrong. Kate didn't know what it was. In truth, she didn't want to know what it was, but there was something unusual. The shapes were… urgent. Frustrated. In pain, or under pressure, or something. She had even seen the ghost of her computer, for God's sake!

She hadn't seen it since. She had a feeling she wouldn't. But she had seen plenty of others, and all were expressing the same thing as her PC had been. They wanted to escape. None of them lasted long, either. Within a few moments they seemed to vanish, almost torn apart, as if they were in a high wind.

None of them survived, except… except the ones she had seen clinging to the vet. What was his name? Mr Reece. The ones around him seemed normal, except they looked like they were clinging to him, holding on for dear li… holding on.

Kate had a deeply uneasy feeling, like a person who has heard the creaking and snapping of a falling tree in a forest, and is for the moment unsure of which way to start running. She had a thought that it was something to do with the accelerator in Kent, but whether her brain had connected these just because it couldn't cope with too many horrid things happening at once, or whether there was genuinely some connection that she could instinctively but not logically see, she did not know.

She had emailed, written and telephoned the scientists in control of the accelerator, to try and warn them of her findings. The response had been predictable, if understandable. Kate wondered what she would do if someone had phoned her and told her she was about to cause the end of the world.

The telephone conversation had got no further than the receptionists, who had told her they would pass on her messages, and had told her to have a nice day, with an undertone in their voices indicating that they believed that the secret to her having such a nice day would involve her not phoning the laboratory again.

The email had provoked a short, if polite, reply, indicating that all the hazards and potential dangers of the project had been thoroughly assessed, and noted in the health and safety folder in the lab. So that was all right, then. The letter had got the same response, five days slower and with a stamp.

Kate wasn't sure what to do next. There was no way her project could be up and running again before the accelerator started accelerating, which would be right before the New Year. She toyed with the idea of visiting the lab, but without evidence she imagined it would be an expensive repeat of the telephone calls (which had, of course, been paid for by the University). Professor Lattman sympathised as far as he could, but he was unwilling or unable to back her up. Still, she had to do something, didn't she?

She picked up the glass of sherry in front of her, and sent it the way of the first four. There was a tiny scream from the glass, which only the dog heard, and it didn't care. The doorbell rang, interrupting Kate from her reverie. Her mother stood up, smiling.

'Ah, that'll be Colin and Margaret!' She bustled off towards the door.

Kate looked forlornly at the empty glass. She hadn't drunk nearly enough sherry to cope with Colin and Margaret.

The sound of the door opening was followed by the sounds of middle-aged women performing the strange high-pitched shrieks they make whenever they meet anyone of a similar age that they haven't seen for forty-eight hours. This was mingled with the low-pitched rumbling noises that middle-aged men make in the same circumstances, and soon after this Colin and Margaret bustled into the room.

Margaret was tall and only slightly podgy, with a pretty face absolutely ruined by the inches of make-up that were spread across it. Colin was small, thin, bald and angular, and walked the nervous walk that men like him developed after having been married to women like Margaret for a certain number of years.

Margaret made her high-pitched noises and rushed forward to hug Kate, while Colin rumbled in the background. Kate did her best to emulate the noises being made.

'Oh, look at her, Colin, look at her, hasn't she grown?' Margaret was saying, as she did every time. It seemed such a cliché that Kate hadn't really believed that anyone actually said it, even as a young girl, until she met Margaret. Margaret had said it, every time, without fail and without a hint of irony, despite the fact Kate had stopped growing twelve years previously.

Margaret looked back to Colin, who shrugged as he looked at Kate. 'Don't think so, Margaret. She's twenty-six, now.'

'Oh, Colin, for God's sake, you always have to bloody argue about everything, don't you,' Margaret snapped back. Colin's mouth clapped shut like a mantrap and his eyes drilled into the back of her head, with a gleam in them that suggested he wished he was actually using a drill to do it.

She turned back to Kate.

'Sorry about him, dear,'

Kate tried to smile as they all settled down, Margaret uncomfortably close next to Kate. Colin and Margaret's marriage seemed to be one of such constant warfare that it made the hundred-years war look like a brief skirmish. Anything that Colin said was immediately and automatically contradicted by Margaret, who then felt the need to glance around the room and roll her eyes, simultaneously apologising and begging for help for having married such an idiot.

Colin, on the other hand, was, as far as Kate could see, simply a miserable git. Whether this was due to the years of warfare, or the cause of them, Kate didn't know or care.

Polite conversation began to float genially around the lounge, and Kate let it wash over her, saying 'yes' whenever anybody offered her another glass of sherry. Apparently Colin had been promoted at work to something or other, which meant he was now in charge of stationery, or toilet roll, or something like that at his workplace, but he wasn't happy about it because someone or other had told him something about someone else. Margaret said all this, of course. Colin knew his place, and simply grunted in a displeased sort of way at the points where it seemed he should do so. He got them right. He was an old hand at this by now.

Kate's mother and father bustled in and out of the kitchen. Margaret ran out of things to say about herself and her husband after an hour or so, and Kate was horrified to find the initiative was suddenly on her.

'So, how are you, dear? All OK? How's that lovely Trevor?'

Kate smiled politely. She managed to do this because of the sherry, which was now giving the room a nice warm glow. It made talking seem remarkably easy.

'Oh, yes. Lovely. Lovely. He's very well. Dumped him yesterday, dreary bugger.'

Kate smiled politely again. She could do this small-talk thing, no problem.

There was a polite pause, in which Colin cleared his throat. Kate wondered if she should fill the polite silence before it turned into an impolite one, but fortunately Margaret knew how to handle the situation.

'Oh dear,' she said, her expression filled with a dreadful mock-dismay. 'Oh, that's a shame, isn't it, Colin, isn't it, though, 'cause he was a lovely lad, so interesting.'

Colin grunted. 'What was that, dear?' Margaret asked him.

'Yes, he was,' Colin agreed.

'What would you know about it?' Margaret snapped back, rolling her eyes at Kate.

'So, dear, anything new to tell us? Anything happening with you? How's that lovely cat of yours? How's work?'

Kate smiled politely again. Here there was something she could talk about. She just had to phrase it correctly. She paused to allow the jumbled thoughts to rearrange themselves in her head.

'Well,' she said, 'my cat is recovering from minor coffee burns, my computer has blown up but seems to be haunting me, along with anything that dies within a ten mile radius, I've lost three months' work and the end of the world is nigh.'

She stopped, and ran through the last sentence in her head, to see if she had missed anything out. Nope, she thought. That about covers it.

There was another one of those polite pauses. It lasted most of the rest of the day.

III

The lock jumped around in front of the key, and it took Kate several attempts to bring the two together. She eventually succeeded only by moving the key very slowly towards the lock, like a docking procedure from 2001. It seemed to work better with her eyes shut. Her father had wanted to stay with her until she had managed to get inside her flat, but she had sent him away, insisting she would be fine.

The dinner had been fun, largely because Kate had managed to keep the alcohol at exactly the right level in her bloodstream. The turkey had tasted particularly bland, almost as if it had not been cooked properly, but Kate had enjoyed it anyway because she got to watch Colin and Margaret have to chew their way through the tough, tasteless meat, very politely of course.

The door jumped open more quickly than Kate was expecting, and she flopped into the flat. She closed the door and fumbled for the light switch for a few moments, then decided that it wasn't that important, anyway. Roger appeared from the lounge. He had been hanging back to make sure no cups of coffee were in evidence. They weren't, so he went and said hello. Kate said hello back to him, and explained she was sorry she was a bit drunk, but it was because she had drunk a bit. Roger didn't seem to mind, and purred, pushing his face against hers. Any confusion thus cleared up, Kate struggled her way out of her coat, and went into the lounge.

There were two blinking red lights on the table. She tried to think what she had that flashed with two blinking red lights. Nothing. She closed one eye, and one of the lights disappeared. Ah. The answerphone.

She tottered over to it as carefully as she could manage, squinting at the nasty beige plastic, trying to find the right button. She jabbed at the one she thought was the most likely, but fortunately missed it, hitting the one next to it, thereby playing the messages rather than deleting them and, although she didn't know it, saving the entire planet as she did so.

'You have... two... new messages,' came the strange Bride of Frankenstein voice from the machine.

'Wednesday... One... oh... seven am.' it continued. It was wrong about this, of course, as all answerphones are. Owners of them never manage to set the date and time on them properly, except for that very special golden period in the hours before a power cut.

'Oh... erm... hi,' Trevor said, sounding, as he always did, slightly surprised. 'I... erm... am just... erm... ringing to erm... interesting answerphone, by the way... sorry... erm... just on my way out to... erm... oh, Happy Christmas, by the way... erm... I was just wondering if erm...'

Kate sighed and reached for the fast-forward button, managing to hit it first time. Even his messages were boring.

'Wednesday, Two-fifteen am,' said the Bride of Frankenstein.

'No, it wasn't,' said Kate, now lying on her back beside the sofa. The answerphone did not argue.

A new voice filled the room. It was familiar, and it sounded very scared.

'Hi. It's Alan here. Alan Reece, the vet. I hope I've got the right number. I think... I think I need your help.'

Chapter Ten

I

Colonel Rickenbacker uncrossed his legs, shifting his not inconsiderable bulk around on his buttocks, then recrossed them, left leg on top of right this time. The chair was damn uncomfortable. Sometimes he thought the caretakers made them deliberately so. None of them knew what actually went on in this room, of course. Only a score of people across the globe knew that, including Colonel Rickenbacker. You would have thought that, this being one of the most secret rooms on the planet, in which some of the most secretive meetings in history occurred, the bastards in charge would have found the money to put in comfortable chairs, not this cheap plastic crap.

He sighed and looked at his watch. They were half-an-hour late already. They would probably be at least another half an hour yet. For all their technological advancements, they didn't seem able to keep to a timetable.

Colonel Rickenbacker knew there were many people in the world who would give several of their vital organs for a chance to sit in this room. He grunted. Perhaps, one day, he would let one of them in, just to see their faces fall when they realised how things really were.

He clicked his neck from side to side a few times, then shifted his weight again. Right on left now. He reached across the wide table to the magazine that had been left there. A copy of the National Enquirer. The first page suggested that two celebrities failed to marry each other once more. This time, apparently, they were warned off tying the knot by small blue creatures from the Horsehead Nebula. The Colonel snorted. What a load of crap. As far as he knew, they had been a dullish-purple colour.

He flipped through the pages of the magazine. Stuck at the back there was an article about the Fermi Paradox. The Colonel closed the magazine. He knew all there was to know about it.

The Fermi Paradox had been postulated by the Italian physicist, Enrico Fermi, he of the Manhattan Project fame, and as paradoxes went, it was fairly simple to understand. In a nutshell, it said 'Where are all the aliens, then?'

The theory behind it was also simple. The Galaxy is a big place, never mind the universe. In the Milky Way alone there are one hundred billion stars, which is a large number for anything, let alone immense infernos hundreds of thousands of miles across. Now, if only a tiny proportion of those stars had planets (and recent theories suggested that actually quite a lot of them did), and even if only a tiny fraction of those planets supported any life, then even given the fact that the Galaxy was pretty big (one hundred thousand light years, side to side, to be precise, though only a couple of thousand light years wide for most of its surface) it would take even a fairly stupid civilisation probably no more than a few tens of millions of years to colonise the entire galaxy. And that was without any excitingly science-fiction-type technologies like Einstein-Rosen gates, hyperspace or even the ridiculously badly thought out 'warp' drive. A smart civilisation could probably do it in under a million, provided of course they weren't so smart that they didn't blow themselves back into pond sludge before they got that far.

Not only is the galaxy intimidatingly large, it's also very, very old, certainly more than ten billion years, which is plenty of time for some smart-arse race to do the whole thing a thousand times by now. If they existed, they would be here.

So where were they? This was the question posed by Enrico Fermi. It was the question posed by the back page of the National Enquirer. By a curious coincidence, it was the question running through Colonel Rickenbacker's mind as he glared at his watch again.

If they existed, he thought, they would be here. Well, he knew they existed. Where the hell were they?

There was a creaking noise from the corner of the room. The colonel glanced up. In the corner, there was a small raised platform, with a circular disc of aluminium set into it, about three feet across. The disc was highly polished, and surrounded by a strip of plastic. Inside the plastic strip, a small string of lights had appeared, and begun to circle around it, slowly at first, but then more and more quickly.

A glass panel had also lit up behind the platform now. On its surface, blue flames appeared and began moving quickly and silently across it, jolting and jumping as the lights around the platform began to move so fast that they blurred together.

To Rickenbacker it looked like a cheap prop from Star Trek, which wasn't really a great surprise because that is exactly what it was. All completely unnecessary, of course, because the Epsonils' transference beams were powered directly from the ship's power core, and they could materialise wherever they wanted. The politicians liked a sense of occasion, though, and the Epsonils indulged them to keep them happy.

A second later, two of the Epsonils appeared on the aluminium disc. The engineers were still working on a way of making the lights flash brightly when the aliens arrived. They hadn't managed it yet, and so the slow build-up with the lights and everything, increasing the tension that one was actually seeing a being born on a different planet, was always slightly ruined by the double anticlimaxes of having no special effects or anything, and by the physical appearance of the Epsonils themselves.

Of all the appearances humankind had ever imagined for extra-terrestrial beings, only the tightly-budgeted fifties science-fiction movie directors had come up with anything duller than the Epsonils.

They were about five and a half feet tall, squarish, squattish and a tedious beige colour. They looked, inexplicably, like small men in rubber suits. Rickenbacker knew they weren't, of course. He had seen the medical tests, the DNA profiles with five sets of base pairs, none of which had ever appeared in any life form on planet Earth. The blood was different — strictly speaking, it wasn't blood at all in the sense that humans understood it. It was simply a reaction medium, containing organic... whatever. In all honesty, Rickenbacker couldn't give a crap. He just wished the aliens looked a little more... well, alien.

The two Epsonils looked around the room. One of them blinked slowly, huge heavy lids sliding over the large black eyes. The other one did not. Something to do with the atmosphere. It was humid enough that the Epsonils didn't need to blink at all when on Earth, and only did so out of politeness.

They stepped off the platform, a little awkwardly. That was another thing — aliens, Rickenbacker thought, should be slow, graceful, balletic. The Epsonils lumbered around like... like short, sweaty men in rubber suits. Their heads jiggled as they moved, as if they couldn't quite see properly through their eyes. When the Epsonils had first appeared to the humans, some fifty years previously (though apparently they had been aware of us for thousands of years before that — why they picked the 50's as a globally stable enough time to reveal themselves was anybody's guess. Perhaps they liked the shape of mushroom clouds), it had been assumed that their clumsiness was part of the Epsonils reaction to the difference in gravity between their home world and Earth. When the first humans were taken up, breathless with excitement, to the Epsonils surprisingly dull mother ship, they had discovered that they were always like that. They were simply naturally clumsy.

The first Epsonil stepped towards Rickenbacker, extending its hand shakily. It was wearing a shiny silver one-piece suit, the kind that all the Epsonils seemed to wear all the time. As far as Rickenbacker could work out, it was all that any of them had worn ever. Fashion was not a word, or even a concept, that the Epsonils were familiar with.

Rickenbacker took the dry hand and shook it. The alien watched this ritual with an air of polite bemusement, turning to the other, who wriggled his hips in a way that Rickenbacker assumed, correctly, was some form of Epsonil shrug.

'Greetings, human known as Rickenbacker,' the Epsonil said. They even spoke in the way that aliens spoke in old science-fiction movies. Because of the shape of their larynxes, they spoke with a peculiar accent, which somehow managed to make everything they said sound boring. Eventually this accent had been identified, with the help of a visiting British scientist, as almost identical to that spoken by people who lived in Wolverhampton.

'Good to see you,' lied Rickenbacker.

'Yes,' said the first alien, simply. The second one wiggled its hips in a different manner than it had before. Rickenbacker had no idea why.

'So,' he said. 'What can we do for you?'

The aliens looked at each other. The first one blinked, very slowly. The second wiggled its hips. Rickenbacker tried to keep the smile on his face. It was going to be one of those meetings.

Humanity had very little to do with the Epsonils. The flurry of excitement, and the effort in keeping their arrival secret had kept governments across the globe busy for a while, but eventually it became clear that the Epsonils had very little to offer. They did have hyper-advanced technology, but repeatedly said that the humans were not ready for it, no matter how much the governments begged, pleaded and stamped their feet. Scientists were disappointed to discover that all they were willing to reveal about the cosmos they had explored so far was that it was 'all right'. It was teeth-gnashingly frustrating. It was like having an extremely rich neighbour move in next door, and then proceed to live a simple and dull existence, not even having the decency to show off that he was enjoying his money. No one, thus far, had worked out exactly what it was the Epsonils enjoyed, or even why they had visited Earth in the first place. It was the greatest mystery humankind had ever faced, but in all honesty everyone who had ever studied it had ended up getting so frustrated with the astounding tediousness of the creatures that they had given up in disgust.

The Epsonils rarely visited Earth, anyway. They showed little interest in the planet, or its inhabitants, but still they remained. No one could tell if they had a colony, or a base, or were planning an invasion, or what. Occasionally they flew ships above people's houses. Sometimes they abducted people for a while, then gave them back. Sometimes it was cows.

No one knew why. When asked, the Epsonils would wiggle their hips, and say that it was something that had to be done. As it never seemed to harm anyone the governments eventually let them get on with it. Recently they had taken to trampling around cornfields. If there was some reason for this, it evaded the finest minds on the planet.

So Rickenbacker, being one of the Chiefs of Staff and current head of the Majestic project, found himself in the unenviable position of having another baffling meeting with these, the greatest and dullest of mankind's discoveries. They had requested to speak to someone in charge. This was not unusual. Often the meetings were short, consisting of the Epsonils asking clarification about something in human society, such as the meaning of the phrase 'How's it hanging?' or why men never made eye contact with each other in a public lavatory. Rickenbacker readied himself for a question along these lines.

'We have come,' said the first alien, in its slow, mournful accent, 'to say goodbye.'

Now it was Rickenbacker's turn to blink.

'What?' he said.

The first alien looked back to the second. More wiggling of hips. 'We have come,' said the first, louder and much more slowly.

'Yeah, I got that,' Rickenbacker said quickly. 'You're leaving?'

'Yes,' said the first. 'We have perceived things.'

'Things?' Rickenbacker said. 'What things?'

There was a pause. 'Certain things. To do with your planet. There are changes coming.'

Rickenbacker glanced at the second alien. Wiggle wiggle. A cold feeling began to creep up his spine slowly, readying itself for the big finish at the back of his neck, where it would make the hairs stand up on end.

'Changes?' he managed, half turning towards the big red telephone on the desk behind him.

'Yes. It would not be wise for us to be here. We are sorry for you.'

The hairs on the back of Rickenbacker's neck were standing up. 'You're sorry?' he said, his voice rising. 'What do you know? What's going to happen?'

'We cannot say. We cannot help you. We are sorry.'

Rickenbacker couldn't believe it. What were they talking about? Just humanity's luck to get the Epsonils as first contacts. It would have been better to be invaded. He stopped. Was that it?

'Are we going to be invaded?' he said.

The first alien blinked, infuriatingly slowly. 'Yes,' it said. A pause. 'No,' it said. Another pause. 'Sort of.'

'Sort of?'

The second alien nudged the first, which then tilted its head to one side. They stepped back onto the platform.

'It is time for us to go,' it said.

Rickenbacker stepped forwards. 'But, wait... wait goddammit! Can't you tell us what...'

The two aliens vanished. Rickenbacker, trembling, turned, picked up the large red phone, and began shouting at people.

Chapter Eleven

I

There were very few reputable cafés, even in Bristol, that were prepared to open on Boxing Day. This did not apply to the Great Relish in Clifton, as it was neither reputable nor, in the strictest sense of the word, a café — at least, Alan had never been served with anything that in the outside world would have been recognised as food. It was as if physical laws behaved differently inside the small, yellow and greasy walls of the place, as if the chef was a frustrated physicist who spent his working days experimenting with new ways of producing exotic forms of matter. It didn't matter what you ordered — what invariably came out of the kitchen (on a small chipped white plate with a sad brown salad next to it) was neither solid, nor liquid, but some strange kind of pseudo-state in between the two. If Einstein had ever visited the Great Relish on a day off from writing the Theory of Relativity, the future of physics would have followed an entirely different path.

The bizarre thing was that despite the unrecognisability of the constituents and even the unusual state of the food, it was strangely compelling. Inside the café, to which George insisted on taking Alan on every Sunday that he couldn't avoid it, Alan found himself putting things inside his mouth that normally he would drop in a clinical waste bin, and in a horrible sort of way, actually enjoying doing it.

This state of affairs disturbed Alan so much that he tried to avoid the café as much as he could. Today he couldn't. It was perfect for their purposes. First of all, it was open, unlike seemingly everywhere else in the county. Secondly, it was neutral territory for his meeting with Kate, who had finally phoned him back earlier in the morning. Thirdly, it was unlikely anybody would take too much notice of them. You didn't notice what other people were doing in the Great Relish. It wasn't that sort of place.

Alan shifted uncomfortably in the plastic chair. The tables and benches in parts of the café had been done up to look like an American diner, but the effect had been spoiled by the cheapness of the furniture, and the diminutive size of the café. It only had room inside for six tables, and the owner had given up on the attempt to go upmarket halfway through, creating a hybrid of cheap new plastic tables along with greasy and dirty old wooden ones. Alan preferred the plastic tables when he could get them — they seemed cleaner. Hygiene was something that happened to other eating establishments. Alan had no idea what strings the owner had pulled to prevent the café from being closed down by the Food Standards Agency, but he was grateful of it now.

He looked around at the tattered posters and once brightly painted indeterminate objects that seemed to grow on the walls of places like this, and wondered what he was going to say to Kate.

George sat down opposite him, placing a cup of tea in front of Alan and a coffee in front of himself. George had decided to come along on the basis of having 'nothing better to do'. Alan had started to try and explain about the voice to George, then had got nervous and simply asked if he would come along for moral support. George had naturally got a bit suspicious at this point, thinking Alan was trying to set him up on a double date, but Alan had said that it had something to do with what was happening in the world. George had looked unconvinced, but agreed to come anyway. Alan had been relieved despite himself.

'Thanks,' he said, taking a sip of the lukewarm liquid that George plonked in front of him.

'Really,' George said, peering into his own brew, 'Don't mention it.' He took a swig of it. A pained look crossed his face, followed quickly by a paradoxical pleased one. 'Sure you didn't want anything to eat?'

Alan shook his head, glancing at one of the other patrons spooning forkfuls of God-knew-what into his mouth.

His stomach rumbled treacherously, but he didn't want to sit through the half-hour of queasy almost-sickness that always followed a meal in the Great Relish.

'Suit yourself,' George shrugged. 'When's she coming?'

'She said around one o'clock,' Alan replied, glancing at his watch. Still ten minutes yet.

George rummaged in his coat, and took out his battered Dictaphone. Alan raised his eyebrows.

'Come on, George, put it away. We're not here for a scoop for you.'

'But there's no...' George began, but caught Alan's stare. 'OK, OK,' he said, putting it away again.

A waitress, who was, like the café, small, greasy and unpleasant, and as such fitted right there, plonked a plate of material in front of Alan, and then stomped off back towards the kitchen. George reached across the table and pulled the plate towards him, and drowned the stuff on it in ketchup. He had already selected the knife and fork from the stand that stood the best chance of getting somewhere near the dictionary definition of the word 'clean'. He picked them up and set about the plate with them. Alan watched him with the gruesome fascination that people stare out of their side windows at car crashes with.

'So,' George managed between mouthfuls, 'What's all this about, Alan? What's going on?'

Alan sighed. 'I don't really want to go through it all twice. Let's just wait until...'

The door opened and the young woman from Alan's consult room walked in. She was small, dark-haired and pretty. She was trying to look relaxed, but was betrayed by her intense blue eyes, which flicked around the café like someone watching the final at Wimbledon until they settled upon Alan — or, more specifically, on a point just behind and above Alan. Then her deep blue eyes met his, and she smiled. She walked over to where they were sitting, her gaze still wandering every now and then to the empty space behind Alan's head.

'You've picked up another one, I see,' she said.

II

Kate sat down opposite Alan, next to George, and ordered a hot chocolate, ignoring George's frantic sub-vocalised warnings against this course of action. She turned and smiled at Alan. He tried to smile back, but he couldn't. Instead he mumbled at her.

'Erm... Kate, this is George, he's... well, he...'

George did manage to smile at Kate; too widely, in Alan's opinion. It was the smile he used when he was on the pull.

'I lodge with him,' George said. Kate smiled back, slightly puzzled. George shrugged. 'I'm interested in this kind of stuff.'

'What kind of stuff?' Kate asked.

'We were hoping,' Alan interrupted, 'that you could tell us.'

Kate looked back at Alan. Her eyes flicked over his shoulder again. Alan had to fight the urge to turn and look himself. He knew there was nothing there — or, at least, nothing that he would be able to see.

'Is she looking at me?' the Gandalf-voice suddenly echoed inside his head. Alan jumped. The voice had not said a word since the car journey the day before, although he had been able to feel something lurking at the back of his mind, like a half-remembered dream. It took him a few seconds to notice that Kate had jumped as well. Her mouth had opened.

'Did you hear? Did you hear it?' Alan asked, urgently. A small part of him hoped that she did not, actually hoped that he was insane, and making all of this up, because if he wasn't... well, the world would be different. He could already see the answer to his question in her expression, though.

Slowly, she nodded. 'I... I used to be able to see things. A long time ago.' She winced as she spoke, as if embarrassed by her own words. She took a deep breath and looked Alan in the eyes. 'I see dead people,' she said, as seriously and gravely as she could.

George snorted some tea out of his nose. It plopped back into his cup. 'You see dead people?' he smiled, half-amused, until he caught Alan's expression. The smile faded.

'You're seeing one of them now, aren't you?' said Alan.

'Oh, for heaven's sake,' the Gandalf-voice said. 'Do we have to be quite so melodramatic about it all? I think we've established that this young lady can see me.'

Kate's lips twitched. Alan mumbled 'Sorry' under his breath. George looked from one to the other. 'Really?' he said. 'Can you really see something?'

Kate nodded. 'Oh, yes.'

'What does it look like?' George asked, now peering at Alan's shoulder himself. Alan gave in to the urge to glance around. There was, of course, nothing to see there.

'It's hard to say,' Kate said, looking even more self-conscious. 'It's not clear.' She shook her head, and looked down at the table.

'What's wrong with her?' the Gandalf-voice said.

'I'm sorry,' Kate said, looking up. 'I haven't done anything like this for a long time. I never used to hear any of them speak. I just used to…' she tailed off, and cleared her throat. 'It seems a little… strange.'

Alan was inclined to agree.

'You said you could help me,' he said, leaning towards Kate. 'What did you mean?'

Kate shrugged. 'I'm not sure. I just thought…'

A thought struck Alan. 'What does he sound like to you?'

Kate looked puzzled. 'He?'

'Look,' said the Gandalf-voice, 'I'm sure this is all very interesting, but…'

'She,' said Kate, emphatically, 'sounds very much like the voice of my Aunt Mallory. She's been dead for ten years.'

Alan raised his eyebrows. 'To me it sounds like Gandalf out of Lord of the Rings.'

'I'm everything you associate with wisdom,' said the voice, sounding irritable. 'It's complicated, of course, but I was hoping it would be the best way to get you to listen to me.' The voice paused. 'It seemed like a good idea,' it added, sounding as though it thought it didn't any more.

George had pulled out his notepad from some hidden place, and was scribbling furiously. 'Sounds different to both parties,' he muttered under his breath. He looked up, aware at the lapse in conversation. 'Is it talking now?' he said.

Alan nodded. 'Keep quiet,' he said.

'Does this idiot really have to be here too?' Gandalf asked.

'Since you're being so talkative,' Alan asked, 'perhaps you could tell us what you're doing, and why you haven't spoken to me for hours until Kate walked in?'

There was a pause, presumably while the voice gathered its thoughts from wherever they were. Alan felt the mental equivalent of a sigh pass through his mind.

'You're right. You're right, of course. I was waiting for the girl.'

'Why me, particularly?' Kate asked.

'Well, since you ask,' the voice replied, 'not you, particularly. Just someone else. Someone who could hear me too, so I could convince this young man he wasn't completely insane. At least, not yet.'

'OK,' said Kate. She looked annoyed, though whether it was at the voice, or at Alan himself, Alan couldn't tell. 'I'm here. We're all ears. What do you want to tell us about?'

The voice cleared its throat. How it did this, Alan had no idea. He was not about to ask.

'What's it saying?' George interrupted. His face was drawn with frustration.

'Is there any way,' Alan asked out loud, 'that George could hear you as well?'

There was a pause before the voice responded. 'You want him to hear this too?' There was a hint of incredulity that did not sit well with the deep tones of the old wizard.

'We'll only have to tell him anyway,' Alan said. 'It's easier this way.'

George looked excitedly around the room. 'All right,' the voice said, irritated. 'I will try. All of you join hands.'

Alan and Kate exchanged glances. There were not many people in the café, and those that were there were minding their own business; or, at least, they were putting a lot of effort into looking like they were minding their own business. They spread their hands on the table. Alan looked at George.

'He wants us to link hands,' he said.

'No way,' muttered George, half smiling and gently taking Alan and Kate's hands in his. Alan took Kate's hand, reaching across the table. Her fingers were cold. She didn't look at him.

For what seemed like a long time, nothing happened. Then, after a few moments, nothing continued to happen. Alan felt increasingly aware that they were three people sitting in a disreputable café looking for all the world like they were trying to have a séance. Then he realised that this was because it was precisely what they were trying to do.

'Erm…' said Alan.

'Just a moment,' the voice snapped back, irritably. 'I'm trying. It's hard to find… ah… there we are. Can you hear anything now?'

George's eyes widened.

'You can hear it?' Alan asked. George nodded quickly. Alan was interested despite everything. Who did George consider to be the pinnacle of wisdom? 'Who can you hear?' he asked.

'It sounds like… like Yoda,' George replied, in a voice full of awe.

'Can we get on with it now?' said the voice.

'Of course,' Kate said.

III

'I died. A long time ago. How long, or who I was, I cannot say. I am not these people whose voices you hear. That is merely the easiest way for your brain to interpret the thoughts I project. I was… someone important, I think. Or I did something important. It is hard to say. In the… the other place… time and memory blend into one, and it is hard to keep hold of either without losing yourself completely. One survives by taking what bits of memory one can, stealing it from the others lost there. There is a vast sea of the lost ones, ones who have finally broken up under the pressure, who have no sense of self at all, no sense that they ever were anything more. It is… difficult… to keep afloat.'

The voice was filled with a deep, tragic sorrow. Alan, listening to Gandalf's voice, was surprised to find himself moved almost to tears. To judge by the expression on Kate's face, Aunt Mallory was doing a good job of the narrative too.

'I have lost a great deal of myself. I think all this is new to me.' As the voice spoke, images of modern technology — mobile phones, aeroplanes, and computers — flashed through Alan's mind. 'But I have also stolen many memories, some more recent than others, so I know what is happening in the world.

'All we have are memories. There is a great hunger for them.'

The voice paused again. Alan saw that a tear had formed in one of Kate's eyes, and had started the long journey down her cheek. She did not seem aware of it.

'I don't think it was always that way. Perhaps it was, but I think something has gone wrong. Perhaps we are all meant to join with the sea. But I did not have the courage.'

Another pause. When it spoke again, the voice was stronger.

'All that is unimportant, however. You will find this out for yourselves, later.' A chill passed up Alan's spine as he realised what the voice meant. 'Something has changed there. Something that has already started to cause changes here, too.'

'Do you mean the... the transparencies?' Kate asked. This was the name the papers had given to the string of bizarre animal births across the world.

The voice nodded. Again, Alan had no idea how it did this, but just knew he was aware that somehow the thing inside him had nodded. He decided to relegate his feelings about this to the back of his mind, along with the several dozen other things he didn't understand, but which were lesser mysteries.

'Yes,' it said. 'That is the first sign. There will be others. Something has taken control of the sea, of the lost ones. It is hoarding the energy.'

'How is that causing these... things we are seeing?' Alan asked. In his mind's eye he could see again the calf at White's farm.

There was another pause. 'I don't know,' said the voice, simply. 'It is something to do with the connection between the worlds. Somehow the natural transfer of energies has been blocked. These things, these creatures, are being born without it.'

'Without a soul?' Kate asked.

'If you like. That is one way of looking at it. There are many. Whatever you call it, these energies are necessary for life to survive. We are merely seeing the first ripples of the effect. Soon, nothing will be able to be born.'

The three around the table were silent for a moment.

'Well,' said George, 'at least we're all right, eh?'

'I'm afraid not,' the voice said. An abstract part of Alan wondered if George heard Yoda's twisted syntax as well as his voice, but this didn't seem the right time to ask him.

'This... thing... is gathering energy to itself. I am not certain what it intends to do with it. Maybe with enough energy it would be able to break through the normal divisions between the dimensions.'

The voice paused for dramatic effect, but this was ruined

by the waitress walking over to the table, casting a half-interested glance at the trio sat around it, and proceeding to smear grease across the surface of the table with a rag she kept for the purpose on her belt. She took George's nearly empty plate and walked away.

'It would be born again,' the voice said, sepulchrally.

Another pause. 'Wait,' said George, 'are you saying it would be an end of the world job?'

'Very probably,' the voice replied, 'it would be the end of two worlds.'

'Bloody hell,' breathed Kate.

'There's something I don't understand,' Alan said, understating things somewhat. 'What has all this got to do with me? Why come to me? What's been happening to me these last few weeks?'

'You — your energy — stands out in the other world, like a beacon,' the voice said. 'I don't know why. The energies are drawn to you. You are a conduit, a channel. The things you have experienced were the energies channelling themselves through you, thoughtlessly, mindlessly. Somehow you are a connection between the worlds.'

'This all sounds a bit X-filesey to me,' said George, looking doubtful. He was clearly upset that it was Alan that was having all the exciting stuff happen to him. 'Why Alan, then?' he added, with a silent 'Why not me?'

'I don't know,' said the voice. 'I can only tell you how he appears to the other world. Have you had any connection with anything like this before?'

They all turned to look at Alan. He could even feel the voice staring at him.

'Well...' he said awkwardly. He suddenly felt terribly guilty, although he wasn't sure why. His cheeks turned red. 'There... there was a call out I went on, a few weeks ago. It was to a calf, and it was like these others that are being born. Or, it was at first. I touched it, and... well, it got better,' he finished, lamely.

'That hasn't happened with the others,' said Kate. 'All of them have died within a few hours. None of them have got better.'

Alan shrugged. 'It was nothing,' he said.

'That is it,' the voice said. 'That is when it happened. This calf, it must have been the first. Somehow, when you touched it, you opened a channel between the worlds. You gave it the energy. This is bad. This is very bad news.'

'Bad?' said George. 'Bad why?'

'Because this is a threat to whatever is gathering the energy,' the voice said. 'Don't you see? I am here because I was drawn to Alan, because he stood out like a beacon in the other world. I am filling the channel now. Perhaps it is no longer visible with me here, but it was for a long time. And as long as Alan is a conduit, it will prevent the thing in the other world from monopolising the energy. It may even see him as a way through. Either way, it will be trying to find him.'

Alan got the distinct impression he did not want to be found by this thing, whatever it was. What exactly was it, anyway?

'What exactly is this thing, anyway?' he said out loud.

'I don't know,' said the voice, a little embarrassed. 'I can feel its presence across the other world. Even here I feel the enormity of it. I think... I think it was once human. There are floating memories here, segments of things long forgotten. I have found a part of a name, something I think it was once called: "Cranmer".'

The three looked at each other. 'Mean anything?' George asked. Kate shrugged. Alan was annoyed to see he now looked extremely relieved that the exciting stuff wasn't happening to him any more.

'So what do we do?' Kate said.

Alan looked at her. 'You don't have to do anything,' he said, trying to sound brave, but not sure he was managing it, what with his voice trembling and everything. 'It's my problem. I'll deal with it.'

'End of the world!' interrupted George. 'I think that might fit into the category of "our problem" too.'

Kate smiled. 'Come on,' she said, squeezing Alan's hand. Alan was greatly pleased by this, until he remembered his circumstances.

'We'll help,' Kate was saying. 'I've got nothing better to do. You got my cat better for me, didn't you?'

'OK,' said George. 'That's that sorted out. So what do we do?'

'I don't know,' the voice said, anticlimactically. George was disappointed. Isn't this the bit where they get their quest? he thought.

'I think the best solution is to stay together,' the voice continued. 'We don't know if this Cranmer is looking for Alan yet, but if he is we need to be ready.'

'Just "stay together"? What kind of a bloody plan is that?' George complained. 'You sound like my mum and dad.'

'In the meantime,' the voice continued, ignoring him, 'you need to find out more about Cranmer. There must be an answer to what is happening now somewhere in the past. This thing was alive once, I am sure, just as I was.'

Alan nodded. 'Any idea,' he said, trying to sound matter-of-fact about something that was scaring the life out of him, 'how I might be attacked?'

'I don't know,' the voice said, in what was rapidly turning into its favourite phrase. Alan was sure Gandalf had a few more answers than this in the books. 'But it is possible that attacks could come from anyone, anyone in this world. The thing could connect with any living thing as its power grows. It might even be strong enough to control them. I might be able to detect it, but I might not.'

It paused again for effect.

'Trust no one,' it said.

'I told you it sounded like the X-files,' George muttered.

Chapter Twelve

I

They decided to make Kate's flat the base of operations. It seemed the sensible thing to do — it was closer to the centre of Bristol, and so closer to the University and the library. It also seemed unlikely that anybody would come looking for Alan there, unless they were taking persistence to a truly spectacular level and working their way through his client list. They still weren't sure if anyone would come after Alan at all, and to him the precautions seemed foolish. Gandalf was unwilling or unable to elaborate any further than he had been in the café. Kate had offered to lodge them in her flat for a while. George had agreed quickly, and so Alan had little choice but to go along with it. He felt he had little choice about anything at the moment. Having made the momentous decision to leave his job, he now found himself swept along a completely different path, just as helpless as he was before.

He had gone back with George to pack a few things from his house. There had been several messages on the answer-phone, but Alan didn't listen to them. None of them could possibly have been good news at the moment. He would ring his parents from Kate's flat.

He had been mildly depressed to discover how little stuff he actually had. He was sure he used to be more interesting than this. He tried to remember the sort of person he had been when he had been a student. Fun, he decided. Interested in things, more things than just… just… what was he interested in, anyway? He felt as if his life had been put on hold since he started work. Since then he was simply existing, surviving from one day to the next, never looking ahead. Perhaps that was why this latest disjunction hadn't affected him as much as he would have thought. Then again, perhaps it simply hadn't sunk in yet.

He had put a few clothes in his BSAVA bag. It was the

only bag that he could find, given to him for free at a conference. At least that was something about being a vet. Nobody had ever given him anything for free as a student except abuse. As he packed, Alan had a strange detached feeling, as if none of this was real. Even the news reports he glimpsed on the television or heard on the radio did nothing to remove this feeling, remarking as they did on more and more of the mystery births. Even though he had seen one for himself, even with the voice in his head, Alan found he was having trouble believing it. Things like this didn't happen, did they? Not in Britain. Nothing ever happened in Britain, did it?

On the news, doctors were, of course, baffled, but this was to be expected and worried no one. The problem was that everybody seemed baffled, even the strange people who lived in Cornwall and still believed you could forecast the weather by cutting open an apple. There was a sense of muffled panic in the reports that were constantly played, a tension. It wasn't normal. What was, these days?

The only thing that gave Alan any grounding in reality at all, bizarrely, was the constant awareness that he was sharing his mind with someone else. The Gandalf-voice rarely spoke, but Alan was starting to get heartily sick of its ominous doom-mongering. He just wanted some time to himself, to sort things out in his own mind. Unfortunately his own mind was no longer the private place it had been a few days ago. The voice warned him to be on his guard at all times, that the servants of the enemy could strike at any time. Alan ignored it as best he could.

So now Alan found himself alone (in a manner of speaking), in the flat of a woman whom he hardly knew, hiding from something he still didn't understand, while the world went to pieces around him. He sat listlessly on the sofa, wondering if there was something he should be doing. The cat jumped onto his lap and he tickled its ears absently. At least I've made one friend, he thought, trying not to think of George and Kate out together.

The reason he was on his own in the first place was that George, Kate and the Gandalf-voice had decided it might be too dangerous for him to venture outside at the moment, in case a passing servant of the enemy took the opportunity to do to him whatever they intended to do to him when they found him. If indeed they were looking for him at all.

'Be on your guard at all times,' the voice said, ominously, as if it was reading his thoughts, which it was.

'Stuff it,' said Alan, getting up to look in the fridge for the hundredth time. Nothing had appeared in there since the last time he looked. He wasn't hungry anyway. He took out a carton of orange juice and tried to take a swig from it, but because of the ingenious opening mechanism at the top, he instead poured it down the front of his shirt. He swore.

Roger the cat rubbed itself against his legs, purring, and started to lap up some of the spilt liquid, then realised it was orange juice. He looked up at Alan with the expression of one betrayed. Alan put the carton back in the fridge and stroked Roger's ears, who seemed to think this made up for it, and purred. Alan cleaned up the juice.

The evening before had been awkward. It should have been exciting — these three strangers, drawn together by events beyond their control, on a quest to save the world. Instead it had been strange, full of silences. Even George had been subdued. They had chatted politely and tried to find out a little about each other, but Alan especially was not in the mood for it. What exactly do you talk about in a social grouping when you have a quest to save the world?

They had decided, between them, that they couldn't do much more without finding out something about what was going on. Kate had set off to her computer at the Physics building this morning, to trawl the Internet for references to 'Cranmer', and then to head to the library. Alan had offered to accompany her, but at that point the Gandalf-voice had done its ominous bit about the servants of the enemy, so George had gone with her instead. Alan wasn't sure how he felt about that.

Here he was, charged with saving the world and everything, and those two were out doing the important stuff. He was bumming round a flat with a cat and a dead person for company. George had seemed quite keen to accompany Kate, and Alan wasn't sure what he felt about that either.

Shouldn't he be doing something? Planning? Making some mighty weapon? Making phone calls? Something? He hadn't realised saving the world could be so boring.

Kate's flat was not the tidiest in the world. It didn't exactly look as if a bomb had hit it, but it looked as if a few grenades had. Alan had made a half-hearted effort to clean it up, but as he didn't know where anything was he found he was just moving clutter around different piles. He gave up, and had sat on the sofa instead. The Gandalf-voice seemed nervous, agitated, but when Alan quizzed it, it kept warning him to be 'on his guard'. Short of standing next to the front door with a cricket bat, Alan wasn't quite sure what else he could do. He got so bored he actually tried that, but after a few minutes it made his arms ache.

He tried watching the television but the news reports worried him, and the daytime television drained his will to live, so he turned it off again. The radio was no better — in between music, presenters kept bringing on experts in fertility, medicine, paranormal events or whatever, but as none of them had a clue what was happening, they spent their whole time trying to define the problem rather than explain it. Alan tried reading a book, the new Iain Banks that he found in Kate's bedroom, but he couldn't shake the feeling that someone was reading it over his shoulder, so he gave up, and finally resorted to wandering around the flat, peering out of the window, and swinging the cricket bat around the lounge, trying to be on his guard. After a while he went and stood by the door again, brandishing the bat in front of him, much to the confusion of Roger. Alan felt stupid. It wasn't like a servant of the enemy, whatever the hell that was, was just going to come up and ring the doorbell, was it?

'I give up,' he said out loud, dropping the bat and heading back to the sofa. 'I'm going back to sleep.'

The doorbell rang.

II

Kate and George headed for the University library first; it was the closest to where they had parked Kate's car. The streets were busy, as trade began to pick up after the Christmas lull. It would take more than strange births to keep the people of Bristol from missing the sales.

George found himself looking at the faces of the shoppers as he walked. There was something different, he could see. They looked harried, nervous. They didn't look at other people except with short, darting glances. They rushed on with their business, trying to get it done and get home as soon as possible. It reminded him of the days immediately after the destruction of the World Trade Centre in New York, what everybody now seemed to call 9/11, as if they couldn't bring themselves to actually say what happened. People had the same look on their faces then — shocked, suddenly scared. George remembered it well. All his life he had been excited, looking forward to the future and what new technologies and excitements it would bring. 9/11 had changed all that. It had made people scared of the future again.

He looked over at Kate as they walked. She had the same expression on her face.

'Hey,' he said, 'you OK?'

She glanced at him nervously.

'Do you think we did the right thing leaving Alan at home?'

He shrugged. 'Can't see anything happening to him there. Besides, it's what Yoda said. I'm not going to argue with a Jedi master.' He flashed his best grin at her, but she had already looked away.

There were bollards in front of the door of the library.

Several students hung around forlornly outside, bags over their shoulders, like bees looking for pollen in winter. Kate and George climbed up the steps and approached. George peered through the glass windows but there was no sign of life inside. Kate approached a thin student with a fledgling beard.

'What's happening?' she asked. 'Is it closed?'

'They all are!' the thin man said, urgently. It was obviously the most important thing in the world to him. 'The medical library too!'

'Why? Aren't they supposed to be open today?' George interrupted.

The man nodded. 'That's what I said!' he whined. 'They won't tell me why!'

'Will they open tomorrow?' asked Kate.

The student started jiggling urgently, as if he needed the toilet badly. 'I don't know,' he said, 'I don't know, they won't say, they won't say!' He looked at Kate, really jiggling quite badly now. 'They won't say!' he repeated.

George turned Kate away from the library junkie.

'Well, there goes plan A,' he sighed. Kate nodded, chewing her lip, her brows furrowed.

'The library was supposed to be open today,' she said, sounding worried. 'Do you think it means anything?'

'I think it means,' George said, 'that we're getting a little paranoid. You can still access the database from work, can't you? We'll check the Internet while we're there.'

Kate nodded, but she looked unconvinced. They headed over to the Physics building, not far from the arts library. Kate had, of course, forgotten her card, and it was a more difficult tussle than usual to get past the security guard, but after fifteen minutes of haggling with him, they made it inside.

The building was much quieter than the streets. The science library was closed as well as the others, so nobody had much business being in the building. The professor was not in his office — not a surprise, but Kate was still hoping to see him, and maybe ask him his opinion about what was going on.

Instead they headed for Kate's small room.

'Wow,' said George as they entered. 'I didn't know we had many earthquakes around here.'

'Tee hee,' said Kate as she swept a pile of junk from her chair in front of the computer. George did likewise.

'Nice place you've got here,' George said. 'Do you come here often?'

'Oh, smeg!' Kate suddenly said, as she switched on the computer. George was used to responses like this to his lines.

'What is it?' he said.

The computer was slowly flaring into life in front of them. 'I've just remembered,' Kate said. 'The accelerator! They start it up next week!'

George nodded intelligently, but this didn't seem to get him anywhere, so he tried a more conventional 'What?' instead.

Kate ran her hand through her hair. 'I'd forgotten, I'd totally forgotten.' She turned to George. 'They're testing a new particle accelerator in Kent next week. A massive ion accelerator.'

Something about this set a tiny bell ringing in George's mind. 'Oh yes, I've heard about this. We had a report about it a few months ago. A group of protestors are saying it could end the world if it's switched on.' He smiled. 'There's a lot of it about.'

'They could be right,' Kate said, ashen-faced.

George caught himself halfway through another intelligent nod, and resorted to 'What?' again.

'I did some studies, a simulation, before all this started. It showed there's a chance of increased ion interaction, forming mixed strangelets. The strangelets could start a chain reaction, converting everything around them.'

George didn't even bother with the nod this time, but tried 'Eh?' for a bit of variety.

'The strangelets could convert everything around them. Everything. They could, if unchecked, consume the whole world.'

'Oh. Right,' George said. One end of the world scenario in a week was exciting, but getting two together just seemed silly. 'So we've got to save the world twice, is that it?'

'Not necessarily,' said Kate. 'What if the two are connected? It seems quite a coincidence, doesn't it?'

'Erm... what is a strangelet, anyway?'

'It's... well, it's a particle. Well, no, it isn't. It's the sort of things electrons are made of.'

'Like an atom?'

'No, no, much smaller. Like a quark. You've heard of quarks?'

George nodded intelligently. It seemed easier.

'A strangelet is like that, a group of quarks. Some have been seen, or at least, their effects have been seen, but the ones this accelerator might make could possibly have the power to convert anything they touch to the same as them. And anything the newly created ones touch do the same.'

'So... what has this got to do with Yoda and the dead?' George said, trying to steer the conversation back to one where he might at least look half-knowledgeable.

'Well,' said Kate, 'suppose these strangelets don't take over the whole world, but form a chain reaction in another direction. In another dimension.'

'You mean...'

Kate nodded. 'Into the... dead world, or whatever you want to call it. Chaos. What if it forms a connection? What if this is exactly what this Cranmer is trying to do?'

They were silent for a moment. 'Is it possible?' George asked. 'I mean, scientifically?'

Again, Kate nodded. 'Yes. At least, I think so. Assuming this other world had some physical boundaries, and is infinite in at least one extent, so that it passes through all points in our...'

'OK,' said George. 'So, if you're right, what do we do about it?'

Kate shrugged. 'I'm not sure. We still need to find out

more, about this Cranmer. It might be that there's another way in. Just stopping them turning on the accelerator won't stop what's happening, will it? There must be something else.'

George nodded. 'OK. But half a plan's better than no plan at all. Let's see what we can find.'

They turned toward the computer.

III

Alan stopped in mid-step, his back to the door. He could feel his heart hammering away in his chest.

'Gandalf?' he hissed under his breath, feeling very foolish. He still hadn't got used to the idea that he could just think things, and the Gandalf-voice could pick them up. Some part of him still wanted to believe that it could only hear him when he spoke aloud. There was silence, broken only by the soft purring of Roger as he brushed between Alan's legs, and a fresh ring from the doorbell.

'Gandalf?' Alan said again, more loudly this time. There was no reply. Why was the old fool keeping quiet now? He'd had been quite happy to sound ominous all morning, so why was he not communicating now Alan needed him?

Alan couldn't quite remember what the door looked like as he turned, and was hoping to see a huge oak door, covered in iron reinforcements, preferably with a heavy iron grille and a little window. It was optimistic, true, but he was still extremely disappointed to see the flimsy thin wooden frame, like all the internal doors in the flat. It was painted with a white gloss that only seemed to outline how flimsy and thin it was. It didn't look like it could withstand the blows of a mildly irritated nonagenarian, let alone the attacks of whatever might be out there. There wasn't even one of those little round spyholes to peer out of. There was just a thin golden chain, which looked like it would stand up to the aforesaid pensioner for all of five seconds.

Whoever it was outside had now obviously become sick of ringing the doorbell, and started knocking on the door. As if to underline the feebleness of the portal, the door shook in its hinges with each knock.

Alan told himself to calm down, and took a step towards the door. All this business with the babies, and the voice, was getting him unnecessarily wound up. It wasn't as if the knocks were the slow, heavy thud of some indescribable monster, or the massive shuddering of someone trying to knock the door down. If anything, the knocks were the quick, impatient raps of someone who had something better to do.

He approached the door cautiously, unsure of the best plan of action. He looked again at the chain. It looked like it had been made out of paper clips. The knocks came again. He wanted to ignore them, like he had the answerphone messages, but this was much more difficult somehow, much more personal. He reached the door as the knocks resumed, followed by a questioning but undeniably human voice from the corridor outside.

'Hello?' it said, unthreateningly. 'Anybody home?'

Gandalf remained obstinately silent. Alan was on his own. Apart from Roger the cat, of course. He reached up to the little latch, and turned it, slowly pulling open the door, aware of the number of times he had seen people do this sort of thing in the movies seconds before receiving a sharp and usually short-lived surprise in the face. He peeped out of the smallest gap he could make into the corridor beyond.

There was a young man outside. He was dressed in a blue and red uniform, with a baseball cap on, also in red. There was some kind of logo on the cap but Alan couldn't quite make it out. The man was dressed in the kind of lazily untidy way that suggested he didn't really care about the company he worked for. He was holding a clipboard, and turned towards the gap, his face changing in a second from irritated to falsely friendly.

'Ah, good afternoon, Sir. I'm here from PowerFlow. I'm here to read the meter, if it's convenient.'

Alan paused for a moment, looking the man up and down. He opened the door a crack more. 'Oh, really?' he asked, thinking as he said it that this perhaps wasn't the best riposte in the world. The young man obviously shared this assessment.

'Erm... yes,' he said, slightly nonplussed. 'I was just... erm... wondering if now would be a convenient time...'

'No,' Alan blurted, reaching for the small lifeline the man had offered him. 'No, it isn't. I'm... erm... I'm busy.'

'That's all right, Sir,' said the man, cheerily. 'Won't take a jiff. I'll be in and out in no time.'

Shit, Alan thought. Are they supposed to be persistent like this?

'Well, the thing is,' he said out loud, 'the thing is... I don't live here.' He was going to add something more but the man seemed to be considering this.

'Right,' he said at last. 'Well, if you could just let me in, it won't take a second.' He placed his hand on the door. Alan wasn't sure if he was imagining it, but a note of menace seemed to have crept into the man's voice.

'No, really,' said Alan, 'I'm afraid I've got lots to do. I could ring the meter reading over to you.' He made a move to start to close the door, but the other man held it firm.

'It won't take a moment,' he said. All the false cheerfulness had vanished now. He looked very serious.

Alan decided now was the time to get nervous. He pushed the door again. It didn't move. The man pushed the door back to the limits of the chain. Alan looked into his face. There was something wrong with it. He couldn't say what, but there was an expression there that was... alien. The eyes flashed at him. The man took a deep breath, and let it out. Alan thought he could hear voices in the breath, lots of voices all shouting at once. The man's legs began jiggling in a peculiar dance that would have been funny if it wasn't terrifying.

'I'm coming in,' the young man said simply. Alan jumped against the door, slamming it shut. Shit, shit, shit! This was actually happening! There was a man out there that actually wanted to cause actual damage to him! Alan had never been in anything like this situation before, not even at school. He looked desperately around him, hissing 'Gandalf!' under his breath. His eyes fixed on the cricket bat, which he had dropped by the side of the door. He picked it up, keeping one foot firm against the door as he did so, but his arms were shaking so much he couldn't be sure that if he swung it he would hit the man or himself.

The door suddenly shook under a heavy blow. It splintered the wood and broke the lock. Now all that was keeping it shut was the tiny metal chain. Alan turned and ran down the hall, jumping over Roger as he did so. The cat was seemingly unperturbed by all the excitement. Alan reached the end of the hall, and foolishly turned around in time to see the little chain snap under the second blow, and the door fly open. Alan dropped the bat in panic. Shit, shit, shit!

In the doorway stood the now enraged technician. His baseball hat had fallen off. He wasn't holding any weapons, but he still looked to Alan like he could cause quite a serious amount of damage with the force of his fury alone. His whole body was twitching and jerking as if it was at war with itself, although he looked like he would much rather be at war with Alan. For a second their eyes met. Alan shuddered. It felt as if someone had just walked over his grave, only much worse. More as if someone had just rolled over his grave with a large steamroller, followed by the percussion section of a light orchestra. The eyes were completely dark.

Alan froze in sheer terror. The man gave a bestial howl of rage, charged forwards, tripped over the cat, smacked his head hard on the fallen cricket bat, and came to a sliding halt in a jumbled pile of limbs on the floor in front of him.

Chapter Thirteen

I

Alan took a step back, his mouth a wide 'O' of horror. The young man from PowerFlow lay sprawled like a millennium celebrant. Roger, unfazed by all the excitement, sauntered up to the man in that special, unconcerned manner that only cats and people who have just smoked something illegal can manage, and pushed his face into the fallen man's upturned nose, purring like a steam engine.

'It is gone,' said a voice in Alan's head. He jumped and, as always, had to stop himself from looking over his shoulder.

'Where the sodding hell have you been?' Alan asked out loud. He found it difficult to get as annoyed as he would like with the Gandalf-voice simply because he couldn't see it. To give his anger some focus, and to stop it dissipating before he had a chance to really enjoy it, he shouted at an aspidistra on a nearby table.

'I could not reveal myself,' said the voice, in heavy, sepulchral tones.

'Oh!' said Alan, looking down at the man, then back to the aspidistra. 'Oh!' he said again, but felt this wasn't getting anywhere. He went for sarcasm instead. 'How convenient! Didn't occur to you while you were cowering in the back of my skull that it might be about to get broken open, did it?'

'Are you annoyed with me?' the voice asked.

Alan actually jumped an inch off the ground in rage. He started shaking his fist at the aspidistra. It wasn't too difficult. His hands were shaking badly anyway, so all he had to do was bunch one up into a fist and hold it towards the innocent plant. It made him feel a little better.

'Do you know,' said Alan, his voice just below a shriek, 'I think I might just be! I might be a tad narked that you left me on my own to deal with... with...' he waved his hand over the young man, 'with this...'

'Electrical company representative?' the voice suggested.

The anger left Alan all of a sudden, leaving him with the shock of sudden violence. He sat down against the wall, staring up the corridor to the ruined door.

'Shit,' he said after a moment. 'What just happened?'

'You were attacked,' said the Gandalf-voice, simply, but Alan was too shaken and drained to think of a sarcastic riposte to this. 'Could you not sense something was wrong with him?'

Alan thought of the black, staring, furious eyes and the weird dance the man had been performing. 'It was a little difficult to miss, actually.'

'He was being controlled. By the enemy.'

'How do you know?' Alan asked. The voice paused.

'I could... sense something arriving. I could feel it. Not here, but resonating in the other world. I took care to hide myself deep within you. If it doesn't know you have an ally then it may help us in the long run.'

'It was odd,' Alan said, master of understatement. 'It was almost like he didn't know what he was going to do next. Like he was arguing with himself. I think that's why he tripped up.'

The voice remained silent, keeping its thoughts to itself.

That's more than I can do, Alan thought bitterly. 'So... it's gone now? That's why you're talking again?'

Inside his head, the Gandalf-voice nodded. Alan shuddered. He wished it wouldn't keep doing that. 'Loss of consciousness has broken our enemy's grip on this mind. I don't think he will use this man again. Firstly he would be hard to find amongst the sea of living, and secondly...'

Alan completed the thought for him. 'There's plenty more fish in the sea.'

'Yes,' agreed the Gandalf-voice.

A horrible thought struck Alan. 'Could... could you do that to me? Take over, I mean?'

'No,' said the voice. It paused long enough for a cold

sensation to crawl up Alan's back. 'The enemy is much more powerful than I am. He is gathering the power of all the souls to him.'

'So, was that him?' Alan pointed at the man. 'Was that Cranmer? How did he find me here?'

'I don't know,' the voice replied. 'I don't know how they found you. I thought I was blocking you. I must think on this further.'

'Was it Cranmer?' Alan repeated.

'I don't think so. More likely an ally. A servant.'

'Now what do I do?' Alan asked. I've got an unconscious electrician in the hall of a flat that isn't even mine, and we don't know how long it's going to be before another one finds us.'

'We need to remove this man,' said the voice.

We do, do we? thought Alan. Bet you won't be doing any bloody lifting.

'No,' he said out loud. 'I'm going to call the police.'

'That would not be wise. We should avoid contact with any outside agency.'

Reluctantly, Alan saw the wisdom in this. He was feeling strangely calm in the aftermath of the attack, though he didn't know why. Probably his brain was just worn out. All he needed was a good rest, and then he'd start panicking.

'Right,' he said, looking down at the still form. 'Let's get working.'

II

The morning had proved, so far, to be a total waste of time. They couldn't access the Internet on Kate's computer. It let them connect, but all the sites and search engines they tried to use failed to work. Of course, this was such a common experience of the Internet for both of them that they were unsure if there was anything sinister going on, or if things were simply working exactly as they always did. It didn't really matter. Without any information at all gleaned from their morning's searches, they fell back on plan B.

George's workplace, the offices of the illustrious journal 'Mysterious World', were in a particularly nasty part of Redland. The streets were quieter there, darker too. Kate was on edge, and found herself glad to be with George. He marched through the grime with a kind of pedantic cheerfulness, which he somehow managed to extend a few feet from his body.

'Don't you get nervous around these streets?' Kate asked him.

George shrugged. 'Nah,' he said. 'I'm a journalist.'

Kate was unsure if this meant that journalists were braver or just less observant than normal people, but she decided not to pursue it. Within a short time, they were standing in front of a dilapidated building. The shutters were pulled down in front of the glass windows. A red sign with blue letters sat sandwiched between the glass and the metal shutters. Kate almost expected it to read 'CONDEMNED' but it actually said 'My.teri....Wor.d'.

'Mysterious World,' Kate translated.

'Yes,' George said, fumbling with a key ring. 'Rubbish, isn't it. Martin called it 'Illuminated World' at first, but he kept getting phone calls from Christians, so he changed it. He still gets the phone calls though. Beats me why they think his soul is worth saving. Perhaps word has got around about his reincarnation.'

Kate ignored this cryptic statement on the grounds that she didn't want to get involved with whatever George was talking about. She steered the conversation in a different direction.

'Illuminated World? It does sound a bit religious.'

George rolled his eyes good-naturedly. 'It's a reference to the Bavarian Illuminati. They're a secret society that's supposed to control the world.'

'Oh, right,' said Kate. 'Are they nice?'

George glanced sideways at her, eyebrows raised, then looked around the street. 'What do you think?' he said. He jiggled the keys in the lock, swung the door open, and stepped inside. Kate followed him, glancing over her shoulder as she did so.

The offices of 'Mysterious World' were similar to the offices of many other small magazines around the country — small, grimy, dingy, and thoroughly unpleasant. There was a strange smell in the air which Kate couldn't readily identify, but it smelled something like damp mixed with cigarette smoke mixed with God-knew-what. A few sad little wooden chairs, covered with dust, moped around the tiny reception area, where stood a once-white desk, with a brown telephone on it.

'Is no one here?' Kate asked. George shrugged.

'Perhaps they think there's no point reporting at the moment.'

'No point reporting?' Kate asked incredulously. 'But what about everything that's going on?'

'Just the problem,' George said, as he stepped behind the desk into the back room. The 'back room' was only a room by dint of the paper-thin partition between it and the reception desk. It continued the theme of griminess and murkiness, but managed to bring it to new levels. 'What's the point in bringing all the latest paranormal, extranormal and conspiratorial news bulletins to the public, if they've already been reported in the broadsheets and deeply analysed by the Sunday papers weeks ago? Besides, it's just after Christmas. It's usually a quiet time for the paranormal.'

Kate mulled this over. 'Is it?' she asked. 'Why?'

George shrugged. 'Don't ask me. I only work here.'

He leaned in front of a large lump of grime that turned out to be his PC and flicked the on switch, then settled down to wait.

'Fancy a coffee?' he called across to Kate, who was staring resolutely at the screen of the computer, trying not to look at anything else in the room in case she regretted it.

'Erm… no, thanks,' she said politely, horrified at the possibility that somewhere in this office was a fridge for the milk. Her brain suggested what the inside of such a fridge might look like. She shuddered.

'So,' she said, as the computer lumbered into life, 'think we can find anything here?'

Again, George shrugged. 'Well, even if the Internet is still down, and we still can't access the universities' library archives from here, there may be some information about this in our back issues.'

'How long has the magazine been on the market?'

'Well,' said George, slowly, 'about eighteen months.' Kate rolled her eyes. 'But Martin's got a lot of experience at this sort of thing. This isn't the first magazine he's edited. The archives for those will be around, too.'

Homer Simpson shouted 'Woohoo', indicating that George's computer was now able to be used. Kate raised her eyebrows as the screen flickered into life.

'Interesting wallpaper,' she said.

George smiled in an appalling attempt to conceal his embarrassment. 'There's got to be something nice to look at around here.'

Kate looked sideways at him. 'The Teletubbies?' she said.

'Ah, bugger off,' George said. 'Listen, looking at those little guys reminds me of how strange the world actually is. If those bizarrely deformed television aerials can be a success, there's got to be something more to the world than meets the eye.'

Kate had to concede he probably had a point. She shifted some papers from a nearby desk, and sat down on it. One of the papers she had lifted up caught her eye. She read the headline out loud.

'Alien Creatures from Nearby Star in Secret Discussions with World Governments.'

George turned and looked at the paper. 'Ah, that. Been getting those for months. Total bollocks, though. Have you ever seen such fake-looking aliens?'

Kate looked down at the picture with the story. It

showed several small fat men in very false-looking brown rubber alien suits. They appeared to wiggling their pelvises at another man in military uniform. She dropped it next to her and George began tinkering with the computer.

'Now then, let's see what we can find here,' he said. He fished about under a pile of papers, pulling out a CD, and placed it in the computer's tray.

'OK,' he said, turning to Kate. 'What was that name? Cranmer?'

Kate nodded. 'Not sure how we're supposed to spell it, though.' She picked up a pen from a nearby desk and scribbled a few variations on a piece of paper.

'I guess try these to start with,' she said.

George tapped away on the computer for a while. 'Hmm... nothing. Let's try... well, ice cream, probably not the right spelling... what about... ah, here's something. Couple of different entries here...'

His eyes scanned the screen.

'Archbishop Thomas Cranmer 1489—1556. There's nothing else. Mean anything to you?' He turned in the chair.

Kate thought for a while, then nodded. 'Yes... yes, it does. I thought the name rang a few bells. Cranmer was...' she closed her eyes in concentration. 'He was one of the leaders of the Reformation, when Henry the Eighth broke the English Church from its links with Rome.'

'Well, could it be something to do with him? What happened to him?'

'He was burnt to death,' Kate said.

'Oh, lovely.'

'Mary Tudor, Henry's daughter, forced him to recant his words once she became Queen, to declare that the Pope was the true head of the Church.'

'And did he?'

'Yes.'

'And Mary burnt him anyway?'

'Yes.'

'Well,' said George, 'that's gratitude for you. I'd have told her to piss off.'

Kate nodded. 'So did Cranmer. As he was about to be burnt, he turned to the gathered crowd, and denounced the pope as the Antichrist. Then he thrust his right hand, the one which had signed his recantations, into the flames, and as it withered in the fire, shouted "This hand hath offended".'

George wrinkled up his face. 'Enlightened times.'

Kate nodded.

'Well, he could be our fella. Certainly he's got reason to be annoyed.'

'Yes…' said Kate, doubtfully. Something didn't seem right about it. 'What's the other entry?'

'Not much there, either… let's see… Charles Ellis Cranmer. 1890—1921.'

'Any story attached with it?'

'The story isn't archived, but it's in an article for 'The Beast', Martin's last magazine. The article is called "Crowley, Black Magic and the Hermetic Order of the Knights of the Seventh Sword." Hmm… quite a mouthful. I wouldn't like to be their secretary. Imagine writing all the invites to parties. I suppose you could use the acronym… H.O.K.S.S. Hokss.' He shook his head. 'Naah. Sounds like you're clearing your throat.'

'That's it,' said Kate. 'It must be. Black magic, Alistair Crowley. Sounds like the right sort of thing.' Kate was reluctant to pursue this line of enquiry. It felt like she was taking a step backwards, a step back into a world that she thought she had turned her back upon. 'What did he actually do?'

'Doesn't say. Let me have a look elsewhere.'

George tinkered with the computer for a while. Kate sat still. Cranmer. Charles Cranmer. Something about that struck a chord with her. Had she heard about him before? She had used to read a few books about black magic. She felt she had to, being a medium, but they had always been full of quasi-religious nonsense, stuff that had bored her to tears. It had probably been that sort of thing that made her finally decide she didn't want to do it any more. But still... the name resonated. Had she read about him then?

'Nothing on the Internet,' said George. 'Lots of it not working anyway, most of the other sites are about this medieval guy. Well, that and porn, of course.'

'There's a surprise,' said Kate.

'Here's something, though. This is on the library server for Bristol. A newspaper article. Well, several, actually. The last headline is "Tragedy in Bristol — Mass suicide of Hermetic Order." It's dated 10th June 1921.'

'The year Cranmer died,' Kate said. 'Can you get to it online?'

George shook his head. 'It's in the library. We need to get in there.'

'It's closed,' said Kate.

'Well, we'll have to find a way to get in, won't we?' George said. 'If we have to wait for the University of Bristol to get its act together, I think we can safely wave goodbye to the planet.'

'OK,' said Kate. 'I... I might know someone who can help. Let's get back to the flat. I'm worried about leaving Alan there alone.'

III

It was surprising how much the unconscious man weighed. It was the same with animals, Alan reflected as he half lifted, half dragged the man down the corridor outside Kate's flat. It was like the brain had some strange anti-gravity property when it was switched on, and that things suddenly got heavier when their brains went out. There was a probably a research paper on it somewhere.

Gandalf had reassured Alan that the man would have no memory of what happened when he woke up, or probably of the previous few days. Most likely he would just go home.

How the voice was so certain about this when it seemed a little iffy about everything else, Alan wasn't sure, but in truth he was too tired and stressed to ask. He wondered, if the man would have no memory of the events, why couldn't he just pretend the man had fallen over while checking the meter? Gandalf seemed to have serious doubts about this, and Alan wasn't really sure how easy it would be for the man to believe he had just happened to fall head first onto a cricket bat, so he reluctantly agreed to leave the man in the laundry room two floors down, where he could hopefully wake up undisturbed. Doubts kept pecking at the back of his mind, trying to get his attention (What if someone sees you? What if he calls the police and they find where he went?), but he told them he was busy dragging the unconscious man downstairs, and to shut up.

In fact, there were two difficult moments as Alan was moving the man. The first was just outside the door of Kate's flat, when a small old woman had walked right past him. Alan had decided to brazen it out, saying 'Good morning' as cheerfully as he could. The woman nodded and smiled benignly, not seeming to notice the unconscious form on the floor between them. She carried on down the corridor to a flat a little further along, and Alan headed for the lift, thanking God for the human capacity not to see something it really doesn't want to.

As Miss Marple opened the door to her own flat, Alan got in the lift, and pressed the button for two floors down. The lift stopped on the next floor and a young man in a suit entered. He was talking on his mobile phone and acknowledged Alan and his burden not at all. Alan got out on the next floor without the man noticing anything. He peeked into the small laundry room. There was no one present, and all three of the washing machines had 'Out of Order' signs hanging from their doors. Alan draped the man over one of the chairs. The man grunted and stirred a little. Alan checked his head again. There was a large lump, but no other obvious damage. Feeling guilty, but not knowing what else he could do, Alan shut the door and turned the light out.

'There. Happy now?' he said as he headed back to the lift.

'There will be more,' the Gandalf-voice uttered, but Alan did his best to ignore this latest doom-mongering.

He got out of the lift at Kate's floor, to find Kate and George staring at the splintered door. George turned as the lift opened.

'What the bloody hell...?' he said, but Alan shushed him as he hurried down the corridor.

'I'll explain inside,' he said, as Kate unlocked the now largely useless door, and they all stepped into the flat.

Chapter Fourteen

I

The idea of souls has been around for... well, probably for as long as the human race itself. They were the first creatures (on this planet at least) that were able to perceive their own identity. It could hardly escape their notice that this perceiving didn't go on for nearly as long as they would have liked. In short, that they were going to die.

There is not a human that has yet been born that didn't have a quiet, sneaking hope that perhaps the rules didn't quite apply to them, and death might see its way round to letting them off, for good behaviour, say. In fact, this has happened only to a very few beings on Earth, and only a small number of them were human. Those that are still around tend to keep quiet about it, not being especially keen of the whole burning-at-the-stake thing of previous eras and even less enthusiastic about the modern equivalent, the media frenzy.

This belief that they may be the lucky one to cheat death is not reassuring enough for most humans, and so to make themselves feel better they have come up with hundreds of individual coping mechanisms; ways of trying to ignore the very obvious facts and pretend that something else entirely is going on. These are known as religions, or sometimes philosophies. They have at their heart one thing in common.

They are all completely and utterly wrong.

The difference between the idea that most humans have in their minds, however vague and indistinct it may be, of a soul, and the actual reality of the existence of souls, is as different as the promises the revolutionaries make to the peasants before the revolt, and the actual realities of life afterwards; i.e. it bears no relation whatsoever.

Souls are bandied about in the language of humans as if they understand what they mean: soulful, soul-searching, soul music, soul food, All Souls' Day.

They are just starting to discover what souls really are. They are starting to find out what it is really like to live without them. While it is difficult to argue against the idea that there is something missing from the music of the publicly manufactured pop bands, or from meals on aeroplanes, or from Michael Howard, to call these things soulless is to totally misunderstand the true nature of life on the planet.

Humans are about to find out the true meaning of the word 'soulless'. Unfortunately, it may well be a terminal experience for all concerned.

II

'...Minister denied that officials were unsure of the nature of the plague that seems to be sweeping the world's hospitals. In a press conference this morning he reassured all journalists present that there was no cause for alarm, and that Government Scientists were working on the problem. He once again affirmed that discussions were under way amongst all the major nations of the world, and all major health organisations. A solution was only weeks, possibly days away, he said.

'Meanwhile, the epidemic of strange births continues to rise. It is estimated that almost five percent of all human births now show 'transparency sickness', a condition for which there is still no known cure. Data from animal studies suggest this figure is similar in all other species, and some scientists suggest bacteria and even fire seem to be affected by the mysterious condition.

'In other news, several protestors strapped themselves to the railings of Buckingham Palace, wearing large rubber...'

'It's getting worse,' said George, flicking off the television. 'We've got to do something quickly. How long does Yoda reckon before it all goes wrong?'

Alan stood silent for a moment, then sighed. 'He doesn't know.' He was sitting morosely on the sofa, staring at the blank screen. 'Maybe I should be doing something. I cured the calf I touched. Maybe I could go out and...' He stopped, worrying he was getting a little messianic.

George sat down next to him. 'Oh yeah, the old laying on of hands. Never goes out of fashion.'

Alan refused to be deflated. He stood up. 'Well, it's something, isn't it! Helping people, instead of sitting around waiting for more of them to find me!'

'They managed to find you in this flat, didn't they?' George said. 'How long do you think it'll take them to find you doing a Mother Teresa around the major hospitals? Besides, how many of them can you touch? Not all of them, that's for sure!'

'I don't...' Alan said, then stopped, his eyes flicking to the side. George had learned that this generally meant he was getting instructions from his spirit companion, or whatever you were supposed to call it.

'He's saying it wouldn't work,' Alan said miserably. 'He's saying it only worked the first time because I was the first to touch one. It wouldn't work now.'

George frowned. 'Why not?'

Alan sat down next to him again. 'I don't know,' he said wearily. 'He says it just wouldn't.' Alan didn't want to admit to how relieved he felt.

George rolled his eyes. 'So what do we do now?'

Kate entered from the kitchen. 'We get into the library. There's got to be some clues there to what's going on. That's where this document that was mentioned on George's computer is stored. The newspaper article. Maybe there's something more.'

'Look, are you sure that's the best idea?' said Alan. 'I mean... even if we find out about this Cranmer, where is that going to get us?'

'If he, it... whatever... is causing this somehow,' said Kate, sitting down in the easy chair opposite the pair of them, 'maybe we can find out how he's done it, and maybe that will tell us about what we can do to stop it.'

'What about this reactor thing?' said George.

'Not a reactor,' Kate said, for what felt like the fifteenth time. It was actually only the twelfth. 'It's an accelerator. A relativistic massive ion accelerator.'

'Whatever,' said George. 'Shouldn't we be looking into this as well? Shouldn't we see if we could get there?'

Kate shrugged. 'It won't help if we don't know what to do there. Alan is the key to all this. Alan and Cranmer. He's already tried to find him once.'

'Well,' said Alan, modestly. 'It wasn't the most sophisticated attack in the world, was it?'

'Not this time,' said Kate. 'What if next time they send someone with a gun?'

Alan shut his mouth. He'd been trying not to think along those lines.

'Well,' he said after a pause, 'I'm coming with you next time. If they can find me here, I'd be better off with you.'

Kate nodded.

'So, how do we get into the library?' George asked. 'They're not likely to open it again at the moment, are they? Not with all this going on.' He waved his hand at the television.

'Leave that to me,' said Kate.

III

'Erm. Hello… erm. Sorry. Erm… Trevor speaking.'

'Trevor? Is that you?' Kate winced as she spoke. Of course it bloody was. Aside from the fact he had just said his name, who else answered the phone like that at home? She had no idea why he had said sorry. Trevor was the kind of man who apologised for everything.

'Erm…' said Trevor from the other end of the line. 'Yes. Erm. It is. Is that. Erm. Is that Kate?'

'Yes, Trevor, it's Kate. How are you doing?'

'Erm,' said Trevor. Kate was remembering exactly why she had dumped him before Christmas. Trevor seemed to treat every question he was ever asked like it was a question in a scientific survey, to be pondered over at great length. She always got the impression he never really understood what other people were talking about, and he spent his life 'erm'ing and hoping that revelation would come to him somewhere in the pause. He also said 'erm' more than any other human alive.

'Who is this idiot?' George mouthed at her from across the room. He had picked up her other handset and was listening intently. She waved at him angrily to put it down, then cupped her hand over the receiver.

'Trevor, an ex-boyfriend. He works at the library.' George put down the phone. 'He's all right,' Kate added, doubtfully.

'Erm,' repeated Trevor. 'Well. Erm. It's been a nice Christmas. I stayed...'

'That's nice,' said Kate. He seemed to respond best when she rudely interrupted him. Trevor seemed to expect it, and Kate suspected that unless you did this, the only other way to finish a conversation with Trevor would be to die.

'I was thinking,' she said, when the 'erm's had retreated into silence, 'that perhaps you could help us out with something.'

'Ah. Erm,' Trevor said.

'There's a lot of strange things happening at the moment,' Kate continued before he could get in to full swing. Unfortunately she paused for breath at this point, and Trevor leapt at the opportunity.

'Erm. Yes. Lots of strange things. Do you think. Erm. Do you think that is could have something to do with the relative effects of...'

'I don't know, Trevor,' Kate said, rudely. Perhaps, she thought, this was why Trevor liked her. She never let him finish a sentence. To Trevor, sentences were strange and mysterious things. He didn't even know himself what lay at the end of them, and Kate thought he liked to leave them that way.

'Listen, we need help to get into the library,' she said.

'Erm,' said Trevor. 'Mm. Well, opening hours are...'

'I know when the opening hours are, Trevor. The problem is, the library isn't open at all at the moment.'

'Ah. Erm. Yes.'

'Could you tell me why?'

'Well, erm, Kate. It's a bit sensitive, really. Bit of a secret.' Trevor added this last in whispered tones.

'Right,' said Kate. 'It's just, we need to get in. We need to get into the library very badly. And if you start your reply with 'It's more than my job's worth', Trevor, I will be very upset with you.'

Kate felt a tiny bit guilty about this tactic, and the distressed pause on the other end of the phone suggested that Trevor didn't feel all that great about it either.

'Erm,' he said, eventually.

'Trevor,' said Kate, 'I know it might be very hard for you to believe, but this may be the most important decision you ever make. Please, get us into the library.'

'Erm. Do you have a library card?'

Kate sighed. Oh, screw it, she thought. I'll sort it out when I see him. 'Yes,' she said. 'Yes, I have. I think I might have two of them,' she said, trying to sound enthusiastic. Another pause told her this was a mistake.

'Two of them?' Trevor said. 'But that's not...'

'Trevor!' Kate interrupted. 'Can you get us in?'

'It's not my decision, erm, you see. Erm. There's been a concern that the current situation would...'

'Can you do it?' Kate was getting a little worried they may have to resort to plan B. Trevor did not sound like he was going to be convinced. As much as he liked Kate, asking him to break the rules he lived by was a bit like asking him to strangle a puppy. In fact, Kate was getting concerned he might be more likely to agree to a spot of puppycide than let them in to the library.

Another pause as Trevor wrestled with his conscience.

'I'm sorry, Kate. Erm. I don't think...'

Kate closed her eyes. Great. If only they actually had a plan B. She supposed George's idea of lugging a brick through the window might work, but in her experience burglar alarms and being arrested were not conducive to good research.

She opened her eyes again. Trevor had stopped speaking. She listened intently to the receiver. There was some noise — a muffled cough, like someone clearing their throat under a balaclava.

'Trevor?' she said.

'Ah, Kate,' said Trevor, sounding a little surprised, though what was surprising about her voice coming out of the telephone when she had been speaking to him for the last five minutes was a mystery to Kate.

'Well,' she said. 'Do you think you could help us?'

Another pause. Then that little cough again. 'How many of you are coming?' Trevor said.

'There's three of us,' Kate replied. 'Is that a problem?' He's going to do it! He's changed his mind!

'No,' said Trevor, now sounding very pleased with himself. 'Three's company. I'll meet you by the library at eight.'

With a click and a hum the receiver went dead. Kate blinked at it a few times, then put it down on the table.

'OK,' she said, turning to the others. 'We're in.'

Chapter Fifteen

I

Alan had a great respect for and love of libraries in many ways. He loved the printed word, the idea that knowledge could be passed down from one generation to the next with such a low technology device.

He also loved the idea of libraries, repositories of knowledge, open to anyone with their minds open to human experience. The fact that anyone could go into a library, pick up a book on one of a thousand or more different subjects, and learn about it, was, to his mind, one of the greatest social achievements of mankind.

However, for all his noble ideas about the beauty of truth, and the wonder of knowledge, Alan himself never used a library. The reason for this was simple. Librarians.

Alan lived in fear of these creatures, and had done ever since he had been a student at Bristol. Librarians seemed to have the most twisted and disturbed moral outlook of any people he had ever come across. Once, Alan had returned a paper on some disease or other to the library when it was forty-seven minutes overdue. The librarian on duty had looked at him with something close to disgust as he tapped away on his computer console. He fined Alan one pound for this startling transgression, but the look in his eyes suggested to Alan that the librarian sat up at night thinking of far more suitable punishments for such deviants, punishments that would have made Torquemada shiver with revulsion. When Alan handed the money over the librarian had quickly slammed it into a small till on the side of the desk, clearly not wanting to be associated with the dirty money for any length of time. As Alan had picked up his bag, the librarian had leaned over towards him. His voice had been a dangerous low growl, which sounded even more disconcerting from the small, bespectacled man.

'Do you realise,' the librarian had said, with barely concealed fury, 'that I had someone request that paper half an hour ago?'

'Erm,' Alan had said. The librarian did not look mollified, so he added 'Sorry' as well. The librarian's left eyebrow twitched.

'Do you know what I had to say to the young lady?' the librarian continued.

Alan had shrugged, too terrified to speak. He looked around the library to see if there was anyone there he knew, so he could share a knowing grin and a shrug with them. There wasn't. Alan was on his own.

'I had to tell her,' said the librarian, only just managing to restrain himself, 'that another student,' he spat the word out, as if it was something filthy he had just found inside a chocolate éclair, 'still had it. I had to tell her,' he added, leaning closer, 'that it was late.'

His message thus delivered, the librarian leaned back behind his desk. He looked down at a pile of books by his side, and began stamping their inside front covers with terrifying ferocity.

This was not an unusual experience in a library. Almost all librarians, in his experience, shared this skewed world view; that bringing a book back late to the library was something that even The Marquis de Sade would have regarded as being a bit out of order. Consequently, Alan had decided, whenever he had wanted a book, it was so much easier simply to buy it and thus sidestep the issue.

Kate parked her Peugeot around the corner of the library. The streets were quiet this time of night. Most of the population around here were students, and they had largely returned home for Christmas. She turned off the engine and the two of them sat in the orange glow of a streetlight.

Alan glanced at his watch.

'How long?' Kate asked.

'Hard to tell with George,' Alan said. 'He'd be late for his own funer...' He stopped. 'He's always late.'

Kate tapped her hands on the dashboard impatiently. 'What was he doing, anyway?'

'He said he just wanted to get some stuff from home, or something. Don't know. Maybe he just wanted to see his parents.'

'Well,' said Kate, 'I suppose he isn't high-risk, is he? He should be OK.'

'Mmm,' Alan said, in an unconvinced tone.

'I mean, the voice said that they couldn't get to us three, didn't it? That we were protected?'

'Mmm,' repeated Alan in the same tone. This was indeed what the voice had said, when George asked what was to prevent them from being possessed like the Electrical Company man. When Alan quizzed the voice as to how this protection was done, the voice seemed reluctant to elaborate, saying simply that they would be safe.

The two lapsed into silence. The streetlight flickered a few times, but remained on. Somewhere above them, Alan knew, the stars continued to shine, but that was about the only thing he was certain of at the moment.

'Alan?' Kate said, suddenly.

Alan turned to look at her. When someone said your name in that sort of way, you didn't keep peering out of the sunroof if you could avoid it.

She was looking at him, her face pale. 'Are you scared?'

Alan shrugged in an appalling display of nonchalance, but looking into her eyes he decided to abandon the pretence, poor as it was. 'Yes. The only thing I'm not sure of is which thing to be scared of first.''

Kate nodded. Alan thought she understood. 'Everything's changing,' she murmured.

'You were a medium once, you say?' Alan asked.

Kate nodded.

To Alan, her expression changed to something like guilt, but it was hard to be sure in the orange glow that was pouring in through the windscreen. 'Why did you stop?'

Kate took a breath, and then another. She looked down into the footwell, but there was no help in there. 'I didn't really believe it,' she said.

Alan was puzzled. 'But you could see it, couldn't you? You could see things like… like…' He half turned his head to one side, to indicate his own invisible companion. Kate nodded. 'Then how could you not believe it?' he asked.

'Because… it wasn't what it was supposed to be. I could see something, all right. There was no question of that. But everyone who told me, everything I read, seemed to suggest that what I was seeing was something other than it was. Something that I knew deep in my heart was not what I was seeing.'

Alan frowned.

'It's like,' Kate said, searching for the words. She looked up through the sunroof. 'Like seeing the stars, and someone telling you they look like a scorpion, or a crab, or a woman pouring water into a jug. You see the same things they do, but they seem to be reading more into it. Making patterns that weren't there. Like… I don't know. Maybe they were right after all.'

She looked into Alan's eyes again. He reached over and placed his hand on hers, because it was that kind of look. They leaned a little closer. This kind of situation really needed moonlight to be shining through the windscreen, but it looked like the nasty orange glow was the best they were going to get.

'Do you think,' Alan asked, 'that there really is such a thing as a soul? Do we really go somewhere when we die?' The voice in his head was muttering something, but for the first time since it had invaded him, Alan managed to ignore it.

'Well, it looks as if we do go somewhere, doesn't it?' Kate said, sadly. 'But perhaps it isn't the place we were promised.'

Alan felt for the first time that Kate was actually looking at him, not over his shoulder. He opened his mouth to speak, but again he caught the look in Kate's eyes. It wasn't time for talking now.

They leaned a little closer. Kate closed her eyes.

There was a harsh rap on the driver's window. 'Come on, you two,' George's voice came from outside. 'No time for that! Let's get on and save the world!'

II

The library was in darkness, like much of the rest of the city. A few bollards still remained outside the doors, but even the most desperate of the remaining students had headed to the pubs by now. The three walked briskly along, Alan and Kate not really looking at each other, George in the middle grinning but remaining quiet. Alan wished he could say the same for the Gandalf-voice. For a few moments back there he had forgotten about the presence in his mind. He wasn't about to forget again soon.

'Plenty of time for all that later,' the old man was muttering. 'Do I have to remind you of the importance of what we are doing? Do I really need to explain the term 'end of the world' to you?'

'All right, all right,' Alan muttered under his breath, but George and Kate still glanced round anyway.

'Trouble with the in-laws?' George asked, cheerfully.

Alan nodded, and then shook his head, hoping that the two conflicting movements might give the voice vertigo and get it to shut up for a moment. It didn't work, but it confused George enough that he kept quiet.

There was a tall figure in a long black coat standing to one side of the library. The three stopped, and George and Alan looked at Kate.

'Is that him?' Alan asked.

Kate peered into the gloom. The figure seemed not to have noticed them. It was concentrating all its efforts on looking inconspicuous, and thus standing out like a greyhound at a shih-tzu convention.

'I think so,' said Kate. As they watched, the figure put its hands into its pockets and began whistling tunelessly. 'It's him,' said Kate.

They started walking towards the figure. Alan remembered the electrician.

'Let's just be careful,' he said, unnecessarily.

'Thanks, Dad,' said George.

They got within twenty feet of the figure when it suddenly jumped, and turned its back on them. The whistling got louder.

'Trevor,' Kate hissed as loudly as she dared. 'It's OK. It's us.'

Slowly, the figure turned round. The whistling stopped. There was a muffled 'erm' from somewhere inside the coat. Kate walked forwards, flanked by George and Alan.

It was hard to see much of Trevor. He seemed to have picked out every piece of black clothing that he owned, working with the theory that the more he wore, the blacker he would get. He was wearing a dark black trilby, and his face was covered with a balaclava, around which was wrapped a black scarf. It was hard to make out anything under the hat but Alan thought that Trevor was wearing dark glasses as well, which would explain why he hadn't noticed them until they were almost upon him. Alan had a sneaking suspicion that underneath the balaclava, Trevor's face would be smeared with boot polish.

He was wearing, as they had seen, a long black cloak, and from somewhere he had dug up a black polo-neck sweater, with black jeans. The overall effect was of Jean-Paul Sartre on a particularly bleak day.

'Nice clothes,' said George, holding out his hand to Trevor. 'Very subtle.'

Trevor nodded once, briefly, then looked at Kate. 'Erm,' he said.

'Oh, sorry,' Kate said, turning to her companions. 'This

is George,' she said, as George dropped his hand, realising it wasn't going to get shaken any time soon. 'And this is Alan,' she said, indicating him. Alan wasn't sure, but he thought Trevor jumped a little again. Kate looked unconcerned. Perhaps Trevor was always like this.

Trevor glanced nervously about him. 'This is highly irregular,' he said, like a technician in a 70s science-fiction series who's just been asked to open the missile silo for the hero.

'If you just let us in...' Kate began, but Trevor shook his head so vigorously that Alan thought for a moment the glasses might fly off. 'Erm... can't do that. I'll need to supervise, make sure there's no...' He tailed off into silence, leaving the other three to imagine what Trevor didn't want them to do in there.

'OK,' said Kate. 'Let's get on with it, then.'

Trevor led them around a side-door to the building, and pulled out a set of keys. George tapped him on the shoulder, then pointed to a camera mounted on a nearby wall. There was a dim green light on it. 'I hope you've already thought of that,' George said, flatly. Trevor nodded, quickly.

'Erm, yes. Yes I have. You see, the cameras are all controlled in the central hub, and there's no way to... erm... to disable them there, so instead I've rerouted...'

George held his hand up. 'OK. Thanks. So long as it's done.'

Trevor turned back to the door and unlocked it. Alan looked at Kate. She was looking back at him, and he could see the stress in her eyes. Why were they all so tense? It was only a library, for God's sake.

He knew, though. There was something in the air, something intangible. Something bad was going to happen.

IV

It was dark inside the library as well as outside. Trevor dared not turn on any lights in case it drew attention, so he pulled out a torch. He had difficulty leading them through the corridors even with the beam of the torch, so Kate suggested he take off his balaclava and dark glasses. Trevor did so, stuffing them into his pocket, but kept the trilby on. His face was smeared with boot polish. In the dim light he looked like a zombie on its way to work.

He led them down into the basement level, where the newspaper archive was held. The room was large, and their voices echoed around the walls and empty shelves. There was a small reception area, and several desks, in front of the stacks of documents. It was quiet, even for a library. The stacks loomed half-seen in the darkness like totems from a forgotten race. They were illuminated only by the faint blue glow of the computer screens on the desk.

Kate persuaded Trevor that they could risk one light on down here, the one over the desks. Trevor said he would keep watch at the reception desk, and pleaded with them not to be too long. Kate gave him a brief hug and the three of them passed into the library proper.

'Well,' said George, refusing to whisper as if in defiance of the empty room. Kate and Alan couldn't help but wince as his voice bounced around the shelves. 'Here we are. Think we'll find some answers?'

Alan said nothing.

'Let's hope so,' Kate whispered. 'Let's hope so.'

She sat down in front of one of the computers, which jolted into life when she pressed a key. She fished in her pocket, and pulled out a crumpled piece of paper.

'OK,' she said, tapping away at the keyboard, looking much more relaxed now.

George craned over her shoulder. Alan decided to leave it up to them. He'd be no help, anyway. He looked back to the reception desk, where Trevor was standing. Something was bothering him. He didn't trust Trevor at all, certainly didn't like him, but whether this was more to do with his past association with Kate he wasn't entirely sure. He didn't think so. There was something about him that Alan couldn't express. Something strange. Alan felt guilty for disliking Trevor, then remembered he was supposed to be paranoid, wasn't he? He decided to clutch at the excuse, to go ahead and dislike Trevor anyway, just for the hell of it. He was going to keep his eyes on him.

The dark figure was standing by the desk, looking as tense as it is possible for a human being to be without actually snapping. Despite his feelings, Alan couldn't convince himself that Trevor posed any kind of threat to anything except his own cardiovascular system. Still, it might not hurt to check. He took a step towards Trevor.

A sigh of triumph followed by a 'Got it!' from Kate broke his line of thinking, and he turned back to the computer.

'Here we are,' she was saying. She wasn't whispering now, lost in the excitement of discovery. 'Cranmer. There's an article still here, and a few more things besides.'

She turned to Alan, her eyes lit with excitement. 'Got it!' she repeated.

Chapter Sixteen

I

George flashed his torch beam along the stacks of papers in front of them. Alan took a step forward but George put his hand on Alan's chest.

'Stop,' he said, looking dramatically into the darkness. 'I'll go first.' He grinned. 'Always wanted to say that.'

Alan waited. George frowned at him. 'I'm not actually going first, you know.' Alan sighed, taking the torch from George's hand, and stepped into the stacks.

'What was it again?' he called back to the terminal.

'Che 45:17,' Kate called back. 'Under 10th June 1921.'

Why did library references always sound like passages from the Bible? Alan shone the thin beam of light along the row of stacks, back and forth, until the light fell on a yellow label with 'Che' written in sharp black letters. He headed towards it. George followed him. Alan briefly thought that he should send George back to stay with Kate, but a selfish part of him didn't want to do that. Why should George get to spend any more time with her? Anyway, Alan was the 'chosen one' or whatever. He should be the one with protection, shouldn't he? Plus, he was half-scared to death, though he didn't know why. The more scared he got, the more nervous he became, which in turn made him even more scared.

George was nervous too. He was trying to brazen it out, Alan could see, but he jumped like a man wired to the mains when his arm brushed one of the rows of books.

They turned the corner of the 'Che' stack, and headed down it, each checking the rows of large plastic-bound papers on either side. About halfway down George called to Alan, who hurried over and knelt down next to him. George was pulling out one of the bound rows of papers.

'In here, somewhere,' he said.

He flicked through the pages of the paper until he reached the 10th of June.

'Here we are,' he said. Alan glanced down at the paper. The story had made the front page.

'SEVENTEEN DIE IN SUICIDE PACT' the headline read.

'This looks promising,' George said.

'Hadn't we better head back to the table?' Alan asked anxiously.

'Let's just have a quick shufti,' George said. 'Think this is it? What does Yoda reckon?'

Alan froze. The voice! It hadn't said a word to him since they had been in the library! That was what was niggling at him. He rewound his thoughts to the last time he remembered the voice saying anything to him. It had been when it was whinging to him about wasting his time with Kate, right before... right before they had met Trevor!

'Shit!' he said, jumping up and running back to the reception, leaving George crouching in darkness in his wake.

II

Trevor paced nervously backwards and forwards, up and down the length of the reception desk. For a moment, he stopped, and looked at Kate sitting in front of the library terminal. Then he started pacing again.

This was crazy! He could lose his job! What was all this for? Did he really want to get in Kate's good books that much? He liked her, that was for sure, but... he couldn't shake the feeling that there was something else driving him, something he couldn't quite identify. When Kate had phoned him he was going to dismiss the idea out of hand, and instead suggest they went out somewhere interesting to clear the air — somewhere like the Bakelite Museum. However, he had found that a strange compulsion to help her had gripped him before he could get the words out. He decided that he should help her;

that he needed to take her to the library.

He had tried to resist the impulse, one which was very unlike him, but it had grown stronger and stronger as she talked to him, and finally he had given in and let her talk him into it.

Far from getting rid of the impulse, however, agreeing to help had simply transformed it. He found himself gripped with odd thoughts all throughout the day. Even more peculiar had been the completely contradictory nature of the thoughts. At one stage he made his mind up to drive round to Kate's, just to see her, though he couldn't really have explained why if anyone had asked him. Minutes later he decided it would be better not to go around at all but continue with the meeting as they had planned earlier. It was as if his brain was having an argument with itself. Somehow it had convinced him that his best interests would be served if he broke into his own place of work and allowed two complete strangers and a girl who had recently dumped him to roam free within it. What on Earth was he thinking?

He looked at his watch, annoyed to see that one minute had passed since he last looked at it. Only one minute? It felt like ten. It must be ten. His watch must have stopped.

Right, that's it. Enough was enough. It was time to go. He wasn't going to risk… He stopped midway through his pacing. Suddenly a different idea had popped into his mind, and it wasn't one he liked at all. He shook his head. Where had that come from? Was he going mad? He found himself taking a step towards the computer terminal before he knew what he was about, and forced himself to stop. The thought came again, much stronger this time, as if the arguing parts of his brain had finally resolved their differences and were ganging up against him. He found himself taking another step towards the terminal, and tried to make himself stop.

With a growing sense of horror he realised he couldn't. The impulse was too strong. With the horror of this came a terrible revelation.

The impulse that was driving him was not his own.

There was someone else in his head with him.

III

Kate sighed and tapped her fingers on the desk while the computer in front of her began its achingly slow search program once more. It made an annoyed squeaky whine every time it did so, like an old shopkeeper being asked time after time to retrieve an item from the highest shelf in his shop. Still, even with the Neolithic computer, she was making some progress. She had identified several references to this Cranmer character as well as the article that George and Alan were currently retrieving. He made cameo appearances in several occult reference books of the day, such as *Chambers' Dictionary of Fables and Folklore*, and Golden Hind's *Wizards and Witches of the Twentieth Century.* Both books were, of course, out on loan, and both were overdue. She had managed to find one reference to him online — a brief biographical note written apparently several years after his death by a chronicler of such things. It was this note the computer was currently, if begrudgingly, trying to locate for her.

She leaned back from the screen. In front of her, in the stacks, she could see flashes of torchlight bobbing up and down as Alan and George searched for the newspaper article. Kate steepled her fingers in front of her, and thought about what Alan had been saying in the car.

Could this all really mean the end of the world? It seemed such a boring phrase, now, overused. Just about everything seemed able to end the world these days. But as she had thought about it recently, she had begun to realise what the phrase really meant. The end of everything she knew, everyone she knew, everyone she had ever met. Not only that, everyone that she would ever meet. The Earth would continue in some form, but humanity would lose its past, its present, and, perhaps worst of all, its future.

Kate shuddered, and leaned forwards again. The computer seemed to be about to find the article.

The screen of the computer went black, just for a second, and as it did so the computer whine dropped into silence. With the sudden quiet Kate thought she heard several voices all shouting at once, sounding at the same time right behind her and very far away. In that startled second she also saw reflected in the black screen a dark figure standing right behind her, one arm raised as if about to strike.

Her ears and eyes set alarm bells ringing inside her brain so quickly that for a second all she could do was sit dumbstruck. In that second she watched the reflected figure's arm begin to drop towards her head. Then the blackness on the screen was replaced with the article the computer had been searching for. Kate never saw it. An ocean of pain flooded her head, a fireworks display danced in front of her eyes, and she slumped, unconscious, onto the keyboard.

III

Stupid, stupid, stupid! Why hadn't he thought of it before? It was the first thing that had happened when the electrician had arrived at the flat. Why didn't he notice this time? He hadn't trusted Trevor, and then he had left Kate all alone with him. Tit! Still, he had realised now. There was still time…

He skidded to a halt at the end of the stacks, emerging in the terminal area. The lights were out. Shit! Alan had to wait for a second and make an effort to steady himself, then raise the beam of the torch to where Kate had been sitting. The broken swivel chair in which she had been sitting lay on its side, one of its wheels still spinning. There was no sign of Kate. Quickly he swung the beam over the reception desk. Trevor, too, was absent.

'Alan?' said an extremely annoyed voice from behind him. 'What in the name of Satan's bollocks are you doing?'

Alan stood stock-still. In a hopelessly optimistic gesture, he shone his light back to the spot where Kate had been sitting.

She still wasn't there. The chair still was.

He quickly ran over to the reception desk, and started heading for the corridor that they had come down.

'Alan!' the cry came from behind him. 'What...'

Alan reached the double doors through which they had entered at a sprint, which explained why it hurt so much when he bounced off them. Kinetic energy explained the theory of inertia to his shoulder and the side of his head, both of which responded almost instantly with large, painful lumps. The torch flew out of his hands and slid across the floor but, in flat contradiction of all horror films ever made, failed to smash.

Alan lay on his back in front of the doors, feeling his face and shoulder swell. He heard footsteps behind him as George ran to catch him up. There was a screech of rubber soles on lino, a sharp intake of breath, and a smashing noise. The light went out. George landed next to Alan, in front of the doors.

'Shit,' he said. 'Slipped.'

IV

They both lay on their backs in the darkness, the room now lit only by the silent azure glow from the monitor screens. Alan blinked up at the ceiling and tried to remember what he was doing.

'They have taken her,' a voice muttered inside his head. Kate!

He jumped to his feet again, turning to the now-locked door. In contrast with the door to Kate's apartment, this one didn't look like the kind you would want to argue with. It was the kind of door that other doors would not like to meet in a dark alley. Alan's face and shoulder quietly but painfully reminded him of their last encounter with it. He looked around for another exit, but there were none to be seen. Shouldn't there be a fire door or something?

'They have taken her,' the voice repeated.

'Who?' Alan shouted frantically into the air. 'Where?'

'The enemy,' the voice replied gravely. 'I do not know where.'

Alan wanted to cry with frustration. He didn't have time for the voice at the moment. He leaped over the reception desk to where the light switches were. As he landed on the other side George began to stand up.

'Alan, what are you doing?'

Alan glanced up at him. 'Trevor. He's taken Kate.'

'He is working for the enemy,' the voice said from the depths of his mind.

'Oh, really?' Alan shouted. 'I'm so glad you're here to point these things out. Why don't you do something useful, sputum-breath, like finding a quick way out of here?'

George looked confused and a little hurt. 'Not you,' Alan muttered. He leant down under the desk, finding a row of switches.

'Let there be light,' he said, and flicked all of them on at once.

The room remained in darkness. Alan frowned, and looked down at the panel. George cocked his head to one side.

'Did I hit my head, or can you hear a ringing sound?' he asked.

There was now a red light flashing at the top of the row of switches. It was only at this point that he noticed the words 'Intruder Alert System' at the top of the panel.

'Bollocks,' he said.

George was looking at the door, frowning. 'Well, I don't think we're getting out this way. I think I saw some windows, little sort of quarter-lights, back in the stacks. They probably lead out onto the street.'

'But what about Kate?'

'We're not going to find her in here, are we? Let's go.'

The two of them headed towards the stacks, George stooping to pick up the shattered remnants of the torch on the way.

'Stop!' the Gandalf-voice shouted in his head. 'You have

forgotten something.'

'What?' Alan asked. George glanced over his shoulder, but Alan shook his head.

'The information. About Cranmer,' the voice replied.

'We haven't got time for that,' Alan said. Was it his imagination, or could he hear sirens as well as the alarm bell now?

'Stop and think for a moment, young man,' the voice said. 'The whole reason we came here was to get that information. They have tried to stop you. Most likely they will be taking her to Cranmer. If we can find out where that might be, we will find your friend. If we leave now we will never have another chance to come back here. At least, not before things reach… what is it called? Christmas?'

'Critical mass,' Alan muttered. Gandalf was right.

'George,' he said, 'have you still got that paper?'

George looked around the floor near where he fell. The folder was lying a few feet away. He walked over to it and flipped through the pages, pulling out the relevant section, which he folded into his pocket. He took the rest of the folder with him.

'I'll slip it back in the stacks. They'll never know,' he explained.

Alan ran over to the computer where Kate had been working.

'Charles Cranmer,' he read. 'A biographical sketch of a genius.'

'That's it!' Gandalf said, urgently. 'That is what we need.'

George joined him at the terminal. 'Erm,' he said. 'There are definitely sirens out there now. It's time we weren't here.'

Alan clicked the 'Print Document' icon. There was an ominous whirr from the machine; the kind of whirr that indicated the computer felt it had all day to print the thing. Alan ran over to the printer and stood in an alert crouch, left leg jiggling with tension.

'Go ahead and see if you can get that window open,' he said to George. 'I'll be with you as soon as we've got it.'

George nodded and headed off into the darkness. The printer clicked, and a piece of paper began feeding into it. Alan's leg jiggled more quickly. A green light began flashing on top of the machine. Alan had no idea what that meant, but green had to be good, didn't it?

There were definitely more noises now, shouting from upstairs.

'Is it Cranmer?' he asked the voice.

There was a pause. 'I can detect nothing like that. But if you are caught by the police…'

Alan didn't need to be Gandalf to work out that things might not go well for the world if that happened. The printer made another clunking noise. The paper had stopped halfway. The green light had turned to a stubborn red.

Alan thumped his fist onto the printer. The red light changed to orange, and there was another clunk. The air around Alan turned metaphorically blue for a moment. All this bloody machine had to do, its one sole job in creation, was to print things. That was it. Why was it having such a hard time understanding this?

'Come on, come on,' he muttered. The orange light turned red again. Frantically he reached down to the piece of paper and jiggled it, simultaneously thumping the printer again for good measure. There was another clunk, and then a whirr. The red light turned green, and stopped flashing. There were heavy footsteps outside the door.

The printer began to splurge out the paper. At least when it got going it was quick. Within a few seconds, five sheets of paper had landed in the out tray. Alan grabbed them. The printer began making some more whirring noises. Alan glanced down at the bottom of the last sheet.

'Page 5 of 5.'

Alan headed for the stacks at a run. Someone was rattling the door. There was a jangling of keys. He heard a thump, and then a tinkling of shattered glass from ahead of him.

'I've managed to open it,' called George.

Chapter Seventeen

I

Once they were on the streets, it wasn't difficult to put a lot of distance between themselves and the library. They headed for a pub that George knew, the 'Monkey and Trowel' at the top of Park Street, and threaded themselves into the maze of happy, drunken punters. They headed over to one of the quieter corners of the bar. George ordered a Stella for Alan and a Cripple Cock for himself. Alan tried to nonchalantly keep an eye on the door. After a few seconds he realised that he wasn't going to be able to do anything nonchalantly at the moment, so he simply stared at the door.

George appeared in front of him, drinks in hand.

'Sorry,' he said. 'Didn't know if Yoda wanted anything.' He handed the Stella to Alan, who took it, trying not to notice how much his own hand was shaking.

'Think we'll be OK now?' he asked George, who took a sip of his amusingly named ale. George shrugged.

'Would have thought so,' he said. 'Who gives a crap about a library being burgled?'

Alan had to concede the logic of this. 'So, what now?' he asked.

George looked up at his forehead, and at the same time the voice echoed again around his mind. 'We must study the enemy. We must find his weaknesses.'

'He says we need to read all this stuff,' Alan translated to George, who raised his eyebrows.

'Great plan. What about Kate?'

'Yes, what about Kate?' Alan asked George, who opened his mouth until he realised that, once again, Alan was talking to his internal tenant. He waited.

The sides of Alan's mouth creased in annoyance, the way a married man's do when he is being told off for leaving the toilet seat up again.

'He says they'll take her to the reactor when it's switched on. They want me and they've taken her to get at me. We can't leave it until then! We've got to find her now! We don't know what...'

'Hey,' said George, gently, 'Yoda's right. We don't know where she is now, and we'll get into trouble looking. We have to find out more about this guy.'

Alan sighed, and nodded.

'So, where are we going to read all this stuff? The pub's not the best place, is it?'

'Well,' Alan said, 'there's only one place we've got left — we'll have to go back to the practice house. Might be a bit of a risk, but what choice have we got?'

George nodded. 'Let's just wait, though. Give the Old Bill a chance to calm down.'

'And you a chance to have a few more?'

George grinned his infuriating grin. 'Can you think of a better thing to do after tonight?'

Alan found himself in agreement with George once again.

'Just one more,' George said, finishing the first.

II

Five 'just one mores' later, George finally decided that they were safe enough to venture outside. After several minutes of extreme effort, George eventually remembered the number of one of the taxi firms in Bristol. It was a very simple, repetitive number, and consequently it only took George seven tries to tap it into his mobile phone.

Alan watched him struggle with the ridiculously small piece of hardware. Aside from George's fine movements not being quite what they should be at the moment, the problem was compounded by the fact that the buttons on the phone were roughly an eighth of the size of a human finger, and so unless absolute precision was used in dialling, one tended to type in four numbers at once. Alan's own mobile phone was one given to him by his practice and, as a consequence, was the size and weight of a lead brick. He had taken great pleasure in letting it run out of battery and not bothering to recharge it since he had left his job.

Eventually George managed to dial a number that was at least close to the one he had remembered. Either he got it right, or he reached the home of some enterprising Bristolian, because within five minutes they were in a car on the way back to the practice house.

George got out of the car the instant they arrived, leaving Alan to pay the driver. He was never sure whether he should tip taxi drivers or not. The only time he ever remembered that he wasn't sure about this, however, was in the seconds leading up to paying them, and so he never asked anyone about it. Sometimes he tipped them, and sometimes he didn't, but whichever he did it always provoked the same reaction from the taxi driver, that of complete indifference and disinterest.

'Twenny-five, mate,' the driver said, distantly. Alan handed over a twenty and a five-pound note. Then, on impulse, he dropped two pound coins into the outstretched chubby hand. The driver looked at them as if they were kippers.

'Keep the change,' Alan said. The driver shrugged and poured the money into the pouch on his belt, muttering under his breath. Alan got out of the car. George was swaying by the front door as the taxi sped off behind him. Alan looked nervously up at the house. At first he thought it seemed to be looming over him, menacingly, threatening to collapse on top of him. Then he realised that this was because he was swaying gently back and forth himself. No lights were on.

'Gandalf?' he called, unable to help feeling a little foolish.

'There is no one,' Gandalf said. 'None of the enemy, at least. Does the girl know of this house?'

Alan stopped. The thought of Kate being interrogated

brought him up short. 'No,' he said. 'No, she never came here.'

'Then,' Gandalf said, 'I think we'll be safe for a while.'

III

The house had the musty smell of a place left empty. This was better than it usually smelled, Alan reflected. He looked through the mail on the mat. Bills and junk mail. He sighed. What he wouldn't give to receive a real letter, actually written by someone who didn't want to sell him something.

The answerphone was full. Alan played it while George checked the rest of the house. Three phone calls from his mother, wanting to know what was going on. Four from his boss, along the same lines. Two from George's parents. One from some guy about some new mobile phone deal, and finally, a peculiar one which consisted of two minutes of fax machine noise, like someone connected to the Internet. A call centre somewhere had obviously got confused.

George came in to listen to the last phone call.

'Bloody fax machines,' he said. 'Never give me a moment's peace.'

Alan sat down on the sofa. He suddenly felt very tired. The room was spinning, only a little but enough to suggest it might really get going around four in the morning, and be followed by a short but eventful trip to the bathroom.

George was taking the paper from his pocket, and unfolding it with some difficulty.

'Can't we do this in the morning?' Alan asked.

'No!' shouted Gandalf and George together in a spectacular internal/external stereo effect that you would have to pay a fortune for at Dixons if you wanted to achieve the same effect without being possessed.

'Think of Kate!' George said, while simultaneously Gandalf berated him on the urgency of it all.

'All right, all right,' he muttered, stomping over to the

table, and pulling out the biographical sketch. George joined him with the now unfolded (but torn) newspaper article.

They leaned over the papers, and began to read about the man who was destroying the world.

IV

The nineteen-twenties had been a good time to be alive; at least, better than being dead. There were an awful lot of dead people by then, as well. Most of Western Europe had only just got round to stopping killing each other for no good reason, and those that hadn't been killed by the war had been killed by the massive flu pandemic just afterwards, like an exclamation mark after a death sentence.

For the lucky ones who managed to survive the twin disasters, it was a time of exuberance, of the joys of simply not being shot at any more. Nobody who had been in it really understood what the war had been about. In something of a break with the tradition of human history, it hadn't been about religion, or about territory. It hadn't even been about someone stealing someone else's horses. It had simply happened. The flu had just been the icing on the cake, though to be honest it was a cake no one really wanted to eat.

At least the survivors could console themselves with one thing. They had fought the war to end all wars, and no one would have to go through anything as horrible as it ever again. And so, it was a time of excitement, and hedonism, and general abandon, at least for those who could afford to ignore all the other horrible things going on at the time.

One such person was Charles Cranmer. Born in the last years of the nineteenth century, he had been just old enough to spend a lot of his early years sitting in a trench, covered in mud, with people shooting at him. Five long years of this tended to give those of a philosophical bent a unique perspective on life, and a somewhat downbeat outlook on humanity in general. Charles had never been over-endowed with optimism in the first place. In a school essay, when he was nine, Charles had been posed the question 'What will I do when I am older?' His one-word masterpiece 'Die' was not well received by his masters. It was also, as it turned out, not entirely accurate.

Charles had been a thin, pale child, the kind of boy for whom the word 'wan' was invented. This was, of course, pointed out to him forcefully, repeatedly and often painfully during his early years in boarding school. It didn't help that he excelled at schoolwork but wasn't good at sports. In all respects, he fitted the stereotype of the thin, pale child that will turn into the thin, pale public servant, the one who never forgets his school nicknames and secretly enjoys making people's lives just that little bit worse with bureaucracy.

The war changed all that. Half a decade in a ditch with death all around him brought Charles to something like an epiphany. He decided that nothing really mattered, and in contradiction to the popular phrase, there was only one certainty in life. Tax officers were not one hundred percent consistent, in his experience, but the Reaper tended not to disappoint.

He returned home to find both his parents dead from the flu, and himself the sole heir of a small fortune built upon the lumber business. Never having to work another day in his life, Charles devoted it to unravelling the secrets of the cosmos, and of death. Naturally, this involved trekking around the world in obscure, dark places, a huge library full of dusty tomes with arcane sounding names and, of course, no girlfriend. Eventually, Charles decided to go the whole hog, and founded himself a secret society, complete with rituals, passwords, secret meetings, altars with suspicious rusty stains on them, and big cloaks. The last, of course, were the pièces de résistance. Deeply mysterious, albeit hell to wash and rather heavy.

The biggest problem Charles faced around this time was coming up with a name for the society. Words such a 'Hermetic', 'Twilight', and 'Dawn' all sounded suitably mysterious, but as England already had one 'Hermetic Order of the Silver Twilight', one 'Knights of the Golden Dawn', and even one 'Confounded Order of the Befuddled Elder Mystics' (held in a tea room in Bournemouth by two old dears who went to church on Sunday and prayed to the Black Goat of the Woods with a Thousand Young on Thursday), it took him a while to settle on a name that hadn't already been used. Eventually, after brief dalliances with other names, he settled upon the 'Mystical Brethren of the Outer Peculiarities', because he found that the 'Peculiar Brethren of the Outer Mysteries' was already taken. To put people off the scent, he kept this name secret, and used the more innocent name of 'The Hermetic Order of the Knights of the Silver Sword' in public. He didn't want people to think he was strange.

During the years after the war, many hundreds of these groups were formed, and they were all broadly similar; all flickering torchlight, mystical muttering, no women and lots of port and brandy afterwards. The heads of these orders told themselves that the fragile mind of the fairer sex would be too weak for the deeper truths of the world, and happily ignored the fact that most of them had no interest in dressing up in silly clothes, muttering mumbo-jumbo by candlelight. Charles' group was no exception to this rule.

All the societies had one goal in common; to discover the answers to some of the deeper mysteries of the cosmos. None of them could really say what mysteries these were, but they wanted answers anyway. There is, however, a problem with mysteries, deeper secrets from beyond the dawn of time and the dilemmas of the outer spheres, and it is this: most of them are dull. Really, really dull. For instance, an ancient Roman sect formed by a group of Elder Senators who had become heartily sick of orgies, gladiators and eating until they were sick, and decided to try to find out, as their members put it, 'what it was all about'. They finally discovered, after many years of careful searching as well as a great deal of luck, one of the greatest secrets of the world. The secret was closely guarded by shadowy pseudo-deities and half-beings, and it was this:

The chosen drink of the creator-being is Dr Pepper.

After all their efforts, dangers, a few deaths, not to mention all the money they had put in to it, to discover this 'astonishing' secret was, to put it mildly, a bit of an anticlimax. It didn't help that the chosen drink of which they had learned would not be invented for two millennia. No ingredients had been included with the mysterious secret, which they had forced from the lips of a Servitor of the Outer God-beings during a particularly long-winded ritual, and when the sect finally perfected the formula generations later they discovered they had created a drink which tasted like fizzy mouthwash. Why the creator-being, whatever it was, would be so keen on it was another of the deeper mysteries, and to be frank the sect was by then completely sick of the whole thing. They finally took to bitter squabbling over who owned the copyrights to the drink, until it was sold to a famous drinks manufacturer, where it inexplicably sold quite well.

The point of the story is this — ninety-nine percent of the time, deeper truths and hidden mysteries are simply not worth knowing. They are all based on a perspective other than ours, and taken out of context they are as meaningless, pointless, and flat out boring as the factoids on Steve Wright's afternoon radio show. Like all secrets, they are more exciting and romantic when they are still secrets, and the reason they remain secrets is because those who have gone to a lot of spiritual trouble to discover them are generally so embarrassed and annoyed that they dare not reveal them to anyone else. Much better to be the mysterious dark-robed holder of dark encryptions, than the one who tells everyone that actually genetically speaking the egg came first, not the chicken.

A few of the more determined secret societies formed between the first two world wars discovered some of the inner mysteries. Many of them disbanded soon afterwards, because, as had already been pointed out, ninety-nine out of a hundred of them weren't worth the planks of wood they had been burnt into by a flaming demon's finger.

The secret discovered by the Mystical Brethren of the

Outer Peculiarities was number one hundred.

V

It came as quite a surprise to Charles when the breakthrough actually came. He was an intelligent, well-educated young man at the time, and as such was realistic about the prospects of actually achieving anything worthwhile with his Mystical Brethren. Still, he liked the robes, and the chanting, and all the business with the goats' blood. He did wonder, deep in his heart, about the mystical significance of it all, but the hours were good, and it beat working.

So when, one especially mystical night involving several goats, a few chickens, and some really intense chanting, with the heaviest robes, the Mystical Brethren managed to actually summon a Dark Servitor of the Outer God-beings into their midst, Charles was somewhat confounded as to what to do next. From the instant it had appeared in their cellar, a dark flickering shape amidst all the requisite clouds of smoke, gradually coalescing into something partially incredibly beautiful, partially indescribably hideous, and wholly inhuman, Charles had realised that he had never really believed a single thing he had done up until that moment. He also realised that he had better start believing in things pretty quickly if he was going to survive the night.

The creature stirred in its acrid cloud of sickly-yellow smoke. Its shape was hard to describe; the eyes seemed to slide off its edges, so that it was blurred and indistinct. It was shaped partially like a dog, partially like a man, and wholly like something Charles didn't want to be standing next to. The sounds it produced were deep, echoing, as well as pant-wettingly terrifying. The thing turned to Charles. Noise flowed from it like a tidal wave. The voice of the beast was deep and guttural, but also singsong and melodious. It was as if the brain couldn't decide anything about the creature, and was changing its mind from one instant to the next. All the mind-altering drugs floating around Charles' system did not improve this state of affairs.

'What do you require of me, my master?' the creature roared. Cranmer crouched in terrified supplication until his ears finally made sense of what the creature had actually said. Slowly he straightened up again.

The rest of the cloaked brethren waited in tense silence. This was the moment they had waited years for, but if they were honest with themselves, now that it had happened they couldn't help feeling a little bit nervous. All eyes turned to Cranmer. It was easier than trying to keep looking at the servitor.

'Erm...?' said Charles. He was acutely aware that he didn't have the faintest idea what to do next.

'Erm?' echoed the creature in its paradoxical growling, singsong voice.

Charles tried again. 'Erm...' he managed.

In the huddled group of cloaked figures in front of him, someone cleared their throat.

The creature turned around to survey the rest of the room. It made another noise that sounded a bit like a sigh. It turned to Cranmer once more.

'First time?' it asked.

Cranmer nodded.

'Nervous?'

Again, a nod.

'Right,' said the creature. If it needed to breathe, it would have muttered something bitterly under its breath. It didn't need to, so it muttered loudly instead.

'Bloody amateurs,' it said. 'OK, here's the deal. You have summoned me, so now you get...'

One of the cloaked figures seemed to gain some courage at this point. 'We have brought you forth from the seventh veil of the night, through the realms of sleep and nightmare, and here to do our...'

The creature looked at the figure, who fell silent. One of his comrades nudged him and glared at him. The creature stared at the figure for just long enough to show complete contempt for all humankind.

'Whatever,' it said, in a voice that shook the room.

Cranmer felt he was losing control of the situation.

'Erm...' he said, then realised he had already said this, and decided to try something a bit more forceful. 'Oh, Servitor of the Outer Planes, we have summoned you here, to our pit of damnation, for...'

'Look,' said the servitor. 'This is all very well, but I've got another six manifestations to do this evening, some of them halfway across the galaxy, so could we just take all the chicken blood and mumbo-jumbo as read if it's all the same to you.'

Charles wasn't sure that it was all the same to him. He was gaining courage now it was becoming apparent he wasn't about to have his body and soul rent asunder. He'd been trying for years to get this done. OK, he had never really believed it, but he hadn't spent ten years pissing about in a cellar with a big cloak on to not do things properly when the time arrived.

'We have summoned you,' he began again, 'for the great task of...' Again he faltered. What were they going to do with it now?

The servitor sighed once more. 'OK, OK, blood and thunder it is, but I'm going to make it quick.'

There was a sudden, terrible, complete noise that drilled through the brethren's ears and made their teeth itch. The servitor suddenly towered above them, hundreds of feet tall. Just trying to work out how it could do this in a room with a twenty-foot high ceiling made Cranmer's brain water.

'You have brought me forth,' the creature boomed, 'I, Valiantrar of Grag, Initiate of the Fifteenth Circle of Pain, Keeper of the Mysteries of Nit, Spawner of Deeper Darkness, Defiler of Plums and Assorted Vegetables, and Master of the Seventy-Eighth Layer.'

The creature paused for dramatic effect. It worked. Everyone in the room was most impressed by this outer-planar show of strength. Even the cloaked man who had interrupted the first time was too awestruck to enquire about the plum-defiling.

'I come upon you feeble mortals,' it continued in its melodious boom, 'and am honour bound to share with you my knowledge. Seekers of the truth, are you ready for the knowledge I am about to share with you? Are you ready for your minds to part the ultimate veil?'

The creature paused again. Cranmer cleared his throat.

'Er… yes,' he said.

'Then,' the creature said, 'prepare!' It stopped, and waited to check which secret internal knowledge titbit from beyond the veil it was due to impart. The servitor always liked this bit. The way the puny creatures' faces fell when he told them that snails were the beloved children of the creator, or the most fashionable planet in the solar system was Pluto. Ah, here it came. Eternal Verity number 100.

'Blimey,' it thought. 'That's a good one.'

It told them.

VI

'So, you're saying a demon told him how to cheat death?' Alan asked, trying unsuccessfully to keep the incredulity out of his voice.

'No, not a demon. A… now, let's see… yes, here we are… a Lesser Servitor of the Outer Gods, apparently,' George said, peering down at the printout.

'Oh,' said Alan. 'Right. Well that's much more sensible then.'

George looked up. 'Well, that's what he claimed afterwards, anyway. Seems his brethren had some kind of revelation.'

'Who did he claim this to?' Alan asked.

'Just about anyone who would listen, as far as I can make out. I don't think that was many people, though. It seems they all thought he was talking bollocks.'

'You're kidding,' said Alan. 'Look, are we sure this has anything to do with what's going on?'

'It has everything to do with it,' the Gandalf-voice said. 'This is where it started.'

Alan rolled his eyes. 'He says that... oh, look, I'm sick of repeating everything you say. Can you do the thing where we both hear you again?'

There was a pause, after which the Gandalf-voice said 'Without the woman? I'm not sure.'

'Can't you try? Please?'

'Very well,' said the Gandalf-voice.

'Do we need to hold hands again?' George said, guessing the relevant bits of Alan's internal conversation.

'Hmm... no, I'm not sure that will be necessary now,' the Gandalf-voice replied. Alan shook his head. 'We have linked minds before,' the voice continued. 'I simply need a focus, a spiritual resonator to appear to project from.'

'Well, we're all out of spiritual resonators I'm afraid,' Alan said, testily. He didn't know why the Gandalf-voice annoyed him so much, but every time it spoke he wanted to jab a pencil in his ear and hope he caught the bugger. Perhaps he just needed some sleep.

'Oh, anything will do,' said the voice. 'Anything you both have some form of spiritual connection with.'

Alan looked around the room. 'How about the telly? We're as connected with that as anything else in here.'

'Hmm,' said the voice. 'Yes. Let's try that.'

Alan walked over to the television in the corner. He had bought it with his first pay packet, straight out of vet school. It was of the widescreen variety, a black monstrosity that squatted in the corner of the room. Its dimensions were such that they were slightly wrong for anything you might want to watch. Normal television programmes were too fat on the screen, so the actors looked like they had been living on Big Macs for three months prior to recording, and films, even the widescreen versions, still had black lines running across the top and bottom of the screen. The man at Currys had assured Alan that this was to ensure authentic and enjoyable picture quality, but quite how you were supposed to enjoy a telly where a third of the screen was pointless was a question the Currys man had not seen fit to bring up.

The screen flickered into life. On it, a Government minister was desperately evading questions put to him by an aggressive looking Jeremy Paxman.

'What are you doing putting...' began George, but at that moment the screen flickered, and a face appeared on it. Alan sat down in front of the grey-robed, bearded man on the screen, and glanced over to George.

'See it?'

George nodded.

'Yoda, is it?'

George nodded again, dumbly, and sat down next to Alan.

'So,' said Alan, 'now that we're all here, perhaps we could find out what happened next?'

He looked at George, who was staring at the screen.

'Oh, right. Well...' he scanned down the paper he had carried from the table. 'Not a lot, really. The group began to say they had cracked the secret to life itself. This sparked off a bit of a trend and so everyone started saying it, which seemed to annoy the brethren. After a while they went quiet.'

The face on the screen nodded once, tersely.

'Then...' George said, running his finger down the paper, 'then, one year after the announcement, they killed themselves.'

'All at once?' said Alan.

George nodded. 'Took some drug or something. They were all found dead in the cellar of Cranmer's mansion, candles still burning, still wearing their robes. Fifteen of them.'

'The start of the journey,' the face on the screen said, ominously. George nodded.

'So it would seem,' he said.

'So what does all that mean? Why would they kill themselves?' Alan asked.

'Well, I've been thinking about this, and about what Yoda said earlier.'

'About what?' the face on the screen asked.

'Well,' said George, putting the paper on the floor, 'you tried to explain what it was like in... in the place we go. If you're not strong willed, you're torn apart, just drift into your component parts, your memories, your thoughts.'

'This is so,' said the face on the screen. Alan rolled his eyes. Couldn't he just say 'yes' like ordinary people? Then he looked at the screen, at the sadness in the eyes, and remembered this wasn't an ordinary person. It was someone who had died.

'Well, I was thinking about an article I wrote a few years ago. Some scientist guy claimed he had come up with a mechanism for the afterlife.'

'A mechanism?' Alan asked.

'Yeah, you know, a theory. A way for it to work. It's to do with quantum entanglement.'

'Ah,' said Alan. There was a reason he had become a vet rather than a physicist. Phrases like 'Quantum Entanglement' were very much part of that reason. He decided to brazen it out by nodding intelligently.

'You don't know what I'm talking about, do you?' George said.

'No,' said Alan. He was surprised and a little relieved when he heard the Gandalf-voice also saying 'no'.

'Well, the point is that in quantum theory, there is a connection possible between particles that seems to ignore time and space. The particles are connected no matter how far apart they are to their quantum twin. No one is quite sure how this entanglement occurs, but it does seem real.'

Alan nodded again, hoping to stay above the surface of whatever was coming next.

'Well, ultimately, thoughts and personality are made up of nothing more than particles and charges. It is possible that if any exact replica of the particles and charges could be made, then the personality would be replicated as well. In other words, it is possible to have a quantum 'twin', an exact copy of our thoughts and memories at some distant point.'

'Right...' said Alan, nodding, hoping he was saying the right thing and nodding at an appropriate juncture.

'Well, this guy's theory was that when we die, the state of our minds is preserved in this quantum twin. Our personality switches to that.'

'So, where is this twin?' said Alan.

'Well, that was the problem. He didn't know. The other problem was, without the structure of neurones and brain tissue to hold the charges and particles together, they would quickly break up. Scatter. Dissociate. Sound familiar?'

'So you're saying,' said Alan, slowly, 'that this quantum twin is in the spirit world?'

George nodded. 'Exactly. And this break up is what happens to everyone and everything that dies. What nearly happened to Yoda.'

Alan sat and thought. 'Doesn't sound that great, does it?'

'Whoever said dying was a good thing?' George said.

'Well...' said Alan, but realised he didn't want to get involved in all that. 'So why,' he asked instead, 'did Cranmer kill himself? What did he learn?'

'Well, it's a guess, but what if he learned some way to keep himself together? To hold his quantum twin permanently? Perhaps if you die in the right state of mind, together with the help of drugs, you can survive, even in a place like that.'

Alan thought about what it would be like, struggling to hold on to your identity, feeling your memories being stripped away. Once more he looked at the sad, silent face on the screen. It seemed to be lost in its own thoughts. He shuddered. He looked at George, but couldn't think of anything to say. George was looking at the screen too. He was frowning.

After a moment of silence, the face on the screen blinked. Why it did this Alan wasn't sure. Probably more habit than anything. Certainly it didn't need to blink.

'That's it,' it said in a low, sad voice. 'That is what happened. What must have happened. Cranmer, alone amongst the ranks of mankind, entered this realm fully prepared for what was to happen to him.'

'So he survived,' said Alan. George remained silent.

'Him, and the rest of his brethren. The enemy,' the face on the screen said.

'And somehow, he found a way to collect the... what? Power? From everything that has already died?'

'Soular Energy?' suggested George, but he wasn't smiling. He was still looking at the screen. On it, the face nodded slowly.

'And that's what is causing this mess? He's taking all the energy for himself, so none can leak back into the world?'

The face on the screen nodded. 'It must be so.'

'So how do I fit in?' Alan asked.

'You were the first to encounter the leeching of the energy. You created a bridge. You are the conduit.'

'So you keep saying,' Alan said, irritated. 'I don't know what that means.'

'It means,' said George, tearing his eyes away from the television, and with them presumably his train of thought from wherever it was heading, 'that you are a connection between this world and the next. It means that Cranmer can use you to get back into the world.'

'Oh, great,' said Alan. 'I'm a spiritual stepping stone, am I?'

'Just so,' said the face on the screen.

'Why does he want to get back here anyway? Why not just stay in the other place?'

The face seemed to shimmer on the screen. Its eyes darkened. 'You don't know what you are saying. You don't know this place, what it is like. An eternity of battling, of fighting against losing yourself, with no prospect of reprieve and nothing but bitter memories to remind you of what you have lost. There is nothing else. It is a false world, a world of lies and tears. Nothing but ashes and wind. He has to return to your world. There is nothing for him here.'

'Hmm,' Alan said, trying not to think about it. After all, wasn't this the place they were all going to end up? 'Well, why don't we just let him? What's so wrong with him coming back?'

This seemed to surprise the face, a course of action that genuinely had not occurred to it. Before it could say anything, George snorted.

'Oh yeah, seems a really community-spirited guy, this Cranmer, if you'll pardon the expression. Look at the world! Do you think it's going to be in very good hands if he returns?'

'It's not exactly in very good hands at the moment,' Alan pointed out. 'And anyway, who's to say that he wants to take over? Perhaps he just wants to settle down in a cottage in Wales.'

'He's a classic megalomaniac personality. He's got all the power in one world already. Do you think he'll be satisfied watching sheep eat grass for the rest of time?'

Alan had to admit George had a point. He felt he'd been doing this a lot recently.

'Besides,' George continued, 'we don't know what the effects of the return will be. Perhaps bringing all the energy with him will end both worlds. Either way, we've got to stop him. With him in power, even if he doesn't re-enter the world, nothing can be born on the planet. Within fifty years, everything on it will be extinct.'

'Hmm. Hadn't thought of that,' said Alan. 'So, what do we do? He wants me, does he? And he's taken Kate to get to me, we're assuming?'

George and the face on the screen both nodded.

'So where is she? We were hoping all this stuff would lead us to her, weren't we?'

'We know where he's going to be, don't we?' George said. 'This accelerator, the thing Kate was telling us about. This is how he's going to get back in. Maybe that's why they took Kate. If they couldn't get you, they figured she'd know something about how to make it work.'

'So what do we do? Drive up there and ask them not to switch it on, please, or the world will come to an end?' Alan asked.

'Something like that,' said George.

'Great plan,' Alan said sarcastically. 'Maybe while we're at it we could ask the Prime Minister if we could stop attacking other countries, and maybe even find Al Qaeda and ask them if they could be nice to us for a change.'

He settled back in the sofa, satisfied that the full assault of his sarcasm had got across.

'Well, one thing at a time, mate,' George said.

'Wait,' said the face on the screen, suddenly. It had been silent for a time, and Alan had almost forgotten it was there. He found it much easier to ignore now it was on the screen rather than in his mind. 'There is more we can do,' it said.

'Really?' said George.

'Yes,' said the face. 'We have one advantage. We now know who we are fighting, and why.'

'Super,' said Alan. 'He might as well just give up now.'

'Look again in the biography,' said the face. 'Does it say where Cranmer was taken after he died? What happened to the body?'

'The body?' Alan said. He had a horrible premonition of what was coming next.

'Erm... let's see,' said George, unfolding the paper again.

'Why would we want to know where his body is?' asked Alan.

'This world, this 'spirit' world, in which I am trapped, is, as I believe I may have mentioned, a place of nothing but memory. It is all we have. The events, the dates, and the objects of our previous lives become things of power. Anything Cranmer was intimately connected with in his life will have some power over him. It may give us some kind of advantage when we encounter him,'

'Intimately connected? You mean like a favourite shirt or something? Buried with him?'

'I mean the body itself,' the face said.

'His body? Can you be intimately connected with yourself?'

Beside him, George sniggered as he scanned the paper.

'Of course,' said the face. 'It is with you from the moment you are born until the moment you die. There is nothing that has greater power in this place. If we find his body, we may be able to stop him entering the world.'

'How?' asked Alan, but George interrupted him.

'Here we are,' he said. 'He was buried in the grounds of his house. There was a small family cemetery there, apparently.'

'Then, our course is clear,' said the face.

'You're not suggesting we... we go round to the house and...'

The face nodded.

'Come on,' said George, nudging him and smiling. 'Where's your sense of adventure?'

If Alan had worn glasses, he would have looked at George over the rim of them at this point. 'Grave robbing?'

George shrugged. 'Beats working,' he said.

Chapter Eighteen

I

The white Ford Transit hurtled through the city streets like a thing possessed, the amber glow of the streetlights flickering off its battered roof. One of the headlights worked only intermittently, so that from the front the approaching vehicle resembled an elderly cat with a cataract caught in the beam of a flashlight. There the similarity ended, however, as even an especially ancient cat with a nasty case of arthritis and a leg missing would not have been juddering quite so badly when it moved as the van was.

The van's jolting was only partially down to the fact that the letters MOT meant nothing to it, and that it hadn't been serviced since the last millennium. It was also due to the fact that the driver of the vehicle seemed to be in need of a service too.

It is, of course, quite natural for white transit vans to be poorly driven. It is an accepted part of life, as is the presumably ironic sign on the back of them that says 'Well Driven?' In this case, however, even the most casual observers (of which there were few at this time of night) felt that there was something unique about the un-well-driven-ness of this particular van.

The driver appeared to be in a permanent state of indecision. The indicators flicked on and off at random as the vehicle shook its way through the streets, and bore no relation to the way the van would eventually turn. The transit swayed from side to side of the road, like a man walking home from a good time in the pub. It looked so much like this, in fact, that the few casual observers who did see it were left with the overwhelming impression that the van was about to lean over in the pavement and introduce its last meal to the paving stones.

Of course, the observers, who had generally ceased to be casual by this stage, especially if they were in a car that the erratic van was approaching, assumed the driver of the van to be drunk.

The truth was actually a little more complicated than that.

II

The swinging, shaking, flashing, braking, accelerating, screeching of brakes and frustrated beeping of horns going on at the moment would, arguably, have been enough to get a mummy out of its sarcophagus and demand to know what all the fuss was about. Fortunately this was not put to the test, but it was certainly enough to rouse Kate from her unconscious dreaming.

She groaned, but the groan was lost in all the other noises, so she tried again, louder. This was also drowned out. She tried opening her eyes but this proved to be a mistake, as her vision was immediately filled with dancing bright lights that would have been enough to warrant a warning about photosensitive epilepsy if they appeared in a computer game. There was enough time for her to get an impression that she was travelling at speed before her brain wisely took over control of her eyelids and snapped them smartly shut again. Her stomach flipped around in her belly, wondering if it would be a good time to pop up to her throat and say hello. Kate politely but firmly asked it not to and so for the moment it decided to stay where it was and see how things panned out.

The back of her head throbbed, as if… well, as if someone had hit her there quite hard, which was presumably what had happened. Automatically, she tried to lift her hand to the pain, but her stomach thought this was a signal to start jumping around again so she left her hand where it was and tried to remember what had hit her.

A sudden stab of fear entered into the mish-mash of confusion, nausea, dizziness and annoyance that was washing around her brain. While she waited for her head to clear she tried to sort through the jumbled memories of the library. This too proved a mistake. Trevor!

The stab of fear quickly rounded all the other emotions up, and told them that it was taking over. Terrified, they filtered away, leaving Kate with a clearer head and a racing heart. Trevor had taken her.

She screwed her eyes up, then slowly opened her left one to let in the smallest amount of light that she could. It was less bright now, or at least it seemed so. She was in the front seat of a car, or a van or something, and the lights had been streetlights. Watching them for a moment she soon worked out that the car she was in was not being handled especially well. Slowly she turned her head to the driver's seat, and her heart slipped smoothly into overdrive.

Trevor was sitting there, but it was the not the Trevor she knew. Physically he hadn't changed, or she didn't think so, although his whole posture was so distorted it was hard to tell. He was hunched over the steering wheel, one of his hands gripping it so tightly it appeared as if he was trying to pull it off. The knuckles of the hand that was gripping the wheel were as white as an agoraphobic's in the Sahara desert, but the arm and wrist attached to it were jerking, pulling, with the result that the van twisted from side to side of the road. Trevor's other hand was hovering somewhere between the steering wheel and the gearstick, making small movements to each but then stopping in mid-air and heading back the other way, as if it couldn't decide where it would be most useful to be. His legs were in a similar state of disagreement, alternately jumping on the brake, the accelerator and the clutch in such a manner that it was a miracle they were moving at all. It was Trevor's face, however, that Kate was drawn to, and it was this that set her ventricles hammering like castanets.

His head was jolting, sometimes violently, up, down and side to side. His eyes seemed to blink independently of each other, so that he appeared to be winking at the road ahead. His nostrils were flared and his lips curled in something that sometimes looked like a snarl, and sometimes a smile. His jaw was working and he seemed to be muttering to himself.

Kate had once seen a programme on an unfortunate young man with Tourette's syndrome. He had been constantly racked with impulses that he was powerless to prevent. He was a mass of nervous tics, and would suddenly burst out in a stream of obscenities, looking tremendously embarrassed and remorseful afterwards, at least until the next attack that would come seconds later. She was reminded of the young man as she looked at Trevor, a being at war with himself. What the bloody hell was going on?

He didn't seem to have noticed she was awake. He didn't seem capable of noticing anything, much less of controlling a speeding vehicle through busy streets. She chanced another look out of the window. The view outside had changed, in that instead of careering down streets they were now traversing darker, smaller roads, with less traffic, more trees and no more streetlights. Kate couldn't help feeling that her situation had not improved.

She glanced back at the jerking form of Trevor again. He was frantically wrestling with the indicator as if hoping it would tell him which way to turn next. She wiggled her body a little away from him, to try and get her hands closer to the door lever without drawing attention to herself. Jumping out of a speeding vehicle was not a stunt she had thought about trying before, but it seemed preferable to wherever her maddened ex-boyfriend seemed intent on taking her. As she twisted, the van hit a pothole on the road, and the whole thing juddered. She fell back into the seat, and suddenly Trevor seemed to notice she was conscious. He turned to her with his twitching, animated face. It was the kind of face Hannibal Lecter would have crossed the street to avoid meeting. His eyes, which had been rotating in his sockets moments earlier, were both fixed on her.

'She's awake!' he said, then closed his mouth again. One of his eyes blinked, then the other one. Suddenly his head snapped back round to look forwards again.

'Keep your eyes on the road, idiot!' he said.

Kate decided to upgrade her mental alert level from

'worried and scared' to 'confused and extremely frightened'. Trevor had never shown any sign of mental illness before — come to think of it he had never shown much sign of anything before. This had been the main reason she had split up with him. She had found herself hoping he could say something, anything that would be interesting, surprising or otherwise out of the ordinary. Be careful what you wish for, she thought now.

She opened her mouth to say something, but pain blossomed from the back of her head, lighting up her vision, so she snapped her mouth shut again. Perhaps it would be best if she kept quiet anyway. Trevor was now frantically glancing at her and then back at the road, like a man with two televisions and an extremely short attention span.

'What do we do now?' he was muttering. 'We have to get away first,' he said immediately afterwards. 'How far is it anyway?' he continued.

'Don't know, just keep going. Can't be far now, can it?'

'Were we followed?'

'Don't think so.'

'Doesn't matter if we were, does it? We've got to get away from the others.'

Kate watched this solo conversation with mounting panic. She had heard of multiple personality disorder, of course. Who hadn't? It was the stuff of a hundred films and mystery novels. But she hadn't heard of the personalities conversing with each other, certainly not occupying the same body at the same time. She squinted at him, and it was then that she saw the haze around Trevor. It was thin, a wispy cloud barely visible in the darkness of the van, but it was definitely there. And Kate knew instantly what it was.

A crowd of spirits, so dense as to be almost formless, surrounded Trevor. There was no separation in the cloud. All the spirits seemed to have merged into one form, but somehow retained some aspect of their individuality. And all of those individuals were trying to control Trevor at once. Revulsion and pity mixed with the fear in her mind. Was Trevor in there somewhere, buried underneath the single horde that had overtaken him?

Suddenly, one of Trevor's legs slammed down on the brake pedal, and the van came to a screeching halt. Kate was thrown into the dashboard and then sank back into her seat. The body that until recently had contained Trevor turned towards her. He seemed to be trying to decide what to do. There was a pause, and a surprised expression appeared on his face.

'What, now?' he asked.

'Yes,' he told himself a second later. 'Now.'

Chapter Nineteen

I

The years had not been kind to the house in which Cranmer had spent his youth, and where he and his brethren had finished their journey through life; in fact, they had been extremely unkind. It was as if the years had not only bullied the house in the playground, but they had also stolen its lunch money, tied it to the railings and flushed its head down the toilet.

When Cranmer died there were no relatives to take on the estate of Hope Manor. The house had been, when Cranmer's parents were alive, a typical country manor, such as could be found in any corner of England in the early twentieth century; a bastion of polite conversation, excellent dinner etiquette and extreme animal cruelty. When Cranmer became master of his own country estate, he had dismissed most of the servants, so that the polite conversation and dinner etiquette died away, although he managed to keep up with the animal cruelty. Members of the brethren did most of the housekeeping. This had been the first of many downhill steps for the house. Members of Mysterious Cults who performed Unspeakable Deeds to deduce the Inner Mysteries of the Cosmos are not renowned for their housekeeping skills, and the most that tended to happen was that the robes got a bit of a wash now and then, and the tomes of Deeper Understanding were dusted twice a week. What with all the Unspeakable Deeds being carried out most nights, which tended to play havoc with the carpets, and the fact that most of the unfortunate farmyard animals which experienced the Unspeakable Deeds tended to be justifiably quite nervous while being led into the cellar, the situation wasn't improved very much.

In fact, by the time Cranmer and his devotees had finally stopped performing Unspeakable Deeds on animals and finally got round to performing them on themselves, the manor was, it could be said, a bit of a tip. So much so, in fact, that the Government of the day, who inherited the house (there being no family members left to give it to), had tremendous difficulty reselling it to anyone, even at a bargain-basement price. Years passed. The gardens became more and more overgrown, the house itself more dilapidated and less pleasant that it had hitherto been. The outbreak of another round of people killing each other just over twenty years after the war to end all wars saved the manor, for a time. Because of its size and convenient location on the south coast, it was appropriated by the Royal Air Force as a training centre. The brief spit and polish it received at this time was unfortunately somewhat ruined by the fact that it then spent an unhappy few months having bombs dropped on or near it on a daily basis. By the time the Battle of Britain was over, the manor and the surrounding gardens looked like... well, like bombs had hit them.

The RAF then handed responsibility for the bits that were left of the manor back to the Local Government. The Local Government tried to hand responsibility straight back to them but the RAF said they had important flying and bombing things to do. The matter became a dispute between the two agencies, each trying to pass the buck back to the other. When, years after the war, the whole mess had been sorted out by an over-enthusiastic public servant, and inspectors were sent to investigate the ruins, they found a thriving community of squatters who had been there for years.

The squatters were polite and friendly but also were not renowned for their housekeeping skills. Their gardening left something to be desired too, and so the rot continued. Eventually, an American company planning to create a theme park bought up the grounds. Unfortunately, no one thought to consult the squatters, and so once more the ownership of the grounds degenerated into first a legal and then an actual battle, with bailiffs moving in to remove the squatters. The squatters politely explained to the bailiffs that they would leave the grounds over their dead bodies. The bailiffs had postulated that this could be arranged, whereupon the largest of the squatters intimated that the bailiffs had better remove themselves from the premises as quickly as possible. The bailiffs had pointed out that the squatters could stuff it, and the squatters mentioned that the bailiffs were a bunch of morons, and added a few points about their mothers. Things had degenerated from this point.

So this was the situation that Hope Manor found itself in; a nearly forgotten ruin. Overgrown. Unloved. And somewhere, deep in what used to be the gardens, buried under six feet of earth and several tons of overgrown vegetation, lay a shell that had once contained the essence of Charles Cranmer. Deeper in the undergrowth, something watched. And waited.

II

Alan squinted at the crude sign, scrawled in white paint on a piece of chipboard, which hung around the rusting iron railings that surrounded the gardens of Hope Manor.

'Trespassers are welcome provided they bring a bag for their teeth,' he read aloud, then looked back to George, who was studying a piece of paper on his lap. George glanced up, and flashed an infuriating grin.

'Ah, that's just for the bailiffs', he said. 'They won't mind us. Besides, bailiffs tend to call round in daylight, don't they, not in darkness.'

'Oh, that's right,' agreed Alan. 'I'm sure anybody who sneaks into the grounds in the middle of the night has a much more peaceful motive.'

'We don't want to cause any fuss, do we? It'll be a ten-minute job, I promise you.'

Once again, Alan wished he was wearing glasses, so he could look penetratingly at George over them. He thought about trying it anyway, but decided it wouldn't really work without specs. Instead he turned and looked dubiously over the couple of shovels and various other bits of vegetation-cutting equipment that they had grabbed during the day on their brief visit to B&Q.

'There is not much time,' said the Gandalf-voice.

'And you can shut up, as well,' Alan said out loud. George lifted his head briefly, but he was getting used to these one-sided outbursts by now.

'The machine is due to be switched on tomorrow night,' the voice persisted. 'We must be there at all costs.'

'What's he saying?' George asked.

'Harping on about the accelerator again. Do you think they'll go ahead and switch it on anyway, with everything that's happening?' Alan asked.

George shrugged. 'Probably. I mean, what else are they going to do? Sit at home and worry? There were still people in the hardware shop, weren't there? People would rather just get on with their lives and ignore the end for as long as they can.' He paused. 'Well, most people, anyway.'

'Are you sure,' Alan said out loud, looking intently at his hand, which was his way of signalling to George that he was actually speaking to the voice inside his head, 'that this is absolutely necessary? I mean, I like a bit of moonlit grave robbing as much as anybody else...'

'If we do not stop this menace, then the world will be bathed in the blood of innocents, and the seas will run red. The air will be filled with the wailing of the dying and the stench of the dead, and the ground itself shall...'

'All right, all right,' Alan snapped. 'I just feel our time would be better spent going to the police, and starting to look for Kate.'

'We've been through this, Alan. The police are busy enough, and we can't trust them! We can't trust anyone,' George said. 'There's no time. Besides, we know where she'll be tomorrow night. We just have to be prepared. You're not nervous about this, are you?'

'Nervous?' Alan laughed. 'Of course not! Why would I be nervous about breaking into a manor house full of thugs ?'

'They're just squatters,' George said wearily, but Alan

was not to be put off.

'...to search acres of ground for a half-century dead lunatic who is trying to destroy the world. What have we got to worry about?'

'Exactly,' said George, determined to ignore his pessimism. 'Let's get on with it.'

III

The day before had been busy with preparation. So busy, in fact, that Alan had not really had time for what they were actually going to do to sink in. George had returned to his office, with a reluctant Alan in tow, to find out all he could about Hope Manor. Alan had been relieved to discover they would not be breaking into a stately home, but not so pleased when he had read the newspaper report on the Internet about the violence between the current residents and the current owners. The report had been entertainingly graphic in its descriptions of broken bones.

From some website that he seemed to know quite well, George had managed to download the original plans of the manor house, including the site of the then proposed graveyard. It was too old to have Cranmer's burial place marked upon it, but it was a safe bet, or so George said, that he would have been interred there or somewhere nearby. Alan wondered why Cranmer hadn't been buried in a tomb, rather than a much more common grave. There was no explanation on the website. He and George supposed the money to build one must have run out.

In the newspaper report, the bailiffs had apparently been repelled once only the previous week, and were planning to return, with police reinforcements and presumably somewhat inflamed tempers, in two days' time. That gave them one day. The article suggested the squatters had spent much of the intervening time building barricades against the return of the bailiffs.

'Relax,' George had said. 'They'll be barricading the

houses. They won't care about the graveyard. They won't go anywhere near it. Probably only use it as a dog toilet.'

This snippet of news failed to relax Alan. Vicious dogs, he thought. Bit of a busman's holiday, really.

The manor house itself was several hundred miles away, near the New Forest. The accelerator, which was a few hundred miles further away again in Kent, was due to be switched on the same day as the bailiffs would descend on Hope Manor.

The rest of the day had been spent buying digging equipment, poring over the articles and plans that George had downloaded, and watching the news. Things were getting worse. There was now not a single baby born, human or animal, which lived more than a few hours, not anywhere in the world. Many countries were in a state of hysteria, but governments had not started toppling. Not yet. The news screens were full of angry shouting people. Religious leaders were trying to appear calm, and were smoothly saying that was what had been planned all along, never mind what it said in whichever book they happened to have told everyone to read and believe in for thousands of years.

'So what happens if this doesn't work?' asked Alan, as they watched the panicked images on the screen.

George shrugged. 'Goodbye, human race,' he said. 'Nice knowing you.'

IV

Getting over — or rather, through — the fence was not difficult. Whatever barricades the current residents of Hope Manor had been working on, they hadn't included patching up the gaping holes in the railings surrounding the estate.

'There you are, see! Difficult bit done already!' George said cheerfully, but quietly, as he wriggled into the grounds. A shovel was tied to his back, along with a rucksack full of bin liners, ready to receive whatever bits of Cranmer they managed to find. He was wearing a thick pair of gardening gloves and a black boiler suit, but he somehow managed to look dashing.

Alan looked back. He could just about see the dark shape of George's Nissan Sunny lurking under the trees on the road opposite. The road they had approached the estate on had been selected for its quietness, and its closeness to the spot marked out for the graveyard on the plans George had found.

He turned back from the hole in the fence, catching a glimpse of his own arm as he did so. It was not difficult to spot. The shop had been out of boiler suits (except for the black one, of course) and so George had bought it for himself, because Alan had one already.

It was the one he had worn during the hazy summer of 2001. He had been working for the Ministry of Agriculture, Food and Fisheries at the time, largely because the pay was better than anything he could have reasonably expected as a veterinary assistant anywhere else. They had provided him with a car (a lovely Mitsubishi Shogun), some buckets, some disinfectant and, of course, a boiler suit. Thus equipped, he had then spent several well-paid months slaughtering most of Devon's peaceful cows and sheep in the name of disease prevention.

Belatedly, far too belatedly, he had realised that perhaps, in some cases, the ends did not always justify the means, and that it was possible the MAFF had reacted somewhat overzealously to the disease. No matter how bad the officials told him the disease was, he had a hard time reconciling the fact that it was harmless to humans (not especially nasty to sheep, either, now he came to think about it) with the piles of corpses that began filling the farmyards and fields of Devon. He left the MAFF that autumn. Because he had been in contact with the disease, he was classified as 'dirty'. This more or less fitted with his feelings at the time. In fact, he didn't feel clean again until the last of the money he had earned was spent (he didn't give it back, of course. Principles only got you so far, after all. He didn't think the MAFF would take it back anyway, but he didn't try).

The most upsetting thing about the whole experience,

(apart from the horrible realisation that it was possible to become numb to death — it was actually possible to perform executions without any sense of moment, or awe, but with boredom, or no sense at all) was the fact that the profession he belonged to, the people who had sworn to uphold the welfare of all the animals under their care, said nothing about it, other than it had all been necessary. Alan, as a vet, had fairly serious doubts about this. Yes, the disease had been stopped, and maybe there had been no other way to stop it. But wholesale slaughter did not fit comfortably with the reasons he had become a vet in the first place. Of course, the animals would eventually have been killed anyway. And, of course, he said nothing himself, but he was upset and disappointed when nobody else did.

It had been about this time that his disillusionment with the profession had started. To gain some small measure of revenge, he had driven his Government Issue Shogun into a farm gate, and dented the front bumper quite badly. In their turn, the MAFF (who had now changed their name to DEFRA, or the Department for Environment, Food and Rural Affairs — this put Alan in mind of a phrase of his mother's, namely 'You can't polish a turd') presented Alan with a bucket and a clean boiler suit when he left.

The bucket was very nice. So was the boiler suit. It was white.

V

'Are you sure,' asked Alan as he squeezed through the gap in the fence, 'that I couldn't just wear a dark-coloured sweater or something?'

George turned to him.

'Look, this is the kind of job where you want a boiler suit. We've been through this.'

'But look at me!' Alan said. 'I stand out like...' He tailed off. There was nothing he could think of that stood out like a man in a white boiler suit against a dark background, so he was temporarily stumped.

'For the last time,' George said, 'it doesn't matter! No one is looking for us, expecting us, or anything. They might be guarding the house, but what kind of idiot would guard an eighty-year-old grave?'

He turned and tramped on through the undergrowth, leaving Alan to wonder exactly what kind of idiot would try and move stealthily in a white boiler suit.

VI

Moon Mountain had been christened 'James Weatherby', but had replaced it with his new name during a ceremony at the Winter Solstice. It had been more of a rowdy ceremony than his Christening, or so he was told. Moon himself had no memory of either occasion, though for entirely different reasons.

He had selected Moon as his new name because, he said, of the deep symbolism of the mysterious planetoid, for its cold solemnity, and for the fact that he thought it was pretty cool. The 'Mountain' part of his name had been selected for him, because he looked as if he had been carved out of a large pile of rock. Behind his back, people whispered that his sculptor seemed not to have been particularly skilled, and had maybe been under the influence of various substances when he had done the job. People tended to say this behind Moon's back rather than to his face for two reasons. One was that Moon's face was one aspect that seemed to have been especially badly done, with very little thought going in to the eyes or mouth, and not much effort made to chisel the nose down to a more respectable size. The other reason was that, despite his name, Moon did not tend to react with serenity and quiet calm to people who suggested such things. When he did react, it was often quickly and painfully, but at least it usually involved a free ride in a white van with flashing lights for the suggester.

Moon was not, currently, in a good mood. He wasn't in

a good mood very often, of course. In fact, usually the only times he felt happy were when he was causing other people to feel miserable, by means of introducing his fist to their face. This had got him in trouble in the past and may, he would have reflected (had he not been the kind of person for whom reflection was only something that mirrors did), have been one of his problems.

He was thinking about hitting people. The bailiffs were due to come again tomorrow, and it sounded like it promised to be more fun than the last time they came. The others were in the ruins of the house, getting drunk and stoned and trying not to think about the morning, trying not to think about where they would be sent on to next, trying not to think about what was happening to the world, and whether there would be anywhere else to move on to. They were all so miserable it was getting Moon down, so he had come out here, to the gardens. He was watching the dogs sleep. He liked dogs. They seemed comfortably simple to him, easy to understand. Not like people.

He sat, waiting for the morning. He knew the next day would be one of those times in his life when he was his own master, when it was him against the world. When people would listen to what he had to say. Not that he was going to say much, what with being too busy hitting people and everything, but he appreciated the fact that if he did say something, people would listen to him.

He sat in the gardens, watching the dogs, and hoping that tomorrow would come sooner. Or, at least, that something interesting would happen so that tomorrow would come more quickly.

It did.

Chapter Twenty

I

The Gandalf-voice was getting more and more agitated the deeper they moved into the grounds of Hope Manor. It constantly badgered Alan about how little time they had left, until Alan and even George told the voice to shut up and let them get on with it. It didn't help. Alan could still feel the voice at the back of his mind, buzzing like a fly trapped in a house on a hot day. It played on Alan's nerves, pushing his already tense mood towards breaking point. The voice was evidently very excited. It was like having a violin playing out a very long, very high-pitched note, the kind played in the scary part of a nasty horror film (right before the zombie/vampire/serial killer jumps out of its hiding place) playing just next to his ear. It was making him very nervous indeed.

'What was that?' he whispered urgently to George, who turned around very slowly, sighing.

'That,' he said, 'was you, standing on a twig.'

Alan looked down. 'Oh,' he said. 'Sorry.'

'What's wrong with you?'

'It doesn't matter,' Alan said. 'Let's just get on with it.'

'Right,' said George, turning back round. This was not the first such interruption of the night. He put his torch in his mouth, and shone the beam down onto the plan that he had printed off the Internet, jiggling his compass with his other hand.

'It 'ould 'e 'ust a'ead,' he said through a mouth full of torch, gesturing with the hand holding the compass.

'OK,' Alan said.

The voice in his head started again as George set off once more. 'Wait,' it said. 'Isn't it off to the right a little more? The graveyard, I mean?'

'How do you know?' Alan whispered as quietly as he could.

'I looked at the map, same as you two,' the voice said. 'It's to the right! Your friend is going the wrong way!'

'All right, all right,' muttered Alan. 'George,' he hissed. 'George!'

George stopped. Ahead of them, a little to the right, a dog barked. George turned around.

'It's to the right, isn't it?' Alan whispered.

George frowned. He looked down at the map, then at the compass, then up at the sky. He nodded.

II

They came to another iron fence, this one only about three feet high, and much more ornate than the one surrounding the estate. On the other side, the undergrowth was still thick, but as George shone his torch in they could make out several quiet dark shapes that could have been tombstones.

'You know what this reminds me of,' George said to Alan as they carefully climbed over the fence into the little graveyard. Alan wasn't sure he wanted to know.

'You've done a lot of grave robbing before, have you?' he asked.

'No, no. I'm thinking of that scene in The Omen. It's a bit like that, isn't it?'

'The Omen, the film, you mean?'

'Yeah, you know that bit when Ambassador Thorne and the photographer, what's his name? Played by David Warner. Anyway, they've gone to find out what happened at the hospital on the night his son was born, so they end up arriving at this tiny little graveyard, somewhere in Italy, just when the sun is going down. It's just like this, isn't it?'

The description rang a few bells in Alan's memory. 'Erm... what happens to them?'

'Well, they're attacked by dogs, aren't they? Bloody great Rottweilers, I think.'

'Oh,' said Alan. 'I don't suppose one of them is wearing a white boiler suit, are they?'

'Erm... no. I don't think so.'

Alan lapsed into silence, in the hope that George would follow his lead, and shut up. It seemed to work. They crept through the unkempt grounds to the first dark shape. It was indeed a headstone, but a very old one. It was so old and weathered that it was impossible to make out any details on it, save that there once had been something written on it.

'Can't be it,' said George. 'Too old. Our man's only been here eighty years or so.'

They moved on. The next gravestone was the same as the last. The one after that had the words

'Mary Elizabeth CRANMER. Beloved wife and mother. 1864—1919.'

'His mother,' whispered George. There was another stone right next to it.

'Jonathon Paul CRANMER. Beloved husband and father. 1859—1919.'

'OK,' said George, 'Now we're getting somewhere. Can't be far now.'

Alan looked around. The voice in his head was quiet. Ominously so. The buzzing had stopped.

'Are you there?' Alan whispered.

'Yes, yes,' the voice snapped back. 'Just find the grave.'

There was a strange feeling that came to Alan when the voice spoke, a sense of... Alan wasn't sure what it was, but...

'Alan!' George called from another headstone a few feet away. 'Here it is!'

Alan turned to look, distracted from his thoughts. George was crouching in front of the headstone. It looked newer than the rest. The ground in front was less covered with foliage and brambles than the rest of the neglected tombstones. He walked over. The inscription on the stone read:

'Here lies the damned and accursed body of Charles Ellis CRANMER. 1890—1921. May he rot in hell for his crimes.'

Underneath this, in much smaller writing, an inscription

read 'Rest in Peace'. Alan got the feeling this last had been written under duress.

'Glad to know he was a well-liked member of the community.' he said.

'Come on,' said George, standing and taking the shovel off his back. 'Let's get on with it.'

It didn't take as long as Alan had feared it might. The work was hard, hindered more by the fact that George did as little of the actual digging as he could possibly get away with, pretending instead to be clearing the foliage around the grave, or polishing the headstone looking for clues, or even simply standing looking at Alan dig, saying he was 'on watch.'

Despite this, after an hour and a half of digging, Alan's shovel hit something that made a satisfyingly wooden thunk. He looked up at George, who was now staring intently at the piece of paper he had brought with him; despite the fact it was far too dark to read it as Alan had the torch himself.

'I think it's here,' he said. George raised his eyebrows and dropped into the three-foot deep pit that Alan had created.

'Hmm,' he said. 'Shallow grave, innit?'

Alan nodded, and pointedly hoisted another load of earth out of the pit. George got the message. Within another ten minutes then had exposed the whole of the coffin. It was well made, of a solid oak that hadn't started to crumble yet. George cleared the last of the earth from the top. They looked at each other.

'Erm…' said George, 'just how rotten are we going to be talking, here? Still bits of flesh hanging off? Or just a skeleton? I think I could cope with a skeleton.'

Alan shrugged. 'Only one way to find out,' he said, and reached down to open the lid.

'Stop!' said George suddenly. Alan did so. 'Can you hear that?' George asked.

Alan stopped and waited. Nothing. 'Look,' he said, 'if you don't want to see, that's fine. I'm used to rotting stuff. I've seen lots worse. But…'

He stopped. There was a noise. A dog barking again. Distant, but not distant enough. And what was that? He thought he could hear the sound of someone pulling themselves through the undergrowth, cursing and muttering as they did so.

'Have you seen Night of the Living Dead?' George asked.

'Oh, shut up,' said Alan. 'Come on, we're running out of time.'

He leaned down into the pit again, and pulled the coffin lid open. A skeleton lay there, lying on its back, still covered in a few rags of clothing. The two of them paused for a moment, silently working out whether they should be shocked, or scared, or what, but as this was exactly what they were expecting to find they finally decided to take it in their stride. The noises were getting closer.

'Well,' Alan asked under his breath, 'are we happy?'

The voice did not reply for a moment. When it did, it was surprisingly quiet and subdued, rather than triumphant as Alan would have expected.

'Yes,' said the voice slowly. 'Yes, that's it. We... we don't need the whole thing. A part should be sufficient.'

'What's he saying?' George asked.

'You don't want to know,' Alan said, and carefully lowered himself into the pit.

The skeleton lay on its back, its arms by its sides. There was a small hole at the bottom of the casket, and a mound of earth had poured in along with, presumably, all the things that had reduced the corpse to a skeleton. Alan was relieved. He didn't know why skeletons were less scary than half-rotted corpses, but they were. They smelled better anyway.

Another noise from above, very close now. Alan quickly bent over and grabbed at one of the arms. He wasn't sure quite what he was grabbing for, because his eyes were closed. He only knew he didn't want to get the skull. Something broke off in his hand. He opened his eyes. The humerus. That should do.

He straightened up, and found himself looking at a large pair of shins. A pair of shins that did not belong to George.

Alan slowly looked up to take in the rest of the figure. This would have taken some time even if he hadn't been standing at the bottom of a three-foot deep hole, but as it was Alan nearly toppled over backwards before he got up to the face at the top. Then he wished he hadn't.

The man was enormous, even without the three-foot difference. The shins were coated in denim, and below them was a large pair of Doctor Martens boots. Above them, the legs continued up like a pair of giant redwoods. They were topped with an enormous torso and a pair of arms that could have given a fair representation of the theory of continental shift when they moved. Above them, a large pair of nostrils was staring down at him from an enormous bald head. The nostrils seemed to have steam coming out of them.

'H…' said Alan. The rest of the word retreated from his mouth, and went and hid somewhere in the deep recesses of his lungs, where it trembled and refused to come out. It did this because the continental arms of the unfeasibly large man moved, quite suddenly, and Alan found himself being lifted out of the pit. The large man made it very clear that this was no effort at all for him. Alan was now face to face with him.

Alan didn't know the man's adopted name was Moon, but if he had he would have thought it perfectly suitable. The man's face was large, hairless, white, and pitted with craters. It also looked like something that would be better studied with the science of Geology rather than Biology. That was if you wished to study it at all, which would be unlikely unless it was in a police line-up.

The man's features were currently all screwed up towards the centre of his face, as if someone had pulled a drawstring around the edge of it tight. He looked very, very angry. Alan's eyes darted around desperately to see where George was, but he was nowhere in sight.

A low rumbling noise began in front of him, like the start

of an earthquake. The large man was apparently saying something.

'What do you think,' the man said, the words tumbling out like rocks in a landslide, 'you are doing?'

'I was just hnnnk,' said Alan as the man tightened his grip on the collar of the boiler suit. He waved his arms vainly to try and indicate that he would be happy to answer the question if only he could get a little oxygen in.

'What were you doing?' repeated the man. He relaxed his grip slightly.

'I was just... erm... doing a spot of... erm...' Alan searched for some way to end the sentence. Grave digging? Bodysnatching? Might not go down so well. What else would anybody be doing in a graveyard in the middle of the night?

'I was just visiting a relative,' he said, rather feebly.

'Oh yeah?' grunted the man. 'Digging them up, too, were you?'

'I... erm... I found them like that,' Alan said.

The man's eyebrows squeezed even further together. They were now joined into a single line of fury. His eyes were sunken into deep pits of rage. They glanced at the shovel by the side of the exposed grave, then down at Alan's hand, in which he was still holding the humerus. It didn't look like the large man was buying Alan's story.

The man took a deep breath, and his expression lightened. At first Alan thought that the man had decided to let him go, but then he realised that the reason the man looked a little brighter was because he had decided that it would now be all right to pummel Alan into mush.

The large man took a deep breath, and lifted Alan even higher.

'His head!' the Gandalf-voice suddenly cried in Alan's mind. 'Grab his head! Quickly!'

'Wh...?' said Alan. The large man was drawing one of his fists back, like a baseball player about to take a pitch.

'Grab his head!' the Gandalf-voice said again. It was

about the most direct thing it had ever said to him. Alan reached down and grabbed the large man's stubbly scalp with both hands. For a second the man's eyes widened in incredulity, then Alan felt a thrill of something pass down his arms into his hands. The effect was instant. The large man howled like a kicked spaniel, and Alan found himself dropping back into the pit. The coffin shattered as he landed in it, and bones flew everywhere.

'Get up,' said the voice. 'Get up!'

Alan struggled to his feet. The large man was on knees, his hands on his head, but whatever the Gandalf-voice had done to him, he was already recovering. He lifted his head. His eyes fixed on Alan's.

'Rarrggh!' he said, staggering up onto his towering legs again. All he needed was green skin and purple ragged jeans, and he would have been the image of the Incredible Hulk. Alan jumped out of the pit but the man was already reaching towards him. Then he howled again, dropping once more to his knees. George emerged from behind the collapsed figure, dropping the shovel that he had slammed between the man's legs.

'Come on,' he said, jumping over the grave and heading in the general direction of the car. Alan followed him, glancing over his shoulder at the man who was once more rising to his feet. Looking down at his own hand, he was relieved to see it was still tightly gripping the bone that had caused them so much trouble.

Alan and George crashed through the foliage blindly, the enraged giant tearing after them. George reached the fence a few metres ahead of Alan, squeezing through the small hole they had found in seconds. He was already in the car by the time Alan got to the hole in the fence, and had started it by the time Alan squeezed through. The gate shook as the large man ran into it. The hole was far too small for him. Alan jumped into the passenger seat as the car's engine reluctantly began to kick into life.

'Come on!' the voice in Alan's head screamed.

'Come on!' Alan screamed at George.

'Come on!' George screamed at the engine. One of the cries seemed to work. The engine shuddered into life. The sudden glow of headlights illuminated the large man, already halfway over the fence, moving fast despite his bulk. George lifted the clutch. The car shot forwards, towards the fence. The man had cleared it now.

'Shit, shit, sorry,' muttered George as he wrestled the gearstick into reverse with several horrible crunching noises.

The man ran towards the car. He seemed to be actually glowing with rage. Alan was sure there was steam rising from his t-shirt. The man jumped onto the bonnet as George swiftly reversed.

'Christ!' Alan said.

Amazingly, the man was drawing back his fist, as if he meant to punch through the windscreen. Whether he would actually have managed to do this, or just broken his fist, or what, Alan never found out, because it was at this point that the man fell off. George changed gear again, spun the wheel, slammed his foot on the accelerator, and they shot off into the night.

'There,' he said, smiling at Alan. 'Piece of cake.'

Chapter Twenty-One

I

They drove like maniacs for five miles, then like lunatics for five more. Finally, their hearts still pounding, they turned into a service station off the M4. George drove into the car park, stopped and pulled on the handbrake. They looked at each other.

'Bloody hell,' said George. He was grinning like a child on Christmas morning.

Alan was not. He was still thinking of the fists, of the rage in the huge man's eyes. He looked down at his hands. They were shaking. His right hand was clamped tightly around the arm bone of a man that had been dead for eighty years.

'Well,' he said, trying to sound relaxed. 'We did it.'

As George turned the engine off there was the blaring of sirens behind them. Alan half-jumped out his seat and turned to look.

'Relax, will you?' George said. 'We've not done anything wrong.' Alan couldn't help but notice that he was also peering nervously out of the back window.

The sirens dropped pitch as they sped past the service station and on down the motorway, in accordance with physics. In accordance with biology, Alan found that he needed the toilet very badly.

The sky was brightening as the sun began its long journey across it, and the shops were starting to open.

'Come on,' said George. 'Let's get something to eat.'

II

The restaurant in the service station was less nasty than Alan remembered service-station restaurants to be. Apparently they had been cleaning up their acts recently, to appeal to families, and so there was a lot of varnished wood and pastel colours. It was also four pounds for a cup of tea.

'What the hell,' George had said, ordering a mega-monster breakfast deal (the deal being, presumably, that you paid through the nose for reheated beans and hundreds of rounds of toast). 'Might as well enjoy it.'

Alan didn't feel all that hungry, and settled for one of those little boxes of cereal which look nice until you pour them into the bowl and find out that a cereal company executive's idea of a 'portion' is not necessarily the same as everyone else's.

Thus laden with food, they sat down at a table near the window, through which they could see the sun slowly rising over a drab artificial lake. George began to demolish his meal. At least, compared with the Great Relish café, it was recognisable as food, although it tasted of nothing at all. Alan opened his own box of muesli, and poured it into the bowl. The flakes and berries barely covered the bottom. He tried to open a carton of milk, failed and spilled it all over the table, then realised the milk he needed for the cereal was in a jug by the boxes. He gave up and simply proceeded to prod the muesli with his spoon, stirring it this way and that, looking out of the window. The bone that had caused all the problems was in his coat pocket. He wondered what scene the sun would illuminate when the Earth had rotated right round once more. The end of everything. Was it possible? Could the world really be about to end?

He knew that this was a selfish way of looking at things, that really it would just be the human world that would cease to be. Whatever else happened, the planet Earth would still be here.

Presently, he noticed that the various gulps and slurps opposite him seemed to have stopped. George was looking out of the window as well, uncharacteristically silent. His eyes strayed over Alan's dry muesli, then back to the sunrise.

'Think we'll stop him?' he said.

Alan shrugged. 'Maybe.'

George fell silent again for a moment. He looked down

at his empty plate. 'All this... all this stuff,' he said, faltering, not quite finding the words he needed. 'All this stuff going on... does this mean that there's a purpose to it all? Does it mean there's a God?'

Again, Alan shrugged. 'Don't know. I don't think so.'

George kept looking at his plate, as if this was the answer he was expecting.

'I mean,' Alan continued, 'just 'cause we go somewhere, afterwards, doesn't necessarily mean anything, does it? I mean, it doesn't sound much like heaven, where we go, does it?'

George remained silent.

'Maybe whatever we call souls, they're just a by-product. Something that happens, like... I don't know, like sweat, or something.'

George looked up, his face wrinkled in distaste. 'Sweat?'

'Well, you know. A side effect. I don't know. All I'm saying is, it doesn't have to mean anything, does it?'

He could feel the Gandalf-voice stirring at the back of his mind, but whatever its thoughts on the subject were, it was keeping them to itself.

'What about the servitors? The inner mysteries? Surely they mean something?' George said.

Alan shrugged again. 'Maybe. Maybe not. Maybe they've just been around longer than we have. I think...'

He paused. George looked expectant. 'I think,' he continued, but realised he didn't know what he thought. He peered down at his muesli again. 'Well, it means that this is even more important, doesn't it? It means we can't take it for granted. It means we've got to find Kate!' He surprised himself with the force of his last statement.

The voice in his head buzzed, but said nothing. Neither did George. They sat in silence, until the waitress came to take their plates. 'Everything all right?' she said cheerfully.

'No,' said George. 'It bloody isn't.'

The waitress gave him the kind of look you should

expect to receive after a remark like this, but decided not to pursue the issue.

'So,' he said to Alan after she left. 'What now?'

'Where else?' Alan said. 'To the accelerator.'

III

Dr Harriet Grey took one last look in the mirror. She was perfect. Not a hair out of place. Not even, come to that, an eyelash out of place. Not an unsightly blemish anywhere. Perfect make-up, applied perfectly. Her teeth shone as if they contained some undiscovered radionucleotide, and her hair glistened like dark matter. Her perfectly formed lips were just the right shade of pink to look intelligent but also dazzlingly beautiful. The cameras, she decided, would love her. There was even a chance she could steal Carol Vorderman's crown as smart totty; the thinking man's crumpet. Or rather, the crumpet of the kind of thinking man who couldn't be bothered to think for himself, and preferred someone else to do it for him.

She sighed. That, at least, had been the plan. There were no cameras waiting for her. No reporters. No press conference. There had been a brief mention in this week's New Scientist, but that was all. No one was interested any more. These damn births had taken care of that, the births and everything else that was going on that people were saying were the signs of the end of the world.

Well, screw them. They had cancelled the press conference, and they had got rid of the cameras. She had given one interview, over the phone, and from it the reporters had only taken a single word. Stunning. Well, she didn't care. She was going to go ahead anyway. Even though a quarter of her technicians were absent without leave, and a further quarter were absent with leave, she still had enough to turn on the accelerator. She could still go ahead.

As she turned away from the mirror, she very briefly wondered why it had become so important to her. Certainly it was important to no one else at the moment. Even before all hell had been let loose on the world, she had received several emails, letters and phone calls about the danger her work posed. She knew all about the risk of killer strangelets.

The experiment had become something like a religion to Harriet. No, that was wrong. Not a religion. It had become a science, and to Harriet that was much more important.

Even so, she had approached this particular project with a zeal that had surprised even her. As soon as the idea had been floated, even before any research grants had been secured, she knew, simply knew, that the accelerator must be built, that the massive ion collision experiments must go ahead. She knew it would attract attention, and if there was one thing that Harriet believed in more than science, it was attention. Other projects would too, but this had been right. She had known that immediately.

It had all been going so well. She had denied the risks skilfully enough to attract just enough attention. Soon, she would catch the attention of the public. Soon.

And then, all this! The end of the bloody world! Who would have thought it? All those miserable virologists saying we were all going to catch superflu from ducks, or the climatologists who said that the Earth's weather system was close to a sudden and unpleasant readjustment, the astronomers who banged on about floating rocks, even the boring pundits who still warned about the risk of nuclear weapons (I mean — nuclear apocalypse? That was so last century). Not one of them had thought to warn of the risk of a sudden plague of transparent babies. Not one. It had happened anyway. All over the world, in every species, even in bacteria, the plague had spread.

So, no press conference. No cameras. One lousy interview, on the phone. Well, screw them. She was going to turn the accelerator on anyway. And she was going to do it tonight. Even though it didn't mean anything any more. She had to. In the name of science. In the name of everything.

Maybe, just maybe, once it was switched on, the voices

would leave her alone.

IV

Mankind, for as long as it can collectively remember, has had a problem. This isn't, of course, as long as it would like to remember. Every discovery mankind has made since it started to realise it was important enough to make discoveries at all, has pointed to the fact that it isn't quite as important as it likes to think it is. One of the discoveries was how little time mankind had been around at all. It was such a frighteningly short time, universally speaking, that even those clever analogies about the whole history of Earth being one day long, and mankind arriving only in the last few seconds, failed to make the point adequately.

This, itself, was not the problem. Or rather, it wasn't the main problem. It was just one of those annoying little things that mankind kept on finding out, like the fact that the Earth wasn't in fact the centre of the universe (it took many more years to discover that the universe was so ridiculously big that even the concept of it having a centre at all didn't really mean anything, but even if it had one, it was most definitely not the Earth), or that the Earth actually went round the sun rather than the other way round, or all those tiny little dots of light at night were actually huge flaming balls of hydrogen just like the sun, only very, very, very far away.

All these things have a tendency to seriously undermine a species' self-esteem. It had been fun in the early days. Then mankind could imagine itself the ruler of the land, the master of all it surveyed. It was dispiriting to discover that almost every assumption that mankind had ever made about anything was completely and utterly wrong.

The real problem, the biggie, as it were, was actually one of the first discoveries mankind had made. The problem was this — as soon as a human settled down, and started to realise that although the place he found himself in was hostile, unfair and often downright vindictive, it was also beautiful, and was actually somewhere that they wouldn't mind staying in for some time, they suddenly found out that they weren't going to stay there all that long after all. There were many, many ways to live upon the Earth, but for each of them, there were twenty thousand ways to suddenly stop living.

In short, death was a problem. It came as little comfort to mankind that it happened to everything else as well, not only them. In a way, that was worse, because it made them feel even less special than they already did. So, it was forced to find a way to cope with the fact that man that is born of woman had but a short time to live. Especially if there were lots of other men also born of women around, who were keen for various complicated reasons to stick their spears through your head.

Mankind toyed with religions to see if they made them feel any better. Most of them tried to explain that dying wasn't so bad after all, and suggested to people just to get on with it, because it all got better in the end. And for a while this worked very well. The problem was that nobody seemed able to agree quite which explanation was the best one to live with. Most of the religions had the same sort of gist (i.e. be nice to each other and you'll have nice things happen to you), but tended to disagree on the finer details, such as exactly who it was who had suggested being nice to each other in the first place, or what type of sandals they happened to be wearing at the time. And, despite the fact that most of them agreed it was probably best not to spend your time on the planet sticking your spear through other people's heads, this is precisely what followers of them tended to do to anybody who felt differently.

In short, in trying to find ways to cope with the reality of death, humankind had simply invented a great new excuse to bring it along to the infidels instead.

And so the problem remained. As time went on, humankind found itself having to insert lots of clauses into their precious coping mechanisms to explain why some of the stories behind them were once more contradicted by the latest observed facts. They ended up moving the goalposts so much that many people gave up on them altogether, and although this generally caused less spear cleaning of an evening, it didn't really solve the fundamental problem.

Well, things were changing on planet Earth. Something had gone wrong. Even though only a handful of people on the planet knew exactly what it was that had happened, even the most devout followers of some of the really holy coping mechanisms could see it was something serious, and it didn't really fit in with any of the explanations that had been thus far put forward. Humankind started to get nervous.

It wasn't just the births, the strange translucent creatures being born all over the world to all types of animals. It wasn't the sudden lack of strange lights in the sky, or the fires that refused to burn. It was something else. There was something in the air. Every human on the planet could feel it. A sense of... of waiting, an ominous sense of doom. The sense that, after all the warnings and misfires, this was finally It. Capital I.

And, like a dog who has pooed in his master's favourite hat and has just heard the front door opening, mankind waited, nervously and anxiously, for It to happen.

Chapter Twenty-Two

I

The radio blared into life with reassuring clarity as Alan pressed the switch.

'...in the streets of east London, along with Birmingham and Manchester. The Prime Minister has urged people not to panic in a special address to the nation, adding his voice to those of the Queen and the Archbishop of Canterbury. In America, martial law has been declared in response to widespread rioting and looting in most major cities. Islamic leaders in the Middle East are advising followers to prepare for the coming of Allah, while in China...'

George reached over and flicked one of the preset buttons, and suddenly the car was filled with the beat of Queen's 'Hammer to Fall'.

'Christ,' said Alan, shocked by the news report. George snorted.

'Oh, not him as well,' he said, half-smiling, keeping his eyes on the road. 'We've got enough to worry about.'

The roads were clearer than they expected. They were taking the long way round, keeping away from London as much as possible. The traffic reports had suggested most of the motorways were clogged. It seemed people had finally decided to stop ignoring what was going on, and try to do something about it. Unfortunately, people being people, they had mainly decided to either run away or smash things. Neither of these solutions were helping the situation very much.

George and Alan had stolen a few hours' sleep in the car in the service station car park. Alan's mental passenger had awoken him just before ten in the morning with a renewed sense of urgency, telling him there was no time to lose. Once he had shaken off the fuzziness of sleep, Alan was surprised to find he agreed with him. He could feel it too. There was something in the air. Something was about to happen.

'Perhaps we should put the news on again,' Alan suggested. 'Y'know, find out what's going on.'

George shook his head. 'Why bother? We already know what's going on, more than they do.' He waved his hand towards the radio. 'Besides,' he added, tapping his fingers along with the steering wheel in time with the beat, 'it'd only depress us.'

Alan fell silent while George headbanged as much as he could get away with without actually driving the car off the road.

'*Just got time to say your prayers, then it's time for the hammer to fall,*' sang the radio. Alan found himself rocking along with the beat.

'You know what this song's about, don't you?' said George.

Alan shook his head.

'Nuclear war,' said George. 'End of the world.'

'Great,' said Alan. 'Very appropriate.'

The song ended. Alan jabbed the preset button again.

'…agree that it's time the World Health Organisation, or Centre for Disease Control in the US told us a little bit more about what's going on?' the radio said. John Humphrys.

'Erm…' replied the unfortunate he was interviewing, but he got no further because George jabbed the off switch.

'I told you, it's pointless,' he said.

Alan nodded. 'I suppose so.' He thought for a moment. 'You know, I read in a book somewhere that one of the ways submarine commanders were supposed to tell what kind of state Britain was in after a nuclear exchange was to tune into Radio 4. If the 'Today' programme didn't come on for more than two days in a row, the commanders were to assume civilisation had collapsed.'

George snorted again. 'Bloody hell. That puts a bit of pressure on the producers, doesn't it? Make sure the show comes out or the missiles start flying.'

Alan smiled. 'Still, that's a good sign, isn't it? The programme's still on.' Doubt crept into his voice. 'Though,

Humphrys did sound a little nervous.'

'Things fall apart,' said George. 'The centre cannot hold. Mere anarchy is loosed upon the world.'

Alan frowned. 'I know that,' he said. 'That's from a poem, isn't it?'

George nodded. 'Yeats. The Second Coming. Don't you remember how it ends?'

Alan thought for a moment. 'Hmm. Something about Bethlehem?'

'And what rough beast,' said George, 'its hour come round at last, slouches towards Bethlehem to be born?'

Alan shivered, and looked at the road ahead.

II

Even taking the long road, it didn't take them very long to find the compound that held the accelerator. George had brought with him yet another map he had found online (Alan was amazed at George's expertise with the Internet. He had tried, several years ago, to get to grips with this obviously ground-breaking new technology, but had grown tired of waiting half an hour for every page he was vaguely interested in to appear on the screen, and then find it was covered with adverts for sites he wasn't interested in. The main problem he had was that he clicked on the links almost on impulse, and by the time the screen had loaded he had either forgotten what he was waiting for or lost any interest he had in it anyway. The net result of his dip into the information superhighway had been sore eyes and a large phone bill. He decided from then on the leave it to the experts).

At two in the afternoon, avoiding several small jams on some of the busier roads, George's Ford pulled up on a grass verge alongside a forbidding ten-foot high wire-mesh fence topped with barbed wire. Every hundred feet or so there was a large white sign with a warning in red and black letters which was much more eloquent but just as unfriendly as the sign outside Hope Manor. Alan was feeling a horrible sense of déjà vu. They got out of the car. Rain drizzled down upon them, blown into their faces by the light wind. Crappy day for it, Alan thought. George picked up a stick from the ground, and tentatively touched the fence with it. Immediately he jolted his arm back.

'Yowch,' he said, dropping the stick and rubbing his arm. 'Well, there goes plan A.'

Alan peered though the misty rain into the compound. Off in the distance he could make out a small cluster of white, flat-roofed buildings and, just beyond that, something large and silver. He could only see a tiny part of it from here, but the shining structure somehow gave him a daunting impression of immensity even through the drizzle. The accelerator. It would have glittered majestically in the sunlight, but this being England, there was none, so it squatted miserably in the gloom instead, like everything else.

'It's close,' whispered the phantom in his mind. 'We must hurry.'

'So,' Alan said out loud, 'how do we get in?'

George smiled the smile that made Alan want to cry. 'Piece of cake,' he said.

'Don't tell me,' said Alan wearily, 'you saw this film once...'

George nodded enthusiastically. 'Oh yeah, not just one. There's always a place like this to break into at the end of any cheapo straight-to-DVD movie.'

'Right,' said Alan. 'So, what's plan B?'

'Ah, the old classic,' said George, still smiling his smile. 'The bluff.'

He headed back to the car. 'Let me do the talking,' he said, unnecessarily.

III

The gates were tall, thick, wiry, covered with barbed wire, and very unfriendly. The large 'KEEP OUT' signs were entirely unnecessary. Even if they had said 'WELCOME, FRIEND' the gates would have given out their decidedly unwelcome message all by themselves. They looked strangely familiar to Alan, and he slowly realised this was indeed because of all the movies he had seen where the heroes had to break in to places like these.

A small security box stood by the side of the gates, inside which was contained a small security guard.

'Bugger,' muttered George as the car approached. 'Small ones are always more difficult.'

'I see,' said Alan. 'You do this sort of thing a lot, do you?'

George ignored him. 'Just let me do the talking,' he said again.

The guard stood up and came out of the box as Alan and George approached. There was something slightly peculiar about his movements, as if he had cramp in his bottom and was trying to conceal it. George rolled the window down as the small man approached. The guard was wearing a blue peaked cap and had a thin goatee beard (of which he was probably very proud, but which gave him the appearance of having covered his face with pocket lint).

He walked, very slowly, up to the open window, and stood there for a moment, swaying uncomfortably from one leg to the other. His mouth was open.

'Yes, hello there,' George began after a small awkward silence. 'I'm Doctor Reese Mathers, this is Aiden Foxtrot, PhD, I'm sure he needs no further introduction, of course, does he? We're here for the initialising, again I'm sure I don't need to tell you this, let's hope they haven't started without us!' George gave a short and embarrassingly false laugh that made Alan cringe and sink a centimetre into his seat. There was no reaction at all from the open-mouthed security guard, who was staring at George like a lobotomised guppy fish.

'Anyway, all a bit last minute of course, can't think how they forgot to get our passes to us sooner. Everyone must have assumed that someone else had already sent them to us. Can't imagine how they thought they'd get anywhere without us. Anyway, the thing is, what with everything going on, babies and so forth, postal service not being what it was, we didn't actually receive our passes until last night, and of course would you believe it first thing this morning we look at them only to discover that...'

It was slowly dawning on George and Alan that the security guard was not really responding in the way that most security guards did in the films they had watched. He had not yet peered suspiciously at either of them, nor had he, in contravention to everything Alan and George had ever watched concerning these matters, pulled out a clipboard and tutted, or shook his head. He hadn't, in fact, done anything at all, except drool a little.

'What's going on?' Alan muttered. George didn't move. The Gandalf-voice in his head replied, to Alan's relief.

'I don't know,' it said. For good measure (perhaps it felt it hadn't been ominous enough) it added, 'There isn't much time!'

The guard had moved his eyes slowly to look at Alan. The rest of his body remained immobile. A rumbling noise began, deep in his chest, and Alan wondered for a moment if the man was about to explode.

'You may enter,' he said. His voice was slow and low, like a record being played at the wrong speed. He turned and headed back to his little shed. George sat nonplussed in the driver's seat.

'Well,' he said. 'That was certainly a bit easier than I was expecting.'

'What are you talking about?' said Alan. 'The guy sounds like Louis Armstrong after a night out! Something's wrong here, very wrong.'

The guard reached the shed and must have flicked a switch, because the gates began to swing open in front of them. At the same time, George and Alan became aware of the sound of another car approaching from behind. The guard looked up the road too.

'They are coming,' said the Gandalf-voice. 'Hurry!'

George didn't hear the command, but he could feel the urgency of the situation. He slipped the car into gear and quickly drove through the gates, which began to close again behind them. Alan looked out of the back window in time to see a white transit van approaching the slow-motion guard before they were out of sight in the drizzle.

'Who?' he asked. 'Who is coming?' There was no answer from the voice. Fear began to caress its icy fingers up and down his spine. His testicles, sensing danger, began to retreat back into his abdomen, hoping that whatever was going to happen, it wasn't going to happen in there.

Alan was right. Something was very wrong.

Chapter Twenty-Three

I

It was another half a mile along the road to the ion accelerator facility. They passed a few prefabricated buildings on the way, all of which were empty. Eventually, with nervous glances in the rear-view mirror, George pulled into the main car park, a wide swathe of tarmac interspersed with the occasional sad-looking tree. A dozen or so cars were parked here. All of them were parked across, beside and occasionally actually in the parking spaces, so that Alan felt the correct description would have been 'abandoned' rather than 'parked'.

George stopped in a space marked 'Visitors' in friendly yellow letters sprayed onto the tarmac, and they got out. It was cold outside the car, cold and wet. Alan found that he was shivering, but it wasn't entirely from the chill in the air.

'Do you think Kate is here, then?' he asked.

George shrugged, his eyes searching the desolation. 'I hope so,' he said. He was, for a change, not smiling. Something about the car park had drained his sense of adventure. The place felt as if it was lonely, and lost.

'Come on,' he said, in as cheerful a voice as he could muster. He turned, and together they headed towards the set of buildings in front of the accelerator.

Beyond the car park was a small plaza, whose centrepiece was a fountain covered in shiny metal and mirrors, the sort of sculpture which is always used to indicate the future and technology, though why a future civilisation would want to build anything so tacky was never explained. It was plastered with bird droppings, and it wasn't working.

George and Alan walked though the silent plaza to the large three-storey building beyond. The square was as quiet as the car park, and though neither of them said it, the often-used comparison with graves was foremost in their minds.

II

The frosted glass double doors outside the reception area slid open smoothly when George and Alan approached. The doors were, like the fountain, impressively high-tech. They slid open at exactly the correct time, just before Alan and George realised they were automatic doors at all (instead, as is usually the case, of just afterwards; leading to the awkward pausing, slow stepping and strange hand gestures which is the normal ritual when approaching such a door, and also dispelling the slight paranoid fear experienced when approaching that the door is not automatic after all, and you are about to a) smash your nose into the glass and b) look extremely stupid. In short, the doors actually worked in the way they should have done, rather than making people wish they were good old simple, normal doors).

The lobby continued the theme of frosted glass, polished surfaces and a complete absence of people. The large, curling reception desk was devoid of receptionists, and no sounds of life could be heard from the doors and corridors beyond. No sounds of any kind at all, in fact, except for a low thrumming, which George and Alan felt through the bones behind their ears. Outside, in the car park and even in the plaza, the lack of people had been unusual and a little unsettling. Here, in the lobby, it was downright unnerving. Alan felt like one of the rescue party for the Marie Celeste.

'Where the bloody hell is everyone?' he asked.

George shrugged, trying to appear nonchalant, but he too was glancing nervously around the empty space.

'Perhaps they're all watching the reactor?'

'What, the receptionists as well?'

George shrugged again. 'Maybe they have a keen interest in particle physics,' he suggested.

Alan looked down at the floor. 'And that humming… do you think that's the accelerator?'

George glanced at his watch. 'Maybe. Maybe it's warming up or something.'

The reality of the situation was slowly and unpleasantly sneaking up on Alan. 'We don't have a bloody clue what we're doing, do we?'

George remained silent. Not a good sign.

'So, what now?' Alan asked out loud. The Gandalf-voice seemed oddly distracted, only half-listening.

'I said,' hissed Alan, 'what now? Where's Kate? Is she even here at all?'

'She must be,' the voice replied after a pause. 'They would not kill her.'

George opened his mouth out of habit, to ask what was going on, but Alan raised his hand.

'It is time,' the voice in his head was saying. 'We must go on.'

'Is that your plan then?' Alan said. 'Just "go on"? What do we do when we get there?' He was waving his hands in the air, again feeling foolish, as there was no one to actually argue with. In his left hand he was gripping the humerus of an eighty-year-dead man.

'We'll figure it out,' said George. 'Let's keep moving.'

'For fuck's sake, George, this isn't Indiana Jones. We can't just bumble along without a plan!'

'Why not?' George asked. 'It's worked so far.'

'I want a plan!' Alan repeated desperately. 'I want to have it all sorted out! I want, very much, not to be standing in a deserted lobby or a particle accelerator with a film-freak, a bone, and a dead man inside my head!'

George sighed, and turned back to Alan. 'You want a plan? OK, here it is. Shut up and come on. Don't like it? Tough. It's the only one we've got. Now stop whinging and come on and save the world.' He turned back round and stomped off down one of the corridors that led further into the building.

'He's got a point, you know,' the voice commented inside Alan's head.

'I've got a very bad feeling about this,' Alan muttered,

and hurried along to catch up with George.

III

Their footsteps echoed eerily through the empty corridors, as all good footsteps in empty corridors should. The effect was slightly spoiled by the lack of flickering wall-mounted candles casting jumping shadows on the walls. The building was lit, in fact, by sturdy fluorescent lights mounted in the ceiling, and although the occasional one of them blinked occasionally as they walked past, it wasn't the same as some good, atmospheric torches. In the same vein, because of the well-lit rooms and the fact that it was daytime, there were no dark corners for horrible things to unexpectedly leap out from. Alan found this paradoxically unsettling. There was something obscene and deeply unpleasant about walking towards the end of the world in a nicely illuminated corridor. It was like descending into hell and finding that the way was down a shiny escalator, with mirrors on either side and muzak pouring from nearby speakers.

It soon became apparent that they were not, after all, totally alone in the building. Here and there, they heard doors shut ahead of them, or saw people shrink back from windows of nearby offices as they passed. Every time they caught one of these fleeting glimpses, the people would disappear, shrinking back from them as if they were the Dead Sea beating a hasty retreat from Moses. This was also deeply unsettling. Alan wondered if it were possible to be any more unsettled without being scared, but when he thought about it he realised he actually was, so he stopped wondering and got on with being frightened.

As they walked, they heard another noise, aside from the humming, which this time came from behind them. It was the roar of an abused engine and the screech of tyres. Apparently the van had made it past the security check, though Alan had to admit from experience that it was not exactly New York immigration control. Both he and George unconsciously quickened their paces.

'Do you know where...?' Alan began, but before he could finish George lifted one hand and pointed to a blue line running down the wall at eye level. It continued down the corridor they were in.

'Shows the way to the accelerator,' George said. Alan didn't bother to enquire any further. George was clearly feeling tense, and was also clearly unaccustomed to such a feeling. The last thing Alan wanted was to antagonise him further. Behind him, he heard the perfect automatic doors swish open once more. They both consciously quickened their paces.

They turned the corner, and both stopped. The white, shining style of the corridor they had thus far been following ended in a large metal door, although 'door' was perhaps the wrong word, as it bore about as much resemblance to the door in Kate's flat as a Yorkshire terrier did to Cerberus. It looked like something that had been left behind when George Lucas had left town after filming the Phantom Menace. It was large, thick, extremely metal, and was covered in the kind of complicated rivets, screws and hinges which suggested that there was no way this thing was going to do anything as mundane as simply swing open. To underline the point there was a large metal wheel mounted in the middle of it, above which there was a pane of glass in the centre of the door, small enough that the only way you would see anything at all through it was by pressing your face right up against it. Just in case any viewer could possibly be in any doubt that something large, important and expensive lay behind the portal, it was painted bright yellow, and the walls, ceiling and floor were plastered with yellow and black stripes. To further clear up any possible confusion that this monster of a door might simply be the caretakers' cupboard, the blue line that they had been following ran above the door where it was interrupted by the enormous red words 'Accelerator Chamber' in the kind of font usually reserved for defence bunkers under the Pentagon. Underneath this, somewhat smaller and entirely incongruously was printed 'No unauthorised access.'

George and Alan exchanged glances. Alan gripped the bone more tightly in his left hand. Behind them were the noises of various surprised shouts and yells, and they were getting closer. There was no time left.

'Let's do it,' said Alan, surprising himself by not feeling foolish at all by saying this. It was that kind of situation. They stepped towards the door. Through the glass they could make out something glittering, shining. There was a kind of reddish glow coming through.

'There,' said the voice in Alan's head. 'The rift. Let's hope we are not too late.'

Still devoid of anything like a plan, Alan and George walked forward to the door. The glow intensified as they approached. If anything, it seemed colder towards the end of the corridor than warmer, though Alan wasn't sure if this was simply because his body seemed to be keeping itself occupied by pumping out as much sweat as it was able to manufacture, presumably to keep its mind off whatever was going on.

They stood in front of the Phantom Menace door. Alan lifted his hand and placed it upon the wheel. He could feel the metal vibrating ever so slightly. The glow was stronger. It was impossible to see anything else through the door now. There was a loud click, followed by several thunks and sliding noises. The wheel began to move.

'Stop!' yelled a voice from the corridor behind them. 'You don't know what you're doing!'

It was Kate.

IV

They both turned around at the same time. The two orange lights above the immense door had started flashing, and the yellow wheel in its centre was slowly rotating. Behind them, Kate had turned the corner of the corridor. Trevor was with her, though there was clearly something wrong with him. His legs and arms were all jerking in different directions at once, as though he was constantly but only lightly being electrocuted. His face was twisted in a variety of different expressions, but the overwhelming passion written upon it was fear. It was mirrored in Kate's own face.

Trevor was bleeding from his nose, but he seemed unaware of this. Kate was holding her left arm with her right hand. Her jeans were dirty and her black sweatshirt was torn and ragged. There were footsteps in the corridor behind them.

Alan was so pleased to see her that he hadn't really heard what Kate had said. His brain only now began working on the problem, telling him to buy it time while it considered things.

'What...?' he managed.

'Kate!' said George. Then a puzzled frown. He glanced back over his shoulder. The door was opening in an excitingly science-fiction-type way, scrolling slowly open like an iris as it simultaneously swung into the ceiling. As well as the orange lights there was now a siren echoing down the corridor. A crimson glow was spilling through the various cracks and openings.

'Aren't you supposed to be in there — with him?' George said.

'Nnnoo!' Trevor managed, shaking his head to try to get the words out properly. 'You'rrrre wrrrooong!'

'It is the servants of the enemy,' the Gandalf-voice said to Alan in his head. 'Pay them no heed. The rift! We must get to the rift!'

'Wait a minute,' said Alan out loud. 'Just wait a minute!' he shouted. Everyone fell silent and looked at him, and he suddenly felt extremely foolish. 'What the hell is going on?'

Kate took a step down the corridor. Trevor did the best he could.

'Alan, you've got to listen to us. Do not go through that door. It's what he wants. He's been playing you from the beginning.'

The sirens intensified. Alan could feel cool air blowing

from behind him, but he dared not look round.

'Who?' he said.

'The rift!' the voice in his head cried again. This time, Alan actually felt a pull in the muscles in his right leg. Something was trying to move him against his will. 'The rift!' said the voice.

'There isn't much time to explain,' said Kate, glancing over her shoulder. 'Alan, you cannot trust the voice. It is not what you think.'

'What?' said George. It was getting hard to hear over the sirens.

'Why do you think no one has stopped you in this place, when we've had to fight every step of the way? Why do you think the door is opening for you now? Did you open it?'

Alan and George looked again at one another. Alan looked down at the hand holding the bone. He was starting to feel the deeply unpleasant sensation that comes along with the very first tendrils of realisation that you may possibly have done something very, very stupid.

'The rift!' the voice screamed in his head. It no longer sounded anything like a curmudgeonly old wizard from Middle Earth. Alan felt the pull again. This time his whole leg moved back one step.

'The voice?' said Alan.

'The voice,' repeated Kate, 'is Cranmer's.'

There was a moaning noise coming from the corridor behind them. The footsteps were very close.

'Shit,' breathed George, looking at Alan.

'He's been trying to get you here from the start. I don't know what he's told you to get him here, but he needs you. He needs you to get into the world. You, and some part of him...' Her voice tailed of as she saw the bone gripped tightly in Alan's hand.

'Shit,' said George again. 'Get rid of it!' he said to Alan, and turned back to the now open door. Alan turned as well. The door had left a huge circular hole behind them, leading into a vast chamber of metal and wires. Crimson light was streaming through the hole, and in the centre of the chamber was a swirling maelstrom of shimmering… something. The kind of something that felt wrong, that felt like it could give you cancer as soon as look at you. Alan and George could almost feel the cells in their skin split under the barrage of photons. The air crackled with an unpleasant charge that felt the same as the light. Alan felt the pull again. It was all he could do to stand still, to resist the urge. He couldn't even release the bone in his hand.

'It is time,' the voice said. It sounded cultured, English, ancient, and quite, quite insane. 'Step forward.'

Alan remained still. George could see something was wrong. He leapt toward the door and hit a prominent red button positioned next to it, praying it would do what it looked like it should. The lights above the door began flashing again. The siren started up. Kate and Trevor began to run down the corridor.

'No!' screamed the voice. 'Enter the chamber, damn you!' Alan's leg jerked again. He took a step forwards. His face was streaming with sweat.

'No,' he cried. 'Help!'

The door was closing much more quickly than it had opened. George must have activated some kind of emergency circuit. Kate grabbed Alan from behind.

'You've got to resist!' she said.

'I'm trying,' said Alan through gritted teeth. With his left arm he suddenly reached up and grabbed a handful of Kate's hair, pulling it hard. His other hand came up and punched her in the head. Her grip weakened. 'Oh, God, I'm sorry. I'm sorry,' he said. The door was almost closed now.

'Enter!' screamed the voice in his head. Alan could no longer resist. He jumped forwards, through George's desperate, grabbing hands, through the closing gap in the door, into the accelerator chamber, where he landed, panting, on the floor. His body was released back to him as he heard the very final clunk of the door behind him. He dropped the bone.

'Thank you,' said the voice. It was no longer in his head.

Chapter Twenty-Four

I

Alan looked up. The swirling maelstrom hovered in the air, only feet away from him. It was even more impressive this close up. To be fair it would have only taken the effects guys at Industrial Light and Magic five minutes to come up with something like it, but given that there were no effects guys around as far as Alan knew, it struck him as pretty spectacular. It twisted and writhed in the air like a snake in a fire, and Alan could feel the same energy that he had felt just outside the door crackling through his hair, his clothes, and the air he breathed.

As he took another breath, the voice spoke again from the heart of the energy storm.

'Thank you for bringing me here, Alan. I could not have done it without you.'

Alan squinted into the red glow. There were objects hovering somewhere in the shimmering mass. The first was familiar to him. It was the bone that he had recently dropped onto the floor. It was now caught up in the centre of the glow, whirling along with the energies. The second object was not familiar, but he knew what it was. It was the rippling visage of a man who had been dead for eighty years.

Cranmer's face was thin, and probably pale, although it was hard to tell in the blood-red light. His black hair was slicked back from his forehead. The eyes were red, like the storm, and they were filled with laughter, like the rest of Cranmer's face. As Alan watched, the face ebbed and flowed, grew and shrank. Then Cranmer closed his eyes and his smile widened. It continued to widen, along with the face, and suddenly Alan found himself in front of an eight-foot wide and fifteen-foot tall projection.

The red eyes swivelled down in their massive sockets and leered down at Alan.

'Your part in this is not yet done,' the massive apparition

began. This shook Alan out of the trance that had so far prevented him from turning around and hammering desperately and futilely on the door. He turned around and began to hammer desperately on the door. He could no longer see through the little window to the corridor; something was misting up the toughened glass. He looked around for a switch, a lever, or even a wheel but there was nothing on this side of the door.

'I still need you for a moment, Alan,' the voice came from behind him.

'Bugger off,' said Alan distractedly, but Cranmer was well into the gloating phase by now, and would not be dissuaded.

'You see,' he said, as Alan felt around the enormous door in the feeble hope that there might be a little crack in it that he could somehow squeeze through, 'It is not enough just to bring the bone here. That gives me my connection to the world, and will allow me to re-enter. But I need the energy. It has all been about the energy.'

'Mm. The energy,' muttered Alan as he began pulling hopelessly at a little pokey piece of metal that was, by no stretch of anyone's imagination except perhaps someone's as stupidly optimistic as Alan at this moment, a door-opening lever.

'I need you.' There was something in the way that Cranmer spoke that made Alan turn around. He decided to give up with the door, anyway. Keep the bugger talking, he thought. Maybe there's another way out.

'What's so special about me?' he asked.

'Nothing,' Cranmer replied. 'Absolutely nothing.'

'Oh, right. Thanks.' Alan said. He was glancing around the rest of the structure. To the left and right, the walls of the chamber extended round, like two arms reaching around an enormous circle, to eventually meet again a mile away from where Alan was standing. Weren't there any emergency exits in this stupid big doughnut?

'You were simply the first to touch a creature without a soul. You grounded the energy I had gathered to myself, formed a conduit. I have been working hard these past years to prevent any of the soul energy from leaking into the world. Gathering it to myself. Closing all the doors. When they all were shut, that was when you found the animal.'

'The calf,' said Alan.

Cranmer's face didn't change. 'It doesn't matter what it was. Only that it was the first. And you were the first to touch it. It created the conduit.'

Alan frowned. 'The mother touched it first, not me.'

'Irrelevant. She was always in contact. Somehow protects her. You were the first. You are the conduit. I need you.'

Alan gave up. There was nowhere to run. He looked up at the giant Cranmer. For some reason, he was not afraid, not now he had run out of options, only resigned to whatever would happen next.

'It took me some time to find you. Even your connection was fading when I did. I entered you, kept it open. Brought you here.'

'Yes,' agreed Alan. He couldn't think of anything else to say. He looked past Cranmer, to the whirlpool of light behind him.

'You see,' continued the massive face, 'You are the only connection now between the two realms.' Cranmer paused, and smiled. 'Of course, it is a more scientific age now. Dimensions would perhaps be more appropriate. But I am old-fashioned. Realms will do.'

'You are the only connection. And I control you. I control the energies of my realm too, now. They are no good to me in that land of memories and ghosts. But I can bring them into your world. Through you. The whole of life, centuries upon centuries, millions of years of accumulated soular energy. All passing through one single point into me. I will break through back into the world, and I will be more powerful than you can possibly imagine.'

'OK,' said Alan. His newfound bravado was giving way quite quickly to icy fear. He was determined not to let the last vestiges vanish without a fight. 'Let me guess. This single point all the energy is to pass through — that's me, right?'

The face nodded.

'And, presumably, millions upon millions of years of this energy pouring through me is a bad thing?'

Again, Cranmer nodded. 'I'm afraid so. You will be torn apart, but born again.'

'Hmm,' Alan said, thoughtfully. He was looking past Cranmer again. Maybe he had an option, after all.

'Still, it is too late to worry. If it helps, I am sorry. But we must be quick. Your friends out there are doing what they can to...' Cranmer paused. Alan had taken a step forward.

'I see. No more talk. If you will just wait...'

Alan took another step forward.

'I said wait,' Cranmer said irritably. 'I'm not ready.'

Alan began to run.

'Wait!' Cranmer cried as Alan leapt into the air towards the storm. Cranmer had forgotten he had left the body, forgotten he no longer had any control over what Alan did. 'I'm not rea...'

Alan hit the centre of the storm. He fell through the looking glass.

II

The door thudded shut behind Alan, leaving George, Kate and Trevor standing helpless, looking at it in dismay.

'Shit!' George said. 'We've got to get it open again!' he added, as though this hadn't occurred to the other two.

'Tttooo laaate,' stammered George, sounding like an acid house CD. He was wiggling his arm frantically and it took George a second or two to work out he was trying to point at something at the other end of the corridor. He looked.

It was not one something that Trevor was trying to point at. It was several somethings, slowly coming down the corridor towards them. George had a better look, and mentally updated the 'somethings' in his mind to 'people'. Then he looked more closely, and wondered if he should demote them back to 'somethings' again.

'Sssoouulless,' muttered Trevor, his body jumping this way and that like a dog who is unsure whether to run for the stick or jump for the ball.

They were, in fact, people, or at least something very like them. Quite what that something was, George wasn't sure. There were seven of them. They looked human. They looked like the kind of people you might find working in a place like this; some men, some women, some scruffy, some neat, all ever so slightly geeky, no matter how hard they tried to hide it. But it was only in looks that they resembled humans. The way they moved, the way they looked at him, was totally alien, yet strangely familiar to George. They all shared the same rocking, slow gait that simultaneously made George think of the security guard by the gate, and of every zombie film he had ever seen. They were shuffling down the corridor towards the three of them.

'What?' said George.

'Soulless,' translated Kate. She was struggling with the wheel on the front of the door, without much success. 'They've had their souls taken from them. Someone else is controlling them now.'

George's first, Pavlovian response was incredulity. Even after all the films he'd seen, he couldn't quite bring himself to believe that he was facing a group of zombies, whatever Kate was calling them. He took a closer look into the eyes of a young woman at the front of the group. She was dressed smartly in a trouser suit, and was wearing fashionable small glasses. Her blouse was ripped and there was blood on her chin. The glasses were slightly askew on her nose, and strangely George found this more disturbing than anything else. It would have taken just a second, only a moment for the woman to straighten the glasses. Instead she left them where they were, one lens higher than the other, out of line with her eyes, and rocked forwards. Horror pushed its way into his brain and forced the incredulity out.

'Controlled?' he said. 'Controlled by who?'

'Cranmer's men,' Kate said. 'Look, are you going to help with this door or stand staring at the soulless?'

George turned back to Kate, and grabbed the wheel along with her. It wouldn't budge.

'Shit, shit, shit!' George muttered as he strained. 'Why won't it open? It opened easily enough before.'

'They… hngh… must have someone in the control room. We've got to get there,' Kate said.

George looked down the corridor. The thought of jostling through the advancing group did not appeal to him. He glanced around the walls for another exit, and saw one. He was so astonished he had to look again before it sank in to his mind. A side-door, only a few metres away, small and flimsy looking. He hadn't noticed it before, distracted as he was by the accelerator chamber. He could have cried with joy, but he pulled himself together.

'There!' he said, jumping towards the door. The soulless were halfway down the corridor now, only a few metres away. He grabbed the doorknob. It didn't turn.

'Try…' Kate began, but George held his hand up, a furious expression on his face. You didn't get many chances in life to be a hero, and he wasn't going to pass this one up, that was for sure.

He took one step back from the door, and squared his shoulder at it, daring it to defy him. Then he ran. He bounced off the door, which rattled in its frame, and landed sitting down several feet away. The breath had jumped out of his lungs and refused to come back in case he did something stupid again. He heard a footstep behind him and sprang to his feet. The soulless were almost upon them.

Kate ran to the door. 'Try turning it the other way,' she said, and did so. The small metal button in the centre of the doorknob popped out as she turned it. She turned it the other way and the door opened, revealing a small, dark room beyond.

'Come on!' she said as she slipped through.

'Ccooome onnnn!' Trevor managed as he locomoted his way through the doorway.

George glanced over his shoulder. The woman with the glasses was reaching for him, her face twisted into snarl, the blood on her chin shining horribly in the overhead light. The others were directly behind her. George leaped through the open doorway, and slammed the door shut behind him, pressing the little button in the centre of the doorknob in as he did so. He looked around in the darkness, praying they were not in a maintenance cupboard.

They were in a maintenance cupboard.

Chapter Twenty-Five

I

Bright light. Pain. Alan's body continued the jump as it had started, arms flailing wildly, the mouth open in a wide 'O' of fear, and it hit the floor on the other side of the chamber physically unchanged, but Alan was not with it.

The light was so bright that Alan tried to blink, or to raise his arms to protect his eyes. He found that he could do neither. In the brief moment of terror this caused he realised that despite this the light caused him no pain either. This was odd. It certainly should have. The realisation of what this meant brought on a fresh surge of terror, which slowly receded as did the light all around him, but unlike the light did not vanish completely. It meant he had passed through. It meant he was... somewhere else.

Cranmer had described the other place as a vast sea, ebbing and flowing. To Alan, assuming that he had indeed arrived where he thought he had, it was more like a whole universe, a vast space of glittering lights. The backdrop to the lights was not the darkness of a vacuum, but a mass of different colours. It was like being trapped inside an enormous Jackson Pollack painting. In one direction, a large patch of white overtook the lights.

He felt himself floating in the centre of it all, an impartial surveyor. He felt, for a moment, like a god must feel. Then some sense of self returned to him, and he remembered he was not impartial at all.

He looked down at himself, and saw nothing but a few faint glimmering blue lines. He could still feel his arms and his legs, but he suspected this was more due to habit than anything substantial actually being there. Briefly, he wondered how he could see or hear anything, having no eyes or ears with which to do such things. Perhaps he was simply experiencing things directly, but his subconscious was interpreting things in a familiar way to prevent him from going insane. He decided to stop thinking along these lines in case his subconscious changed its mind.

Cranmer, in the guise of the Gandalf-voice, had spoken of the horror of being dead, the assault on the mind, the struggle to prevent oneself from being ripped apart. Alan could feel a vague sense of dizziness, but that was all. It must be because his body was still alive. He fervently hoped this would remain the case.

Even amongst the wonder of it all, Alan could feel something was terribly wrong. There was an immense pressure upon him, a feeling of desperation, of need for release. At the same moment this feeling came to him, he noticed that the winking lights in the distance, all of them, seemed to be moving closer. He also realised that the lights were much, much closer than he had initially assumed. Souls, energy searching for a way out. Searching for him.

He looked around again, and began to realise Cranmer's description had not been so far from the mark. Despite his apparent weightlessness, despite the vastness of everything around him, there was a definite up and down feeling to the place. Above him were the stars. They were much closer together now as they advanced towards him. He fixed his attention upon them. They were different sizes, as far as he could tell, and one of them seemed especially vast. This large star, alone amongst the spiritual heavens, was casting long, flickering tendrils out from itself, some of them hitting other stars, splitting them into tiny starlets that quickly faded from view. Now that Alan looked, he could see that most of the other stars were orbiting this one.

Cranmer. Cranmer was looking for him.

Alan now turned his attention to the 'down', or whatever it was. Beneath him, there was an immensity of white, a kind of dull, luminous glow. The surface twisted and swirled around. Large lumps were floating within it. The whole thing resembled a massive pool of radioactive porridge. The lumps had a glow of their own, and Alan realised with a start that they were the same things as the stars above him. Were they souls?

He watched one of them, which was at first hovering above the surface of the gloop. It seemed to be fighting to gain height, to fly away from the white ocean, but to no avail. It was pulled in, twisted and whirled and broken up into tiny pieces. Most of these sank into the goo, but some stayed floating on the surface. Alan knew what was happening. Souls were being broken apart, as Cranmer had described. As he looked, he could see that a new star appeared above the porridge every few seconds, some larger and brighter than others. Most sank beneath the surface within seconds. A few remained, whole and intact, for longer. Some tried to ascend from the pull of the gloop. None of them managed it in the time Alan watched.

The terror, which had slumped down, sulking, in the back of whatever Alan was using to hold his mind together, saw its moment, and bullied its way back to the forefront of his emotions. These were souls, newly released from their corporeal bodies. Freshly dead, then dying again within moments of arriving. A bleakness seeped into Alan, dark and miserable. This was what everyone faced, everything faced, eventually. Lifetimes of pious good works, of contemplation, even of pure evil or total indifference, ripped apart in moments, only a strong-willed few holding themselves together for a kind of terrible half-existence on the edge of oblivion. Welcome to heaven. There were far more lights floating and breaking apart in the soul-porridge below him than in the space above.

Once again, Alan was brought back to reality with a jolt. For all his horror, Alan had little choice. The large star and its orbiting satellites were closing in. Cranmer and his associates. If they reached him, he was dead… or whatever.

He looked down, and dived directly towards the soul-eating porridge.

II

George rummaged in his pocket for his key ring, which he knew had attached to it (along with a small plastic Death Star and a bottle opener in the shape of a pair of breasts) a little plastic LED thing that could never run out of power and could be seen, apparently, from a mile away on a clear night. He had got it free with some rubbish he had ordered on the Internet and had never had cause to use it before. Well, now was the perfect time for a test run. He found and extracted the key ring from his pocket, and squeezed the button. A small, sad light lit the room up for around half a second, before flickering and dying. This had the effect of eliminating everyone's night vision, which had been starting to adjust to the dimness of the room.

'Nice torch,' Kate said.

'It was free,' muttered George, putting it back in his pocket again.

Before the flicker of light from George's key ring had started his dark vision from scratch, he had got a quick impression of the dimensions of the room. It was small. Too small for three people to be jammed into, particularly when the room was already crammed full of cleaning equipment and shelves, and especially when one of the three people in it was constantly throwing their arms and legs out in seemingly random directions.

There was a clatter and a squishing noise as one of Trevor's errant hands pulled a mop onto the floor.

'Will you... ow! Will you stop that!' George said, receiving a kick in the shins.

'Nnnn...' said Trevor.

'He can't!' Kate said.

'What the bloody hell's the matter with him, anyway?' George asked, feeling something whoosh past his ear. He was on edge, and his tension was not being relieved by being repeatedly and randomly attacked by someone he could barely see, and who didn't even know they were attacking him. It was also not helped by the scrapes, thuds and moans of anger coming from the door behind him.

'He's possessed,' said Kate, calmly.

'You don't say,' said George, ducking an elbow.

'It's not as simple as that,' Kate continued. 'There's... well, there's a few people in there. They can't decide who should be in control. They keep taking over different bits of his body.'

'Wee are heeere... to helppp,' Trevor managed through flapping lips.

'Right,' said George. 'Thanks.' He was silent for a moment. The scraping on the door had died down a little now.

'Who exactly is in there?' he asked.

'Wee...' Trevor began, but Kate interrupted him.

'They don't remember. They've managed to survive over there by holding on to their personalities, but they've lost an awful lot. They've banded together but they're all so strong-willed they won't merge. Hence Trevor here.'

'Hee must be sttopppeddd,' said Trevor.

George shook his head, wondering how anyone could manage to say the word 'stopped' with three d's.

'Apparently they formed a group to stop Cranmer, who had already found the conduit...'

'Alan,' said George.

'Alan,' agreed Kate. 'So instead, they found Trevor. He's agreed to be a host for them for the moment.'

'Agreed?' said George, watching the crazily dancing silhouette in front of him with horror. 'Why Trevor?'

'They tried getting to Alan directly, but Cranmer was there already, guiding his actions. They were going to try and knock him unconscious, so they could kick Cranmer out. They failed.'

'The electric company guy?' George said. Before Kate could reply, the scrapes from the door came again. The knob rattled, and the little button popped out with a click.

'Shit!' said George, spinning and pressing it back in, holding it with both hands. 'They're not supposed to do that! Zombies can't unlock bloody doors!'

'Soulless,' said Kate. 'Not zombies.'

'Whatever!' George cried back. The metal was twisting and turning under his hands, and his grip was not helped by his sweating palms. 'Why aren't you panicking?' he called back to Kate.

'I'm too scared to panic,' she said. George could not make out the expression on her face.

'OK,' he said, 'What do we do now?'

'Hee must be sttoppeeddd,' Trevor gibbered.

'Yeah, you said that already,' said George.

'We've got to get to the control room, stop the heavy ions. If we can end the reaction, we might be able to break Cranmer's connection with the world.'

'Might?' George cried, his voice high with panic and incredulity. The door shuddered again.

'It depends if he's... if Alan is...'

'OK, OK, I get the picture,' George said. He thought fast. 'There must be a ventilation shaft, or emergency chute, or something. There always is. See if you can get on Trevor's shoulders, push the ceiling tiles up, and see if there's a grille up there. There's a bottle opener in my pocket — never mind what it looks like — that you can use to prise it off. It might just be wide enough to fit into. Otherwise, we can clear the rubbish from the walls. There might be something there, a trick wall or secret...'

Kate opened the other door to the maintenance cupboard, behind her. Light streamed in from the empty corridor. 'I was thinking of just using the door, actually,' she said with a sweet smile as she leaned forwards and jammed the mop handle under the doorknob. The other end was wedged against the wall. George was silent for a moment, then let go of the door. The other two rushed out into the corridor, while George pulled a shelving unit from the wall to land on top of the mop. The hammering on the door intensified.

'Soulless,' he whispered to himself. 'They look like bloody zombies to me.' He followed Kate and Trevor out into the corridor.

There were a dozen soulless there waiting for them.

III

Alan hadn't realised how large the mush of soul-porridge was until he got closer. The fact that it took him a lot longer than he was expecting to get closer to it was a clue. It was immense; a vast, luminous, lumpy sea stretched out below him, and now to either side, as far as the eye... as far as he could see.

He glanced behind him, somehow managing to do this while simultaneously watching the sea below him and continuing towards it as fast as he could. This phenomenon seemed the least of his problems at the moment, so he ignored it. What he could not ignore was that the stars were still following him, moving quickly, especially the large, tendril-extending blob that Alan assumed was Cranmer.

He moved closer to the surface of the sea. There were strange whispers here, voices of all different languages, all different ages, even different species. Voices of regret, joy, anger, pain, love, all mixed together in one great murmur. A dirge of creatures that had all once been alive, lost in their own memories. The whispers didn't seem to get any louder the closer he got, strangely, but stayed at the level of whispers, almost below his conscious hearing. For this, at least, Alan was grateful.

He was approaching the surface now. There were many, many more lumps here than he had seen from... from wherever he had been before. Some were floating on the surface of the goo, some hovering above it, some being swallowed up. Most of them were very small.

Alan was painfully aware he didn't have anything like a plan at this point. This seemed in keeping with the rest of the day, if time here could be called a day, or anything... Forget it, he told himself. Need to think. The stars were closer still. Perhaps he could lose himself in amongst the goo. Maybe he would be strong enough to prevent himself from sinking into it, something that struck him to be a tremendously bad thing to happen. He had no choice, anyway. If he didn't do something, Cranmer would catch up with him.

Alan tried to take a deep breath, realised he didn't have any breath to take, gave up, and sank down onto the surface of the sea.

IV

...the noise of the bombs overhead had finally stopped. He quivered. Did this mean that it was time? They had been assured there would be no resistance, but they were under no illusions. They had seen what had happened on other occasions. He shifted the pack uncomfortably on his back. Weighed a bloody ton. Well, they could bugger off if they thought he was going to walk across the mud. No chance. He'd be running as fast as he could.

A tense silence filled the air. All around him, the rest of the men were looking ahead. No one would look at anyone else. Ahead of him, Lieutenant Thomas gripped the ladder hard, his pistol in his other hand. It was only shaking a little.

The shrill voice of a whistle pierced the silence, then another, and another. Lieutenant Thomas blew his own in response, and then was up the ladder and away. Alan hurried forwards with the rest of the men, and crested the ladder in time to see the young Lieutenant cut down by machine gun fire. There was a whizzing noise next to his left ear, and a thudding noise in his chest. A bright flash, and then...

...how long had he been lying here? There were tubes in his arm, another under his nose, a third coming out of his mouth. The ceiling was pristine white, and the place smelled of death, of rot and decay. There was a low, steady beep coming from

a machine next to the bed. Alan realised the smell was coming from him. The... what did they call it?... carcinoma, he thought... that was eating him alive was giving him a respite, a moment of lucidity. Why now, he wondered, after all this time, would he regain his senses? He could remember nothing of the last few weeks but a hazy fog, and concerned faces. Why would now be any different? Could he be getting better?

The pain in his stomach, the racking terrible pain that had been with him for months now, intensified. Alan groaned. There were voices nearby, worried voices and shouting. Alan paid no attention to them. The pain was too great. Then... then it was gone. All the pain was gone. There was a cold, tight feeling across his chest. The beeps on the monitor slowed and stopped, to be replaced with a steady hum, and he realised why the pain had stopped. The ceiling began to fade in his eyes...

Alan returned, spluttering. What was happening? Memories. The lumps, the lumps in the porridge, were lost fragments, old memories. They were obviously the kind of memories that people didn't want to hang on to. He had to get out, somehow, he had to...

...the whole place had the smell of blood, of death. The rest of the herd had passed into the room before him. He was the last. Fear gripped him, tightened around his heart, around his front legs. Behind him, the two-legs was advancing. There was nowhere to go but down into the corridor. He passed through a sheet of some clear material. The smell of blood and water was strong in here. Ahead of him was a kind of cage, the sort that the two-legs had sometimes placed him in before, back before this nightmare had begun. He moved towards it. The two-legs behind him followed, pushed him on into the cage. Alan felt his fear subside a little. The cage felt secure, somewhere he knew in a place of surprises. Ahead of him, a two-legs, holding a long piece of bent metal, leaned over towards

him, and gently placed the two sides of the metal on either side of his head. There was a burst of pain, and a flash of light, and then...

Alan spun, terrified, in the goo. Each of the memories tried to claim him, to drag him down into their own world. It was getting harder to escape each time. Why were they all memories of death? Perhaps they were the strongest, the most emotional moments. Perhaps that was why the memories were mostly human. It didn't matter. Alan suspected the only reason he hadn't been dragged down permanently into one of the memories so far was that he still had a body of his own, somewhere. He didn't know how much longer that would protect him. The lumps were all around him.

OK, OK, he told himself. Get a grip. They're not happening. Forget them. You've got to escape. Despite what he told himself, Alan knew the memories had found him, joined him. They would be with him as long as he... no. Don't think about it. Alan looked upwards again. It wasn't working! The stars were still approaching. They had slowed, presumably wary of the memories, but they had not stopped. Alan looked around. More memories were gathering. They seemed to be drawn to him. He could not go up. He could not move across. He had no more choices.

He sank down, beneath the surface of the heaving sea.

Chapter Twenty-Six

I

George came to a dead stop behind Trevor, who had done likewise behind Kate. The twelve soulless stared at them for a moment, seemingly surprised by their sudden appearance. The silence was unsettling. George would have almost preferred them to be slowly moaning 'Brains' as they advanced. At least he would have felt on familiar territory then.

They were in a long, white corridor, similar to the one they had recently vacated, the main difference being that instead of a large door leading into the accelerator chamber at the end of it, there were twelve soulless advancing towards them. George, ever the diplomat, recognised instantly that their intentions were not friendly.

'Shit!' said Kate. George looked up the corridor. There was a door at the end, white and sturdy. There was a square mesh window in it, and the words 'Accelerator Control Room' were plastered across this window. It took George's tired mind a moment to comprehend what this meant, though to be fair to it there was an awful lot going on at the moment.

He pointed up the corridor, and struggled for the words. He settled on 'There!' It seemed to do the trick. Trevor and Kate turned to look at the door. Kate's eyes widened. The soulless were lurching forwards from the other direction.

'Go,' George said, before he realised the words were actually coming out of his mouth. 'I'll cover you.' That stupid heroic instinct had taken hold of him again. George decided to stop being fair to his brain at this point.

'Don't be so bloody stupid,' said Kate, running past him, towards the door to the control room. 'Just come on!'

Trevor lolloped after her. George heard the splintering of wood behind him. Stupidly, he turned to look, and saw the door that he had wedged shut in the maintenance cupboard come crashing down, and the seven soulless from the first corridor begin to pour through the gap. What made him turn to look he didn't know — what had he expected to see? Tarzan swinging through the door on a vine? Darth Vader squashing it with the power of the dark side?

Finally, his brain and himself decided to settle their differences and run down the corridor to the control room. Unfortunately he had delayed too long. One of the dozen soulless in the corridor was reaching towards him. As George turned, the soulless grabbed his left hand and bit into it.

'Arrgghh!' George cried as he felt the teeth clamp against his knuckles. He wrestled it free and began to jump down the corridor to the door, tucking his wounded hand into his right armpit, trying not to do anything too girly like faint or scream. The soulless shuffled quickly after him. He didn't want to look down at his hand. He didn't want to see the blood.

The door to the control room was open. Kate was standing beside it.

'Come on,' she shouted. George ran through, and they both jumped against the door.

'There's no key! There's no lock!' Kate yelled. The door began to shake under the blows of the soulless.

George glanced around the room. It was not the high-tech space age Starship Enterprise kind of bridge thing that he had been expecting after seeing the door to the accelerator chamber. It looked more like his office at the Mysterious World. The room was about the same size, at least. Along one wall was a long desk with several computers on it, and a large flat-screen monitor attached to the wall above them. At least that was a bit Enterprise-like, although George didn't think he had ever seen Captain Kirk facing a viewscreen that had a large panel on it with a little exclamation mark, next to the words 'This computer has suffered a General Protection Fault Z234FFFb. Would you like to create an error report Yes/No?'

There were brown marks and empty paper bags on the desk. It was the kind of place where a lot of doughnuts and coffee were consumed. The rest of the room was relatively bare, apart from several filing cabinets and a few chairs (the type that are great fun to spin around on until you press the wrong lever and they drop permanently to the lowest height setting, making them ever after only suitable for midgets or amputees). There was another door in the wall opposite to the one they were standing against.

'Now what do we do?' George shouted above the hammering.

'We've got to keep them out while I get the computers working again. Probably just need to turn them on and off again.'

'OK,' said George. 'Go on. I'll hold the door.'

Something in his voice made Kate turn to look at him. 'Are you OK?' she asked.

George took a deep breath. 'It's already too late for me,' he said, sadly. Kate appeared confused. He showed her the bite on his hand.

Kate looked at it, uncomprehending. Then realisation dawned on her face. 'Oh, for God's sake,' she said. George couldn't help feeling this was a little unsympathetic.

'How many more times,' Kate continued. 'They're not zombies, George! They're not infectious! You're not going to turn into one just because you've had your hand gnawed!'

George looked down at his hand. There was a nasty bruise and some teeth marks developing along its back. It looked bloody sore. It *was* bloody sore, come to think of it.

'Oh,' he said.

'Hurrrry,' said Trevor, standing behind them. There was no point in his helping them with the door. He would have been more of a hindrance than a help.

'Hmm,' said George. He looked at the other door. 'OK, here's a plan. There's another exit, look. Why don't I sneak through there, get round behind these creeps and get them to chase me. I can outrun them, no sweat. When they've gone, you can start fixing the computer. The old okey-doke.' He smiled.

Kate didn't. She frowned. 'It's a crap plan.' George was crestfallen. There was another thud from the door that they both felt. They would not be able to hold it for long, either of them. 'But,' Kate continued, 'it's the only one we've got. Go on. Hurry.'

George nodded. No more time for words. Time for action. He ran across the room to the other door, and opened it. Outside, there was another corridor, but George couldn't see much of it because right in front him stood the seven soulless that had cornered them in the first corridor. The girl with the still-askew glasses reached for him, a low moan escaping her lips. George shut the door again.

'We may have a problem,' he shouted across the room, pushing himself in front of the second door as the soulless began to hammer against it.

'What?' shouted Kate.

'More of them,' George replied.

A moment's silence.

'Bugger,' Kate shouted.

'Yep,' George agreed.

A particularly hard thud came from the door Kate was holding. One of the hinges gave way. Kate backed away from the door, towards the desk. The door was quickly trampled to the ground under the soulless as they pushed through, arms extended. George didn't want to get separated from them now. He abandoned his door, and ran across to the middle of the desk, where Kate and Trevor had fled to. The second door opened, and the other seven soulless rocked into the room.

George, Kate and Trevor stood and watched as the nineteen soulless formed a rough semicircle around the desk. The semicircle began to shrink. George picked up one of the chairs, and tried to hold it in a threatening manner, hampered in this by the fact that it was a chair. Kate, next to him, did likewise.

'Don't suppose you've got any tricks up your sleeve you haven't told us about, Trevor? Any chance you can zap them all with negative energy or something?' George asked.

'Nnno,' said the despondent Trevor. Even his twitches had died down to the occasional tired jerk.

'Didn't think so,' said George.

The soulless shuffled closer.

'Any more bright ideas?' Kate shouted, waggling the chair at a feral young receptionist.

'Nope,' said George.

'Right then,' said Kate.

'Right then,' said George.

They raised their chairs, and waited for the attack.

II

The goop surrounded Alan, like a wet, sloppy hug, and almost immediately he was lost. Lost to himself, lost to everything. He no longer had any sense of self, of his identity. All of it was washed away in the first moments of the porridge's gloopy embrace. He lost everything he had spent twenty-seven years building up. He simply became part of the whole.

And it was... impossible. Wonderful. Terrifying. Serene. Chaotic. Everything. Nothing. Mere words could not describe it. Where Alan was, there were no words at all, simply a sense of being, a sense of peace. The peace was not complete, however. Amidst it all was a feeling of waiting, waiting for something to happen. Waiting to be reborn.

Alan tried to give himself up completely, to drift in that eternal, ultimate serenity, but he found he could not. Something was wrong. Not with the continuum, but with himself. And as he thought that, Alan realised what was wrong. It was that he still thought at all. Far, far away, in another realm, a part of Alan still existed, still breathed, still lived. And it would not let him go yet.

With a start, Alan returned to himself. It was a terrible jolt, and Alan was left with a terrible longing for whatever it was he had lost. It was the horrible feeling of the alarm clock going off, of being brought back to the waking world when all he wanted to do was sleep. It was realising that he still had to go to work before he could go back to bed. As his own thoughts and memories surfaced, he realised what he was losing. In that dreamlike, serene state he had known everything that had ever been known. Every piece of knowledge, every experience, everything. Now, it was fading, like a dream. He wrestled with it, trying to keep it, desperate not to lose it. It was futile. It was too big. The accumulated experiences of three and a half billion years of life on Earth simply could not fit. Alan understood this; he understood that to know all was to lose his identity, to lose everything that he was and become a part of the knowledge itself, but he didn't care. He wanted it to stay.

It didn't matter what he thought. It was not time for him. Like air whooshing its way out of a balloon, the knowledge drained from Alan's head, leaving him feeling lost and very, very alone.

It took him a moment to realise it hadn't gone; not quite. Whatever the knowledge was, whatever kind of awareness the sea had, it had been aware of Alan, and it had learned what was happening.

It had left him with something. Some tools for the job. And a simple message.

'You know what to do.'

Alan found himself back on the periphery of the goo, surrounded by memories. Shaken and traumatised by his loss, he barely remembered to raise himself out of their way as they clustered around him. He brought himself back up above the surface, and looked around. Cranmer and his stars were still searching for him, down amongst the goop. As he raised himself higher, he realised the message was right. He knew what he had to do.

The first part of the knowledge he had been left with was so simple, so obvious that he was embarrassed he hadn't thought of it himself. Still, no one else here seemed to have realised it, either.

He had it wrong. All of them here had. Physical presence was not necessary here. It was an echo, a hang-up from being alive. Here, Alan was simply Alan, his mind and his thoughts. Wherever his thoughts were, that was where he was. All this messing around with hovering and raising and zooming was exactly that. Messing around. It wasn't needed. It wasn't necessary.

The instant before the stars found him again, the instant before Cranmer became aware that his quarry was near, Alan decided to be somewhere else. And he knew where he needed to be.

III

They grabbed the chair and pulled it from George's grip, one of the zombies tossing it over its shoulder. The chair landed on another zombie (soulless! George pointlessly corrected himself) two rows back, and it fell to the floor. Well, that's a start, George thought. Kate had already lost her chair in a similar manner. The soulless closed in. George tried to step heroically in front of Kate, to protect her from the attacks for however long it took the things to tear him to pieces. Might as well carry on being heroic now, he thought, as I'm going to die anyway.

He found he couldn't step in front of Kate, however. Trevor was in the way. Even out of the corner of his eye, George could see there was something different about him. He had stopped twitching. He had stopped jerking. He was standing up straight. George guessed that the minds controlling him had decided to abandon him to his fate. Bastards.

He opened his mouth to say something to that effect, but something happened that stopped the words. Trevor raised both his arms in front of him, in a distinctly biblical fashion. He then spoke two words, deeply and with immense power, although the biblical effect was slightly spoiled by the fact that the two words were: 'Take this!'

Instantly, as one, the soulless surrounding their small group dropped to the floor as if they had been hit with nineteen slaps. Unmoving. George decided to leave his mouth open for a little bit.

'Wh…?' he said.

Trevor smiled. Kate looked with wide eyes at the neat semicircle of unconscious people laid out in front of them like pins in a game of human bowling.

'I thought,' said George, slowly and quietly so as not to wake up the slumped forms in front of him, 'you said that he couldn't do that.'

'Yes,' agreed Kate, just as slowly. 'I thought I said that too.'

They both turned to look at Trevor, who was doing his best not to look smug, and failing.

'What did you do?' Kate asked.

'Gave them some bad memories,' Trevor said. 'Listen, I don't have time to explain. They've let me have him, but only for a few moments. I need to…'

'Let you have who?' George asked.

'What are you talking about?' added Kate.

Trevor shook his head. 'Sorry, sorry, didn't think. All a bit new to me, this possession or whatever you call it.'

Kate started, and looked into Trevor's eyes. 'Alan?' she asked.

Trevor nodded. 'It's me. I'm OK.'

'Alan!' Kate shouted. 'You're OK!' She hugged him, then stepped back. 'I mean… well, you're sort of OK. Not dead.' Then she frowned. 'Erm… are you?'

George felt it was time for him to make a meaningful contribution at this juncture.

'Alan?' he said, and then wished he'd left it all to Kate.

'I'm not dead,' Trevor/Alan said. 'Not yet. But there's still work to be done. I've got to go again. I'm going to let them back in, but there's something I need to tell you first.'

Alan told them what they needed to do. Then, he was gone.

Chapter Twenty-Seven

I

Cranmer waited while the others searched for the conduit. He was not concerned that he had escaped. There was nowhere to hide, not here. Not from Cranmer. He could still feel Alan's presence, somewhere out there. For one terrible moment Cranmer had thought that Alan had somehow returned to the real world, but it was only for a moment. The conduit was out there. It was only a matter of time.

It was becoming a strain, though, holding in the energies of the souls. Even with the immense power Cranmer had managed to pull to himself, it was becoming difficult holding it all in, stopping it leaking out into the world. Still, only a few more minutes now. Then all that power would flow through the conduit into him. He would be back in a world that made sense. He hated it here. There was nothing. Shadow and memory. The constant tearing, the energies trying to pull him apart, trying to pull him down into... into whatever that thing was down there.

It had been worth it, he told himself. With the knowledge the Thing had given them, he had kept his memories and his identity. Soon he would return to the world, ten times the person he had been. A hundred times. More than human. If only they could hurry up! Where was that wretched conduit?

Something stirred in his mind. One of his followers. They had found him. Not before time! Cranmer could feel the presence of the conduit strongly now, more strongly than before. He turned, and saw the pillar of light that Alan had become, surrounded by the stars of his followers.

'I have you now,' he whispered.

II

Alan had nowhere else to run. He was surrounded. The stars

orbited him, slowly spinning, then one fired off a brief flash of light. Within moments, the bloated, tendrilled Cranmer-thing appeared. It was moving closer very quickly. If Alan had any lips, he would have licked them, for they would have been dry with fear.

'Hello, Alan,' said the voice in his mind, only this time he could hear it outside as well. It was coming from the star. 'You have given up the fight. Sensible.'

Oh, just shut up and get on with it, Alan thought. Who does he think he is, Darth Vader?

Cranmer shut up, and got on with it.

III

Cranmer wanted to savour the moment, to hold on to this victory that he had waited so many years for. He wanted to watch the conduit hanging helpless in front of him before he ripped him open. He wanted some sense of ceremony. Some robes would have been nice.

But the pressure was becoming too great. He couldn't hold on any longer, and so he let go. Immediately, the pressure throughout the world began to be released. The energy began to slowly leak back into the world. It was a worrying, dizzying feeling, relinquishing the control it had taken him so long to gain, but he couldn't hold on to it and open the conduit at the same time. It wouldn't matter anyway. Once he had opened the conduit wide, the energy would be attracted to it, and would come streaming through. All of it. And in the meantime, the energy of the accelerator maintained his presence on the physical world.

The conduit, inasmuch as a pillar of light could, cringed before him. The stars, Cranmer's followers, began circling frantically, like carrion birds over a feasting lion.

Cranmer reached out.

The conduit vanished.

IV

In the control room, Trevor stiffened again. He looked at George and Kate, who stood nervously by the computer console.

'Now,' Trevor said.

V

Panic and fear flooded into Cranmer's mind. What was happening? He looked around, but there was no sign, no feeling of the conduit anywhere. His followers circled more slowly, a little nervously, unsure if this was part of the grand plan. Cranmer could feel the energy he had amassed being ripped away from him, could feel it being sucked back into the thirsty world. He could feel himself shrinking, being ripped apart by the energies.

'Erm...?' said one of his followers, in the polite sort of way that meant they weren't brave enough to say, 'What the bloody hell is going on?' and was hoping someone else would say it.

'What the bloody hell is going on?' said a braver one. Some of the smaller ones had already succumbed. Without the power of the souls holding them together, they had lost their self-discipline, and were being torn apart like everything else that arrived here. They began to sink, with Cranmer, towards the soul-porridge. Some of them plummeted straight into it, screaming like shooting stars.

'Cranmer...?' said the first follower, as the cold touch of entropy surrounded it and began to work its way through his mind.

Cranmer paid them no heed. He was searching for the echo of his physical presence, of the bone. He was losing energy quickly, but he still had enough to enter the world. It was not enough, not nearly enough to be the god he had expected to be, but it would give him time. Time to build this again, time to work out what went wrong.

Amidst a shower of screaming followers, Cranmer headed towards the faint echo of the bone.

VI

'That's it,' said Kate, looking anxiously at George. 'It's off.'

VII

Suddenly, the echo vanished too. Cranmer could have screamed in frustration. The reaction, the energy holding his physical body together, was gone. So was his last hope. He was alone, the last of his followers having plunged into the soul-porridge moments ago. Cranmer could no longer resist, and began to descend.

He still had one last trick up his sleeve. He had been a magician, after all. He looked down at the mass of memories floating on the surface of the porridge. That was his escape. His discipline was still strong enough. If he could hide in a memory, cling to it like flotsam, he could keep himself out of the goo until he could recover some of the power. He simply had to descend into the memory, to live it. If it was not too distracting, if he could have time to think, he could gather his thoughts, and pull himself back out.

He surveyed the mass of memories below him. Some large, some small. So, he would have to live in one for a while. It was even possible he might never emerge. But, compared to whatever was waiting for him in the porridge, how bad could a memory be? How terrible? It couldn't be distracting enough to prevent him from coming out, surely.

He was close to the surface now. There was no more time. He reached out to the closest memory, large and brooding. The memory reached out in return, and embraced him.

Cranmer was gone.

Chapter Twenty-Eight

I

Alan shook his head, opened his eyes, and blinked. It took him a moment to realise he was doing this, or rather, it took him a moment to realise that the reason why he could do this was because he was in possession, once again, of a head, eyes and eyelids. He was back in his body.

There was a roaring noise in his ears, a noise familiar to him. It was the noise of hundreds of people all shouting at once. It was the noise of the trapped souls, and it was getting quieter. The effect was like standing on a train platform when a carriage full of football supporters whose team have just won an especially exciting match rushes through the station. Whatever it was that was in him that had been open, whatever it was that had made him a conduit, was closing. The rushing noise was the sound of the return of the status quo. Or so he hoped.

He struggled to his elbows, then struggled to his knees, realising as he did so that he actually felt fine, and all the struggling and staggering he was doing was simply because it felt like the right thing to do. What the hell, he thought, and, indulging himself further, tottered unsteadily to his feet.

He had been lying on his back on the opposite side of the chamber to the enormous door, and apart from a badly bruised shoulder, which had presumably been caused by his unconscious body hitting the wall when he had temporarily left it to its own devices, he felt fine. Better than fine, actually. It was like waking up one morning after spending a week moaning about what terrible flu you had to find you now felt absolutely normal and would have to rely on acting skills if you wished to continue to receive sympathy and/or sick pay.

He stood up straight, and stretched his neck out. The memory of the other world was still there in his mind, but it seemed unreal, impossible, now he was back home. He remembered willing himself back to his own body at the last possible moment. He remembered the feeling of panic he had picked up from Cranmer, a feeling that had resonated throughout the whole spirit world. And he remembered… something else. Had there been something more? Something about the porridge? What did it mean? He had a feeling that he should feel happy about it, but he couldn't remember why and so he felt twitchy and nervous about it instead. This, at least, was familiar ground for him, as he felt twitchy and nervous about most things in his daily life, and so it reassured him a little. He was aware of a strange feeling of loss, but as he couldn't remember what it was he had lost it didn't seem worth getting too excited about it.

He took a step towards the door, and stopped. There was something on the ground in front of him, a small, blackened lump. He stooped to pick it up, and peered at it, uncomprehending. A moment later it dawned upon him what it was, or, at least, what it had been.

It was the charred and burnt remains of an eighty-year-old arm bone.

II

The whine of whatever it was that drove the reactions of the accelerator began to fade, leaving an eerie silence. George much preferred an eerie silence to the noise of the moaning of the soulless. Kate stood up from studying the console.

'Well,' she said, but was interrupted by a noise from Trevor.

'Mm,' he was saying, looking down at his arms and legs as if he had just picked them off the shelf in a sale at Homebase. 'Hm,' he said. 'Mm,' he repeated.

Kate turned to him.

'That's not Alan in there, is it?' she said.

'Erm,' said Trevor. 'No, erm… I don't think so. It seems that it's all been done, whatever it was. Erm. They've said it's safe to... erm, well, to come back, I suppose. I... erm.'

Kate sighed, but then smiled. 'Welcome back,' she said. She leaned forwards to hug him, but at that moment he said 'erm' again, and she decided not to. She smiled more widely instead.

George raised his eyebrows. 'So that's it, is it? All sorted now?'

'Erm, well... yes. So they tell me. They said that... erm, well, it was a little interesting, actually. You see, it's as if... well, try and imagine that, erm... I'm just trying to think. It's a very interesting experience. Certainly broadens your horizons. I mean, I've read about, for instance, meditation, several times in...'

George ignored the droning, monotone voice. How was it possible for someone to experience the afterlife, to go to the very limits of human consciousness and beyond, and then return and still make it sound boring? That, George thought, took quite a special talent. That was Olympic-level tedium.

'Mm,' Trevor was saying. 'Anyway, they all, all of them, there were a few you see, said thank you for the help.'

'What's happening to them?' Kate asked.

'Hm. Good question. Apparently, though I didn't see it myself, I was speaking to... hard to remember, now, strange that... speaking to...' Trevor caught Kate's expression. 'Anyway,' he said. 'It seems that Alan spoke to them. Something about not being afraid of the porridge.'

Kate screwed her face up. 'What?'

George laughed out loud. 'Brilliant. Wisdom from beyond the grave. Don't be afraid of the porridge. Any other meals it's safe to approach?'

Trevor frowned. 'Mm. Sounds funny now I say it, doesn't it. Odd. Mm. Seemed to... mm... seemed to make sense when it was just in my head.'

George turned and looked at the small pile of bodies surrounding them in a semicircle. The leg of an old man in a white coat twitched. The woman with the now very skew-whiff glasses moaned and made a little snoring nose.

'I think it's time we got moving,' he said.

III

The door to the accelerator chamber was still just as closed as when they left it. Alan's face was pressed into the little circle of glass. George waved at him, smiling. Alan waved back, not smiling. He mouthed some words that even Trevor managed to interpret.

They reached the door and began turning the huge wheel upon it. After an initial inertia it spun quite readily, and very soon began to spiral open in its peculiar, high-tech way. As soon as it was open enough for Alan to squeeze through, he squeezed through, then stood in the corridor and took a long, deep breath. The three others stood back from him, a little unsure of what to do, of how he would be changed by his experience.

'Christ,' he said. 'That was a bit dramatic, wasn't it?'

IV

It was an awkward walk back to the car. No one knew quite what to say. What did you say in situations like this, after the happy ending?

The last time Kate and Alan had spoken, there had been… something in the air. Something that maybe could have turned into something more. Now, with all that had happened in between, it somehow made it more difficult, not less. They had hugged, in an awkward, robotic kind of way, and Alan had kissed Kate's cheek. Kate had smiled and said she was glad he was OK, but that didn't seem enough. They had faded into silence, broken by George's occasional inanities and Trevor's murmuring, both of which had slowly got less and less by the time they reached the car park, so that they ended walking in silence, each lost in their own thoughts.

Alan had briefly explained what had happened to him. This turned out to be very briefly because when he came to talk about it, he found he remembered very little. He knew that he had tricked Cranmer somehow, he knew that he had even been inside Trevor's body for a while, and that was about it. All he could tell them, really, was that he had a feeling it was all sorted out now. There were other things he felt he should have said, important things that he should have told them, but he couldn't find the words. Maybe there were no words.

George asked him about the porridge, but even that was fading from his mind. To be honest, he didn't feel like it was such a loss. They would all find out eventually.

And so, the four of them slipped into silence again, a tense, uncomfortable silence. It was, as usual, George who broke it. Unlocking the car door, he looked at the rest of them and smiled. There were no jokes this time. He looked very tired.

'Right,' he said. 'Let's go home.'

Chapter Twenty-Nine

I

And so, things returned to normal. Not just for the four of them, but for the world. They drove back to Bristol without stopping, and by the time they got back the radio was alive with reports of the first normal babies being born for days.

At least two hundred different groups worldwide were claiming credit for the miraculous turnaround, from scientists who insisted the whole thing had been a global hallucination, to priests who claimed they had sorted the problem out with their respective deities, to less well-known groups such as the NRA and the Women's Institute, both of which independently claimed to have hit upon the solution at their annual conferences.

The four of them knew differently, but whom could they tell? How could they explain it to anyone? They had no evidence except white faces and a burnt bone. Even the readers of Mysterious World would have a hard time believing their story.

On the way home, they made a pact not to tell anyone. It was not a large sacrifice to make for any of them. What would they have to gain by telling their story? The papers would be full of dozens of similar ones by the next morning.

They dropped Trevor off first. He mumbled, 'Thanks,' and scuttled off quickly to his home. He had, like all of them, said very little on the car journey home. It was a strange atmosphere. Shouldn't there be fanfares? Alan thought. Celebrations; at least a feeling of triumph. Instead, there was a cloud hanging over them, like a party on the way to a funeral. None of them could explain why, least of all Alan.

They went to Kate's flat next. She invited them in, and dutifully they sat around, looking at their cups of coffee and not at each other. Alan said hello to Roger, who purred back. Fifteen minutes later they headed for home.

Alan sat and wondered for an hour what to do next. In fact, he wasn't wondering at all, only resigning himself to what he knew he was going to do.

He picked up the copy of the Vet Record on the doormat, and started looking for jobs.

II

In time, the world forgot. Eventually, the only people who really remembered the troubled times at all were those who had lost their babies in the crisis, journalists doing 'Whatever happened to...?' articles for the Sunday papers, and the four of them. They still saw each other. There was a bond forged by their knowledge, a bond they could not ignore, however much they tried.

Alan got a job in a small animal practice in the centre of town. Kate followed him as a client. George left 'Mysterious World'. There didn't seem much point any more. Trevor continued just the same as he always had, and gradually, slowly, normality settled on them.

Alan was surprised to find himself enjoying his new job. Things simply didn't seem as bad as they used to. He still found it stressful, but it was a good kind of stress, the sort that made him feel worthwhile. He saw Kate and George as often as his rota allowed him to, Trevor somewhat less often. He had long since given up trying to remember exactly what had happened that day at the accelerator. Some things were best left forgotten. It was easier that way.

Alan got on with the rest of his life, and was content. The only thing he still wondered about was a question he would never know the answer to.

Exactly what had happened to Cranmer?

III

Cranmer blinked twice and opened his eyes. He was standing in the middle of a long street in bright sunshine. The street was a main street in a city, surrounded by squat buildings. The pavements were busy with people, some quietly walking to work, some shouting in front of their wares. It felt quietly busy, the feeling of a city waking up, yawning, and getting to work. The road, which seemed to be a main road, was steadily filling up with cars and trucks.

The cars were of a fashion Cranmer didn't recognise. He searched his memory — not an easy task. He had stolen so many memories over the years he had difficulty working out which were his and which were other people's. The vehicles seemed old-fashioned to him, but that didn't help. He didn't know what part of him thought they were old-fashioned. Never mind. There would be time enough.

He looked down at himself. He was wearing a neat, dark suit, and holding a briefcase in his right hand. He had a newspaper tucked under his arm. He must be in the memory of some sort of businessman. Well, that was fine. All he needed was a little time, time to gather his thoughts, to build up his defences so that he could burst from the memory and start all over again.

A horn beeped in front of him. He looked up sharply. A truck had stopped in front of him, an annoyed oriental man behind the wheel. He was shouting at Cranmer. A purloined part of his mind told him the man was speaking Japanese.

Cranmer shook his head, angered at the interruption. He only needed time to think. He stepped out of the road onto the pavement. As he did so, a cold feeling passed along his spine, a terrible sense of déjà vu. Had he been here before?

He shook his head. Irrelevant. Maybe one of his stolen memories had visited the city. He looked up the strangely familiar street, trying to place it. He recognised it briefly, but the recognition slipped from his conscious mind like an eel. Where was he?

Once more, he shook his head, to free himself from the distraction. It didn't matter! Concentrate!

He closed his eyes to try and settle his thoughts, but opened them again a moment later. Another distraction. A rumbling, roaring noise — an aeroplane flying, far overhead. It wasn't loud, but the effect on the rest of the people on the street was disconcerting. They looked up, pointed at the sky. A few seemed to be looking for cover. Was he in the middle of an air raid or something?

He remembered the newspaper under his arm. He dropped the suitcase and unfolded it in front of him, but it didn't help. It was all in Japanese. He couldn't begin to understand any of it. He was surprised to find his heart thudding quickly in his chest, and his mouth dry. Some part of his mind made out the date in the corner of the newspaper. August 6. Did that mean anything?

The noise of the aeroplane had faded into silence. Cranmer glanced at the silver watch on his wrist. It was 8.14 am. The people had started moving again now the plane seemed to have passed harmlessly overhead, but Cranmer didn't feel safe. His mind was screaming at him that something was wrong, that he had to get away from here as soon as possible. He tried to turn but his legs wouldn't move. There was a very quiet sound, like a child whistling. He looked up into the sky and saw, high overhead, something dark, falling quickly, silhouetted against the sun.

He opened his mouth to call out. There was a moment of pure white, a burning, dazzling light that felt like… felt like he was looking into the eyes of God. Cranmer wanted to weep at the terrible beauty, to drop to his knees. There was a low thunderous noise, like a giant clapping its hands. He felt the air around him start to burn, and then…

Cranmer blinked twice and opened his eyes. He was standing in the middle of a long street in bright sunshine…

Lightning Source UK Ltd.
Milton Keynes UK
06 November 2009

145890UK00001B/44/A